SNAKE EYES

Susan Slater

Snake Eyes

Ben Pecos Mysteries, Book 9

Susan Slater

Secret Staircase Books

Snake Eyes
Published by Secret Staircase Books, an imprint of
Columbine Publishing Group LLC
PO Box 416, Angel Fire, NM 87710

This book is a work of fiction. Names, characters, places and
incidents are either the product of the author's imagination or are
used fictitiously. Any resemblance to actual events or locales or
persons, living or dead, is entirely coincidental.

Book layout and design by Secret Staircase Books
Cover images Yulia Lelekova, Anton Riakhin, Ezumeimages

First trade paperback edition: November, 2022
First e-book editions: November, 2022

Publisher's Cataloging-in-Publication Data

Slater, Susan
Snake Eyes / by Susan Slater
p. cm.
ISBN 978-1649141101 (paperback)
ISBN 978-1649141118 (e-book)

1. Pecos, Ben (Fictitious character)—Fiction. 2. Native
American—Fiction. 3. Seminole people—Fiction. I. Title

Ben Pecos Mystery Series : Book 9
Slater, Susan, Ben Pecos mysteries.

BISAC : FICTION / Mystery & Detective.
813/.54

When I first decided to add a contest (Miss Teen USA) to my story's plot, I panicked. Who would I use for models? And then it struck me—of course, Alana and Skyler, the granddaughters of a close friend who just happen to be 14 and 17! I've loved watching you grow into young women. I'm so proud to call you friends!

Alana you will always be my "gypsy child" and Skyler, you will always be my Miss Teen USA! My love to you both! And thank you again for letting me bring you into my world.

When playing craps, rolling two ones with a pair of dice is the worst possible throw. It's the lowest combined number and translates to failure.
In slang today, it simply means bad luck.

Chapter 1

The last laugh. When he said it out loud, it sounded like a prize. 'And the last laugh goes to …'; he'd hear his name and walk onto the stage, accept the standing ovation, acknowledging the audience with a bow before forming a heart with his two hands held in front of his chest. A gracious, humbling acceptance speech followed. He would be a hero; his praises sung by many. So, was what he was doing now—cowardice? Taking the easy way out? Not owning up to his part?

Because for all the positives, he was still a villain. There would be those who would understand his reasoning, his motivation for wanting to step away from the finger-pointing, and choose his escape; be his own man, make his own decisions. But an even bigger group would be soundly pissed off that he'd cheated them from taking revenge. How many had secretly planned his death?

More than one or two, he thought. Poison? A gun shot? He was certain both had been considered. And if he had one regret, it would be that he wouldn't be able to see their faces when they realized that they had been taken, their deeds exposed, their actions laid open for all to see. Retribution would be swift. They would be the ones looking over their shoulders, flinching at every loud noise, quaking at an unidentified shadow. He could never have lived that way. The choice he was about to make was the right one—the freeing one.

The morning was still, hot but bearable before the sun was fully up. It was the humidity that seemed to stifle his very breathing, grabbing him by the throat, making filling his lungs laborious. Already he felt clammy and the shirt across his back was sticking to him like a second skin. But there was a beauty about the Everglades. A beauty in stark contrast to the danger—and the danger was everywhere. Sometimes it would glide past him, a slithering column big around as a telephone pole or he would catch a glimpse of huge bright eyes at the end of a long snout punctuated by enormous nostrils as he came into its focus and was being sized up as a possible meal.

It was the snakes that bothered him most. Pet snakes no longer wanted by their owners were released into nature to forage for themselves and grow sometimes at an alarming rate.

Florida had achieved its record-breaking snake capture just this spring. An eighteen-foot Burmese python weighing two-hundred-fifteen pounds hadn't just survived, but flourished by eating its weight in white-tailed deer. The Everglades were threatened by these invasive, non-native intruders. But it wasn't his concern anymore.

He pushed the kayak away from a clump of water grass and continued to paddle slowly, dodging other outcroppings of the green spears pointing upward. Sawgrass, known for its peculiar serrated edges, could reach ten feet in height. It was the mainstay of the Everglades, assuring food and shelter for thousands of permanent and migratory animals and birds. Dying back, it would become peat, rich in minerals offering other plants a chance to flourish. Over a million and a half acres of fresh and brackish waters, it formed a subtropical wilderness. And now it was only half its original size, as much of the land it covered had been cleared to raise sugarcane. Progress. So much was ruined in its name.

But his people had survived. Some tribes had disappeared; others had melded together under the title, Seminole. His ancestors had been Creek and before them members of the Calusa called 'Calos' or the 'Fierce Ones.' What would one of those members of the Paleo-Indians think of their world today? Would they mourn the loss of a sacred way of life? Or maybe laugh in total disbelief at a four-hundred-fifty-foot-high building shaped like a guitar not far from where the swamp becomes solid land? Not far from where these fierce ones had once called home with their platform huts named chickees with open sides and thatched roofs. But now the strangely shaped building cast a crooked shadow across the land where they once hunted to provide food for their families.

The monstrous musical instrument that was really a

building positioned not so far from a city called Hollywood always seemed apt to him. Couldn't the term 'tinsel town,' often used to describe a city in California of the same name, be applied here in Florida? This monstrosity of flashing lights, glittering embellishments, liveried men parking cars and running errands didn't just look out of place in the landscape but cast a jocular pall over its fake environment. Disney for adults? That was also fitting.

He pushed the kayak out into deeper water. Well, the term 'deeper' was deceptive. The Everglades boasted a mere three to five feet in depth—nine feet closer to its source at the deepest point which was always a shock to tourists. He was gazing out not at a static pool of water however huge, but a slowly moving river flowing from north to south from Lake Okeechobee. This was Florida's water—recreational, life sustaining, and endangered. Hadn't the residents dodged one bullet when fracking was voted down? What would it be next time? And would they be as fortunate?

He slowed the kayak, then stopped by sticking the tip of his paddle into a clump of grass. He'd sit a moment. Not that he hadn't had the time to reflect, but there would be no reversing his actions today. He would forfeit his life to save his people. He didn't fear death. It was just another journey. He took the small packet containing a flash drive from his pocket. A year's worth of incriminating evidence—of embezzlement, of killings, of criminal acts so heinous that they went beyond just selling one's soul to the devil. All here in his hand having been carefully collected and authenticated. There were even photos. This tiny bit of electronics was more lethal than a gun, a bomb, or a hangman's noose. It would seal the fate of more than one. And no one suspected. That brought a smile. He liked the element of surprise. Who would have thought that he had the nerve? And he had safeguarded this evidence, placed a duplicate collection of proof in the capable hands of one he could trust. If something were to happen to him ... followed by the instructions of exactly what to do. He'd thought of everything, hadn't he?

He turned his attention back to the environment. He was close to his destination; maybe another ten minutes and he'd be there. It hadn't taken a lot of research to find this place of his youth—the pit of quicksand at the edge of the marsh where the composite of sand and silt was deeper, reaching down to the marsh's rock floor. As a child he'd watched a mule stumble into the treacherous liquefied soil and be sucked up to its neck not able to even thrash about. After an afternoon's effort, the men in his community couldn't save the animal and had humanely ended its life.

It was only in the movies that quicksand was portrayed as pulling its victim completely under. That simply didn't happen in real life. There was a buoyancy that would take a six-foot man down to his chest, maybe his neck depending on the density of his body, but that was it. So why was he willing to step out into a quagmire knowing that death wouldn't be instantaneous? Because it all depended upon who needed to find him, find the body with the small water-proof package resting under his tongue protected by clenched teeth.

This part of the Everglades was patrolled by park rangers. They would take him to the morgue in a neighboring county, not Broward, and outside the jurisdiction of the casino and its supporters. Or should he say 'users'? And it would put his body under government protection. In this part of swampland, he could pretty much rely on only those with official access to this area coming across his body. This place was treacherous and hostile to the uninitiated. There were no tours held here, no groups of brightly colored kayaks skimming along the water, no boy scouts earning a badge by expertly handling a canoe.

The quiet was eerie, but reassuring. Still, shouldn't he fear wild animals? Wouldn't something try to make a meal out of him? Interestingly, gators and snakes gave wide berth to the quicksand pits. Animals were smart. He always thought it would be nice to have that sort of innate knowledge of what was dangerous and should be avoided. Humans might make far fewer life-threatening mistakes. Or not.

Would he suffer? Probably not. He would call upon the gods by chanting. He had been fasting in preparation for his final journey. He would not have all that much time left. He needed to strip to the flesh. There would be less that way to harbor pockets of air and keep him buoyant. He unbuttoned the embroidered encasements for the tiny, hand-made, round circles of bone until the shirt hung loosely on his frame. It was his prized possession, a ribbon shirt that his grandmother had made for his father and it had finally become his. The patchwork and strips of brightly contrasting colored material adorned the front in horizontal stripes. Tucked into his jeans, he wore it proudly.

This shirt was old, from a time when the country store at the edge of the reservation sold cloth—gingham and bolts of cotton in bulk. It was reported by explorers that as early as 1880, there was a sewing machine in every chickee. He wasn't sure about that, but his grandmother had owned a hand operated sewing machine and had refused an electric version years later when they had come available. Her work was slow and exacting. Still, her unique patchwork decoration on garments made them much sought after—literally for generations. He knew that today knock-off fakes were sold to tourists for high prices. It wasn't the same but it kept a tradition from dying.

He folded each piece of his clothing and tucked it into the front of the kayak. He would bring the kayak as close to the edge of the quagmire as he could, anchor it by rope to an outcropping of tall grass to preserve it before he walked toward the pit of liquefied soil that lacked the strength to support his weight. One last look around, a push with his tongue to check the security of the packaged flash drive and he would begin his journey. He stood tall, paused to gain his balance, and took a step forward.

Chapter 2

Oh, c'mon Ben, you're kidding me—an Indian Elvis?"
"Cross my heart. And he's good, too."

Julie still had her forehead wrinkled in disbelief as she asked, "I'm assuming that I'm going to be able to form my own opinion? You'll be taking me to a concert? Am I going to be that lucky?"

"You don't sound thrilled. But, yes, Saturday is a tribute concert and I'm sure Mr. Presley wannabe will be at his best."

"I don't sound thrilled because I'm starving. The food truck in the parking lot had brats on the menu. I'm going to get something to eat and meet you at your office. What can I get you?"

"The same—spicy mustard, no kraut."

"You never did know what's good."

"Doesn't that put marrying you in a bad light?" Ben grinned. It wasn't always that he could playfully land a joke at Julie's expense. She feigned a pout but blew a kiss in his direction before turning and walking back across the lot.

If there was a perk to having been named HR Director for the Seminole's Hotel and Casino in southern Florida, it was probably free entrance to all the shows. Sometimes big-name performers, sometimes the geriatric sets paying tribute—favorites from bygone days like The Beach Boys, The Eagles, Moody Blues, Chicago. He had missed James Taylor and Arlo Guthrie who had both just finished concerts. All, either authentic or copies, were always well attended in plush surroundings that offered a full evening of entertainment and food. He'd had worse jobs.

In a lot of ways, he had two bosses and certainly two offices. One office at the edge of the reservation, and part of the Indian Health Service Clinic, and another as part of the corporate offices serving the casino and located behind the hotel. He was a shared commodity. The casino wanted Native representation. With a high percentage of its employees being indigenous, a Native boss in Human Resources had appeal. He was supposed to be more than just a figurehead. Eventually, he'd hold workshops on timely topics like deescalating potentially explosive situations. Where alcohol was served, there were always opportunities for violence.

Otherwise, it was the mundane. He needed to see that everyone had a current certificate in CPR. A recent incident of an elderly patron having a medical emergency in the parking lot brought to light the lack of uniform training. Plus, one of the kitchens—belonging to one of twelve indoor restaurants—had recently gotten dinged by state inspectors for things like freezers not at the proper temps, fresh produce not being washed when received, and an improperly cleaned coffee machine, among other concerns. He was forming a kitchen committee with regular weekly meetings, for starters, to address the issues.

All hiring would be done through his department, as well as firings. There had already been an incident of a parking lot attendant helping himself to articles left in cars. So, from petty theft to overly ripe bananas, the problems were his. In fact, if he were being truthful, the kitchen's problems weren't confined to just food, its handling, or service. He had a ten o'clock meeting in the morning with a young woman who had reported a groping incident in the walk-in freezer. A truck driver from one of their suppliers supposedly copped a quick feel as he was unloading a carton of frozen sausage patties. The alleged victim and the accused were both nineteen and the young man claimed any "touching" was totally unintentional. He had accidentally backed into the young woman trying to maneuver an overloaded hand dolly through the narrow, double insulated door into the refrigerated unit. Ben wasn't clear on how the incident could have happened, but he was sure he'd find out in the morning.

Being in charge of Human Resources was something new, and maybe not a job he would have chosen. But he liked solving problems and making people's lives a little easier. The tribe had approached Indian Health Service about his hire, and he really didn't have complaints. The casino would pick up his paycheck and it paid for overtime and weekends. Not bad. Didn't the very nature of the business demand some evenings, as well as, Saturdays and Sundays?

If nothing else, he was guaranteed to be in the same place for at least a year. That, in itself, was worth a lot. He and Julie had finally found a house to rent—two stories, big back yard, double-car detached garage, surrounded by old vegetation offering privacy. It had taken a while to find it; rentals were at a premium in the area, but it had been worth it.

An upstairs with adjoining bath and large sitting room would become a dorm-like, bunk area for Zac and Nathan. Both boys would be spending the summer in Florida when school was out in a couple weeks. Ben was hoping to keep them busy by finding age-appropriate jobs for each. There were permanent 'Help Wanted' signs strategically placed in elevators and the parking garage. Kitchen workers, grounds keepers, parking and car care—any and all areas usually had openings. The casino not only had valet parking but offered the opportunity to get one's car washed and even detailed while its owner was enjoying the amenities inside. Ben was pretty sure he could get Nathan on as a carwash attendant.

Of course, he remembered being a teen himself once upon a time, but that was before electronics had ruled kids' lives. Back then making money for sports equipment took priority. He hoped he was right about keeping them busy and giving them some direction. If the carwash didn't work out, Nathan who'd just turned sixteen, would be able to do some other step-n-fetch type of jobs at the casino while Zac, a year and a half younger, might find employment more difficult. Ben would have to be creative, but if Zac was willing to work, Ben thought the two of them together might find something. It was just going to be fun to have both of the boys with him. Already having the ocean within driving distance was a plus and a definite enticement to come to Florida. Ben would have to admit that a little water and sand time appealed to him, too.

Ben was learning a lot about being the father of teenage boys. It was still a bit of a shock to have a ready-made family. The boys were close in age and friendship—Zac, the result of a summer fling when Ben was in graduate school, a young man he had no idea existed until recently. And Nathan, a young Navajo, orphaned and needing a family to belong to had actually chosen Ben. It was a good fit. As Zac's best friend, Nathan gained a mother, father, and brother all at the same time.

Ben had been worried about his wife. Adding children to a relatively young marriage could have caused problems, but Julie was not just accepting of a family she hadn't known existed, she was welcoming. It put their own plans for a family on hold but allowed Julie time to continue to carve out a niche as a reporter. She was good, dedicated to her career. Coming from a newspaper background, she just needed exposure to make the move to TV here in Florida—more studio time in front of the camera. All in all, the move to Florida had been a good one for everyone.

He unlocked the door to his office. As over-the-top as the hotel/casino was, his office was plain—simply utilitarian, nothing fancy. What mattered, the electronics—a desktop computer, a laptop, a printer—all were new and state-of-the-art. A conference room was down the hall and required reservations of at least two to three days in order to count on its use. So, basically, he had a desk job, indoors without even a window. He'd never thought joining corporate America would include duty inside an enormous guitar.

But that's what it was. With six hundred plus luxury

suites and rooms, the building was a design marvel. Built to represent two back-to-back guitars, the front of the building sported brightly lighted 'strings', straight lines of lights running its full length, from the ground to the top of the neck of the make-believe instrument. On top, six high-powered rays of light illuminated the night sky up to twenty thousand feet above the hotel's structure mimicking the strings of an actual guitar. Adorned across the surface with floor-to-ceiling glass panes, Florida's sunrises and sunsets were on full display to inhabitants. LED lights built into the surfaces of the hotel on all sides could change color, flash, and be choreographed to various songs. It was truly a wonder. Even the surrounding grounds were not any less splendid. Spas, and suites between five hundred to over seven hundred square feet overlooked cabanas lining a thirteen-acre recreational lagoon with lush landscaping. It was Florida at its tropical best.

And the cost of all this splendor to the Seminoles? A cool 1.5 billion dollars. Ben had to keep reminding himself that it was billion with a 'b'. Touted as one of the biggest economic development projects in American history, it took twelve years to complete. The tribe's goal? Establish the elite in entertainment along with world-class gaming and dining. And they were on track to do just that. But more importantly, Ben thought, it was proof that indigenous peoples could find their way, even make their mark, in the country's economy. It was a perfect example of fitting in and becoming a productive entity while insuring a bright future for indigenous people.

Yes, it was a far cry from seeing his ancestors' history written in petroglyphs on walls of secluded caves in New Mexico or Arizona where thousands of visitors could reflect on the marvels of antiquity. Maybe today, it wasn't any more impressive to have laser lights shooting out into nothingness where they could be seen from orbiting space craft. In a way, this was a monument honoring more than one people. In fact, a point could be made that a monument honoring the music of this country was probably more equal and fair in its representation than one paying homage to a man or woman of a single tribe.

For example, was this monument of sorts any worse than the six-hundred-foot-high statue of Crazy Horse being carved out of a granite boulder in South Dakota and now in its seventy-fifth year of construction? Ben thought the guitar was a modern touch while giving back to the tribe in the form of revenue. He had respect for the Seminole; he thought they had done things correctly. It certainly was a win-win for the tribe.

And like any corporation, the top echelon included a Chief Executive Officer, a Chief Operations Officer, and a Chief Financial Officer. Being a mere Director of Human Resources put him on a second tier of management. But the enterprise demanded more than one leader at the top overseeing the varied aspects of a billion-dollar business. Big money didn't come close to correctly portraying the amounts of cash that he'd seen change hands. It wasn't just the thirty-one-hundred gaming machines or the one-hundred tables, gambling was only one aspect of the spending that busloads of tourists did on a daily basis. Throw in the steakhouse, gourmet restaurants, bars that offered the best in expensive liquors— there were a myriad of attractions. A hundred dollar a shot single malt? They had it here.

And he couldn't leave out the shows, the best offerings

outside major cities across the state. The Seminole Casino and Hotel was the real deal—a complete offering of vacations for the rich and famous, as well as special nights out for the locals. He was excited about treating Julie to dinner and a show Saturday night. He vowed to spend time as a husband for a change, and this bit of luxury was a good place to start.

Chapter 3

Ben had just sat down at his desk when someone called out from the doorway. This must be the man his boss had mentioned, Andy Thunderhawk. A tall, gangly Plains Native, maybe mid-fifties, was leaning into the room. Other than his name, it was difficult to see much Native blood in him. Like so many who claimed indigenous ancestry, he probably made the registry hoping he wouldn't have a nosebleed. It was difficult to know what Andy's title was or even if he had one. Floor Manager seemed to best cover what he was accountable for. He seemed to have free access to all aspects of the organization. He'd been touted as a go-to person by Oscar Billie, the CEO, if one had questions; so, Ben had made a note of his name and had made certain to meet him at the first staff get-together. Supposedly Andy had been there since the casino's beginning, but that was maybe only ten years.

"Hey, Pecos, got a minute?"

"Sure. It's Andy, isn't it? We met at the new employees' breakfast last month."

"Good memory. I'm just a little late in personally welcoming you aboard."

"With the number of new people hired, it's going to take you awhile to make the rounds. Have time to sit?" Ben motioned to a chair.

"I don't mean to interrupt your day. I won't stay for long. I guess you might call this a heads-up visit." Andy sat, then leaned back, fingers steepling, looking at Ben. "Tough to know where to begin. I just want to give you an equal run at things—maybe keep you a step or two ahead of pocketing the eight ball. If you know what I mean. I don't want you to have a scratch game before you even start."

No, Ben had no idea what he meant, but he thought he was about to be told. He wondered if he'd have to decipher gambling terms in conversation all the time just because he worked in a casino. Ben leaned forward, resting his elbows on the desk. Listening, wasn't that his specialty?

"Any help will be appreciated. It's never easy to walk into someplace new."

"Exactly. And you've walked into some already seasoned friendships, for lack of a better word. I'm shying away from saying conspiracies, but that's what they really are. Let me say it like it is. You're going to be tested—your ethics, your adherence to right vs. wrong, your ability to look the other way—well, you get the idea. Everyone's going to try and figure out whose ass you've got your nose up—excuse my French."

"I know I'm the new kid on the block—some of that is to be expected."

Andy paused. "What I'm talking about might not be

so innocent. More than one person applied for your job. Thought they were entitled—I think you need to know that. One in particular expected to get it. He's an overbearing SOB, and he really campaigned for it. Let me just say he was a sore loser."

"Was he qualified?"

"Loosely speaking but there was a lot about him that made him highly unqualified. So much so that the powers who be around here got the big guns involved. They approached Indian Health Service and made a case for hiring from the outside. They were adamant— no preformed allegiances, no one who was a part of the casino's history, no one from this tribe but he had to be an Indian man. And they wanted someone with your background who had to be able to fix all kinds of minor personnel problems. This is a large operation, lots of different personalities inevitably lead to conflict here and there. Quite frankly, you're perfect for the job."

"Well, thanks for the kudos. I'm looking forward to getting started."

"Speaking of which, I need to get out on the floor. Time for my hourly walk around." Andy stood up and offered his hand. "Just know that I'm on your side. Keep your eyes open and your back covered. I've got your six."

Ben stood and shook Andy's hand. "I can't help but feel you know more than you're saying."

"Well, I've heard some things."

"Can you share?"

"Look, it could be nothing."

"But? Go on." It had suddenly become like pulling teeth to get more.

"I think the boys might try to run you out of here."

"And how would they be likely to try that? And just who are these boys?"

"The boys are connected. Sometimes a little money changes hands—you know, for protection."

"Sounds like the Mafia."

"We don't use that term, but we're talking big money here—booze, gambling, the girls—well, sometimes a casino can be a volatile entity, attracting all the wrong sorts. This place is a little too big to just cater to the retired moms and pops who want to get away for the weekend. You know, spend the Social Security check once a month. In a big money operation there's always somebody wanting to horn in—thinks they're smarter than Indians at running things. Outsiders trying to make a move, that's all. Wanting their own people in place."

"Let's back up. Can you tell me more about running me out? How is that supposed to be done?" Andy hadn't been very forthcoming.

"Nothing overt. More like setting you up to make mistakes. Maybe put money on the wrong horse—that sort of thing. Or worse, not having a skin in the right game at all."

"Are we talking dangerous?"

Andy walked to the door, "I've said enough. You're a nice guy. You mean well. I liked you right off. Just be prepared. Don't take anything at face value; second guess everything and don't be too trusting. Hey, I don't mean to have you panic over any of this; just be careful. Trust your instincts; you're an Indian." After stepping through the door and looking both ways, Andy was gone.

So, a Native was supposed to have better instincts? Ben didn't know whether to laugh or agree. Was he over reacting?

He certainly felt more than just a little unsettled. He knew there was no real reason to give Andy's dire warning any credence. He couldn't even call his information a veiled threat—yet, it sort of was. It was certainly a warning of danger, if not to his job, certainly to his person.

Ben was new to the game of corporate politics. He was a psychologist who had primarily worked in clinical settings, usually on or near reservations or Indian hospitals being assigned these jobs by Indian Health Service. As part of this government program, he had designed and implemented treatment for addicts, along with training interns, maintaining office hours for meeting with patients, researching new meds, speaking at conferences, teaching the random academic class … Nothing in his background said human resources for a large corporation in the gaming field. But that didn't mean that the job was out of his skill range; it wasn't. Still, it was difficult to shake Andy's assessment of what he was in for. Looking over his shoulder, trying to discern danger when there might not be any? Didn't this all add an uncalled-for extra layer to his new job that loaded on pressure just when he needed to be learning the ropes and keeping an open mind?

"You look deep in thought." Julie stood in the doorway with two sacks sitting on a cardboard tray that also held two drink cups. "Did this turn out to be a bad time?"

"No, come on in. A krautless brat sounds great." Ben pulled a roll of paper towels out of a desk drawer, peeled off a couple sheets and spread them over the corner of the desk.

"I love the posters for the Indian Elvis—they're everywhere. He must be popular; didn't I read that this is his tenth concert here?"

"Yeah, I know he comes twice a year. When we finish, I'll walk you out through the front. Coming in from the parking lot you missed all the action."

"It's one in the afternoon. Will it be busy now?"

"This is a business that takes the term 24/7 seriously. Trust me. It will be busy."

When they finished eating, Ben bagged up the wrappers, empty condiment containers, and drink cups. He wasn't sure where he was going to find a place to dump the garbage but he didn't want to leave it in the office. Already the place smelled like onions and kraut. Without a window to open, he had to hope the circulating air would carry most of the smell away.

"Let's go around to the entrance at the back first. I noticed a couple dumpsters next to the building."

They were almost to the back door when a voice boomed out, "Hey there. I need to have you step over here to the side and open that bag." The Anglo man in a brown uniform complete with the casino's insignia on one sleeve declaring he was security police, was motioning toward a wall. All the while Ben noticed the man's hand was on the gun holstered in his wide leather belt.

"Nothing suspect unless lunch remains from the food truck might be cause for alarm." If Ben was hoping for a laugh, he was disappointed. This guy was all business. He handed the black plastic garbage bag over.

"Whew. What'd you have to eat? This could put a horse in a coma." The man had opened the bag and taken a sniff. "You got a name? If you work here, you better be wearing a badge or you'll get stopped at every corner." He tied a knot in the bag of lunch remains.

"Sorry, my mistake. I left it in the office."

Ben could kick himself. The infamous, but apparently necessary nametag dangling from the end of a lanyard was hanging from the hook on the back of his office door. Damn. One more new thing to learn. The barcode on it swiped him inside every morning, but it didn't dawn on him that it needed to be a permanent part of his wardrobe.

"Let this be a lesson. And you." He turned to Julie. "Just showing up for work? You got any costumes? You need to leave them in the dressing rooms. You look like you're new here, too. Well, follow me, I'll show you the ropes."

"I'm with the *Miami Herald*. I just stopped by to see my husband's office."

"You'll be back. To just check up on the mister, if nothing else. The girls here are really pretty. Tough to not do a little looking." He winked at Ben.

"I think I can trust him." Ben noted that Julie's answer sounded more than a little curt. They both had tired of the know-it-all guard.

"You think so? That's what they all say." The guard chuckled.

This time Ben jumped in, took Julie by the elbow but offered, "I know someone who needs to get back to work. I doubt if the *Herald* would be thrilled that its new employee is spending time at the casino."

"Not like we don't have half the working population of the county here over lunch. But you go on. I'm gonna make sure this hubby of yours gets his badge on. Rules are rules, buddy, and you and me didn't make 'em." The man stood to one side waiting for Julie to leave.

Awkward. There was no other word for it. He gave Julie a quick peck on the cheek and a wave as she walked back toward the front entrance. Was this part of what he'd been warned about? Harassment for little or no reason. Would it be constant? Take some other form once he remembered his badge? He dutifully followed the man apparently named Les, if the embroidered pocket of his uniform was telling the truth, back to his office.

* * *

"So, what do you think?" The amount of electronics in the room made it hot and stuffy. The man sitting in front of the screen had loosened his collar and slipped off his tie.

"I say we keep up the pressure—just little stuff, nonsensical, but constant." A second man standing behind him turned away from the screen that had captured the give-and-take of the guard with Ben and Julie.

"The wife's a cutey. I could go for a little of that redheaded stuff."

"Keep your hands to yourself. You're not the one we want out of here. I don't want to have to save your ass. Stick to the waitresses. You've already found out a big tipper gets preferential treatment. You want to get laid; stay with what's working the floor. And this is for Les." He pulled out a billfold and separated two twenties from a wad of bills. "Tell him, good job. Oh, and tell Andy to stop by on your way out."

* * *

Julie handed her parking stub to a young guy working the valet booth. It was warm and humid. An authentic tropical afternoon—a far cry from the dry heat of New Mexico and in sharp contrast to the temperatures inside the casino. She'd left the top down on the convertible when the attendant assured her that she'd have covered parking. Convertibles were great for this part of the world as long as you took precautions. One sunny day left uncovered in this heat and the dash would probably melt. It would certainly be a challenge sitting on the slick, black leather seats. Early afternoon and it was already time to put the top up. Air conditioning sounded great.

She exchanged a five-dollar tip for her key fob when the attendant returned. But he seemed reluctant to walk back to the booth.

"Uh, Miss, I hate to tell you this, but you got nailed by the pigeons."

"I'm sorry, what?" Julie wasn't sure she'd heard him correctly. What pigeons?

"We try to keep them out of the parking areas. We got some of them plastic owls all over the place, corners of the roof, underground garage, perched in trees along the back of the lot. Doesn't seem to do any good. The pigeons have been smart enough to figure out that they're fake."

"I'm honestly not following you. What does this have to do with my car?"

"There. That's what they do when we can't get rid of them." He had turned back toward her car and pointed to the passenger-side front seat.

"Oh my god, pigeons do that?" This was not some nicely formed droppings. There was a runny glob of white mucous smeared across the leather dripping off the edge of the seat closest to the door. How many pigeons had there been?

He shrugged, "I'll get some paper towels. Those birds are wicked bad." Seeing a kid step out of the valet booth, he yelled out, "Got some bird shit over here, need cleanup."

Julie stood to one side as the two kids not only cleaned up the droppings, they followed up their elbow grease with a leather restorer that literally made the front seat sparkle. No one would ever guess it had recently been a bird's toilet. Julie offered two more fives before starting the car.

The air felt good. Even getting on and off of the usually crowded freeway, she couldn't gripe. She loved her job. The hundred- and ten-year-old *Miami Herald* wasn't some small town rag. It was comforting to have landed somewhere with an honest-to-goodness desk with her name on the rolls. Sure, she was just one of over two thousand employees spread across Florida and even Bogota and Managua, but she was among greats in the field—past and present. She pulled into the underground parking garage, got her briefcase out of the trunk and headed toward the elevators.

The first thing she noticed was the handwritten note on her desk chair. 'Check with me when you get in.' The signature was the capital K and U for Ken Usher, her immediate boss. Seemed odd that he hadn't just texted her. Oh well, best to do what was asked. She dropped car fob and purse in a bottom drawer and left her computer in her briefcase. No putting this off.

Ken's office was in the corner across from the roomful of desks. Not every desk had an occupant; the bulk of the reporters were in the field most of the day. It was hard to believe that the paper employed over a hundred and forty reporters. The total newsroom staff numbered four hundred and fifty give or take a couple and included editors, copy editors, photographers, graphic artists, page designers, columnists, editorial specialists—what was she leaving out? Oh yes, news assistants, bosses and critics. But when a newspaper could boast of receiving nineteen Pulitzer Prizes and claim the talents of political commentator Leonard Pitts, Jr., humorist Dave Barry, and novelist Carl Hiaasen, having a huge, talented support staff paid off.

She would bet the next Pitts, Barry and Hiaasen were in this group somewhere. The *Miami Herald*'s bragging rights were pretty secure. Plus, every week the Sunday paper contained over two hundred pages. That fact always blew her away. It took a village to get it out the door.

Ken was on his cell when she walked up so she paused outside the glass-partitioned door to his office making sure he saw her. He looked up and motioned her to wait, then seemed to say a couple words before putting his phone down and waving her in. In his forties somewhere, what he lacked in flamboyant personality, he made up for in dress. The pink flamingos posing bent-legged against the light blue background of his short-sleeved shirt screamed tropics. How do you say Florida without uttering a word?

He pointed to the note in her hand, "That'll brand me as old-fashioned, but I was afraid you wouldn't check your cell. Grab a chair; I've got a favor to ask." Favor? He'd certainly piqued her interest; she pulled a chair up to the front of his desk. "There's an unwritten rule of reporting—do what you have to do to get the story. Trite, outdated maybe, but I'm going to suggest that there's some truth to it."

He paused, picked up a sheet of paper, looked at it then put it aside. "Florida's having a real tug-of-war with its casinos. I personally think it's bonkers, but the legislature is going crazy over Indian rights. A federal judge has just thrown out a gambling agreement that our governor signed with the Seminoles. Says the compact violates the Indian Gaming Regulatory Act by illegally expanding gambling across the state, contending that the tribe stands to rake in billions."

"Doing what? How would they expand what they have now?"

"By allowing the tribe to operate sports betting, in addition to adding roulette and craps to its seven state casinos. All that supposedly adds up to a possible payday of twenty billion dollars over the next thirty years. We're talking big-time money."

Interesting, but what did it have to do with her, Julie wondered. "Isn't the tribe involved with sports betting now?" She was sure she'd read about a plan to add it to current programs.

"You're right. Less than a month ago, the tribe started up online sports betting. A lot of folks had been asking for it—sort of bring the current opportunities to place a wager up to a state-of-the-art level. People from all over the state could download an app and place wagers on professional football, hockey, and soccer games. And these weren't the only sports. They had a pretty complete roster of offerings. And the compact gave the tribe exclusive rights to any wagers placed via the app or other electronic device on these sporting events from anywhere in the state."

"It must have been lucrative for the state, too."

"Originally, the tribe had been expected to pay billions to Florida from this program."

"What happened?"

"What always happens—somebody cries foul, feels cheated. Owners of competing gaming establishments sued. They charged that the agreement with the tribe violated federal laws, causing significant and devastating impact on already established gaming businesses—many of these mom-and-pop set ups had been in operation for some time, years, half a century even. Entire families had prospered from them. In short, they would lose money, bigtime. It would change a way of life that they had grown comfortable with and felt entitled to."

"It does seem to challenge a basic concept of fairness according to the American approach to commerce."

"Yes, right or wrong, the private entities felt Indian gaming interfered with the concept of free enterprise—competition, profit motivation, equal opportunity—you get the picture. The questions seem to be back on the table and being considered once again. And not without rancor, I might add, on both sides. I'm afraid we're going to see this slip over into a possible blood-letting. It will certainly bring out centuries of bad-blood between indigenous people and those who claimed their land."

"Endless ramifications of a touchy subject."

"Exactly. I don't want the paper to get caught off-guard, blindsided by either side. And that's where you come in." He paused, making eye contact, but not speaking; then, "I want to position you to get the heads-up on any discussions that either side has or if anyone even explores finalizing a decision. I don't need to tell you that this conversation stays in this room." He paused and acknowledged her nod. "We have someone on the inside. I'm not going to give you a name or a position. He or she must remain unknown, but I don't want anyone to even guess that we're working undercover. That's where you come in. They'll expect a reporter dedicated to the story. You'll be the paper's rep. You won't raise questions as to why you're there. You'll be in plain sight, asking questions, sitting in on meetings—with permission, of course. And, possibly most importantly, I want you to get the tribe's side of the story. What would the impact be of any change in the current compact? How would change impact the tribe? Do the research. Find the stories no one else has."

"Sounds challenging. I look forward to getting involved."

Ken leaned forward. "I understand that your husband is the new Director of Human Resources for the casino. Is that correct?"

"Yes."

"And it's my understanding that he's an Indian man?"

"A member of a pueblo tribe in New Mexico."

"I believe that this might give you an in, so to speak. But it might also set up the possibility of prejudice."

"I'm a reporter. I've never let my personal life interfere. If for some reason, I feel my actions might be compromised, or find myself in a situation that would skew results, set up one side over the other, you'll be the first to know."

"Good. That's all I ask of you. Work from home whenever you need; take time to get the lay of the land, so to speak. I trust you. I think we'll have a good working relationship." He stood.

Julie followed suit and held out her hand, "Thank you for the vote of confidence."

Chapter 4

She'd dropped her car off at home, dressed, and Ubered back to the casino. The strapless, beaded mini barely brushed her knees, and the stiletto sandals attached to her feet with two, narrow, silver straps. Thank God she was only walking from the parking lot to the casino's front entrance. She wasn't sure what a casino night out demanded in the way of dress, but she thought she was prepared. Even Ben was wearing a suit and tie and looked elegant, dark hair brushed to one side, an escaped lock brushing one eyebrow—the epitome of sexy.

Dinner was in the Council Oak Steak & Seafood restaurant on the bottom floor touted as a sophisticated, classic American steakhouse. It was newly opened after extensive renovations. Ben hadn't stopped talking about the wrap-around kitchen, in-house butcher shop, a dry-aging room complete with Himalayan salt walls. And if that wasn't impressive enough, he bragged about the four hundred labels in the glass-enclosed, award-winning wine room. Julie remembered reading somewhere that the list included numerous varietals, regions, and ranged in price from fifty dollars to over six thousand. Wow! She certainly felt like she was entering the land of the rich and famous.

Ben met her at the door to the restaurant and made her know her choice of dress was perfect for their night out. She was almost embarrassed by his low whistle. His hug and brush of lips on her cheek were reassuring. The dress had his thumbs up. And if their reflection in the mammoth glass entry was any proof, they looked fantastic together. Her red-gold hair spilling over her shoulders held back on one side by a sequined barrette; his six-foot-two frame outlined in a perfectly fitting, natural straw-colored, linen jacket, and slacks. She wasn't immune to the turning of heads when they entered.

Their table overlooked an absolutely iridescent pool twinkling with underwater lighting. But it was the waterfalls that sparkled like jewels. Opulence? The word fit.

"The setting is beautiful." Julie was fighting an impulse to twist around in her chair and look at the open-kitchen.

"Wait 'til you taste the food."

"I can only imagine."

And the entree was superb. Not a big beef eater, Julie marveled at the melt-in-your-mouth perfection she was served after sharing a half dozen oysters as an appetizer. And wine? A perfect, fruity bottle of red, sporting a label from Napa Valley, arrived at their table compliments of Ben's boss.

"I can't believe he remembered that I told him we were

dining here tonight. He did say that he appreciated my learning the ropes, getting a solid feel for what this place stands for."

"Which is?"

"Success. A sharing of enterprise between indigenous peoples and those who came after. I know he sees this hotel and casino, as well as others across the state, as something other tribes could do—even branching out into additional commercial businesses."

Julie didn't comment. This wasn't the time to discuss the current legislative involvement and definitely not appropriate to share the somewhat clandestine work she might be doing in the same arena. The idea of the *Herald* positioning someone totally undercover was a little unnerving. She was glad she didn't have the person's name. She would worry about accidentally blowing the person's cover or somehow being drawn into what the person was working on against her will.

Ben was keeping an eye on the time. The show started at eight, but both agreed that the Cherries Jubilee flamed at tableside couldn't be missed. Coffee, the choice of a liqueur, and a half hour to savor the perfect ending to a perfect meal put this date night in a category all its own.

They were headed to an indoor amphitheater. Another part of the property-wide expansion which included several amenities like the steakhouse where they'd just dined. The 1.5 billion-dollar update saw a fifty-five hundred seat arena grow to over seven thousand seats and play host to the biggest names in popular music, comic acts, and even a Miss Universe coronation.

Their seats in the center section gave them a great view of the stage. The rows around them were quickly filled as the amphitheater lighting dimmed. If not a full house, it wasn't far from it. She wasn't sure why she was surprised, but she hadn't been confident that an Indian Elvis would attract a crowd. Of course, she was probably underestimating the average age of local residents. Recreating one's youth was obviously a money-maker.

"I'm surprised an Indian Elvis is so popular."

"I haven't seen him before, but I hear he's really good. And look at the age of the crowd. These people remember the first Elvis. Tribute acts are usually sell-outs, I'm told."

"I was just thinking that. This is obviously a vintage group. But an indigenous Elvis? Seems like that's a stretch of the imagination."

"There's even a black Elvis."

"Now you're kidding."

"Nope. And he's good—been booked in here a couple times according to some old posters I ran across. Apparently, it's a lucrative field. I even looked it up—worldwide there are supposedly well over two hundred thousand Elvis copycats. Some estimates are twice that."

"Scout's honor? I can't tell when you're pulling my leg."

Ben held up a three-finger scout salute. "On my honor."

Julie realized, over the next hour, that she'd had nothing to worry about—the concert was a good one. Opening with Blue Suede Shoes and ending with a rendition of Heartbreak Hotel with a play on words reflecting where he was; by the end of the concert, he had covered over thirty Elvis hits.

"C'mon, I want you to meet Cal."

"The Elvis? I didn't know you knew him. I doubt he's a Florida native."

"We just signed him to a lounge lizard contract. He'll

be with us for six months in the Starlight lounge, second floor. And, no, he's Cherokee, a Plains Native."

Ben and Julie stood at the back of a thirty-plus person line making its way toward the stage, finally reaching the singer to shake hands and congratulate him on a great show. Caleb Catawnee was personable, unassuming, and signed every fan's program that was handed him. "See you Monday evening? I need you to stop by my office first—I have the copies of your contract." After again congratulating Cal on a great event and giving him directions to his office, Ben turned to go. "How about a drink before we take off? No reason date night has to end at ten."

That sounded great. The very fact that they didn't have to rush because one or both of them were catching a plane in the morning to a job halfway across the US was something she could get used to very quickly. And not only did they have time for a drink, they would be going home to a house. Not a hotel room or some short-term rental, but a place they had even purchased furniture for. Acquiring furniture was always her test for longevity in a place. Living out of a suitcase was a thing of the past. Being separated was also on the shelf. She had never thought she'd call Florida home, but the feeling of permanence was comforting.

The bar that Ben suggested wasn't overly crowded, and it wasn't loud. They sat side by side in a booth toward the back of the room.

"I was put on special assignment today." Now was a good time to share her work orders.

"Just don't tell me you're taking off for, maybe New York or Seattle?"

Julie laughed. "I'm stuck right here. The paper is doing

a series highlighting the Seminole's investment in the hotel/casino trade. I might have to go as far away as Tampa to visit another casino, but that's about it."

Ben was supportive as she knew he would be, even offering to help. Julie was relieved. It would make asking him to get involved all that easier. The conversation soon turned to the arrival of the boys which was just two weeks away. She knew how much Ben was looking forward to having both Zac and Nathan with them.

"I've already gotten an okay to have Nathan work with the parking lot guys. I expect them to keep him busy."

"And Zac?"

"Nothing yet. I was thinking grounds crew."

"What about the golf course? There was a sign out front advertising for help."

"That sounds like a possibility—" Ben was interrupted by Cal walking up to their table.

"Sorry to bother you, but would it be possible to get a copy of my contract tonight? I wasn't thinking earlier but I'm off to meet with my agent in Orlando in the morning and he's been hounding me to make sure everything's in writing and that he agrees. It'd save me another trip if I could get the particulars tonight."

"Sure. Not a problem; we're finishing up here. I'll pay our tab on my way out." Ben turned to Julie, "Why don't you meet me at the car? I won't be long." He handed her the key fob to the Range Rover.

Ben had parked in back on the ground floor of the parking garage in an area reserved for hotel staff. It was a little eerie leaving the glitz, lights, and noise to walk into a darkened cavern of cars. There were still forty or so scattered across an area that usually must hold more than a hundred fifty. The Range Rover stuck out as a misfit among the sedans and sports cars. It was a car that Ben had needed for New Mexico's rough terrain but was a little out of place in an urban setting. Maybe it would come in handy for the beach.

Julie slipped on the jacket she'd been carrying. Once the sun set, evening temps were bearable without so much humidity. She pressed the key fob and the car beeped in welcome, briefly flashing its lights. She opened the passenger-side door and tossed her purse onto the seat. And that's all she remembered clearly. The blow to her head came from behind, snapping her neck forward and down. She tried to grab onto the open car door but was pushed away; she slid down the side of the car, catching the sleeve of her jacket on the door handle and feeling it rip exposing her arm to the rough pavement. Then blackness until she opened her eyes as Ben knelt beside her talking to someone standing behind her.

"We couldn't have been separated more than five minutes—just long enough for me to open my office and hand Cal a folder and walk here."

"It don't take these guys long to get what they want. They can do a house in three. You have a chance to see if anything's missing?" The uniformed security guard had a holster on his belt and the name, Roger, stitched across the flap on his pocket.

"No, I've been more concerned about my wife." Ben knew he sounded short but the guard wasn't exactly jumping into action.

The man turned and leaned into the car. "Understandable. Looks like they cleaned out the console."

"Roger, can we get some medical attention here?" Julie

had slumped against him and he could see the welt rising above her left ear. Why was he needing to prod this guy into doing something?

"Sure. Let me call. It's eleven-thirty; night shift should be just settling in. As you know, we're 24/7." Roger pulled the two-way radio from his belt. "Excuse me." He turned and walked to the back of the Rover.

"Help me up." Julie's voice sounded strained. She held a hand up to Ben.

"Are you sure? I think the medical guys are on the way." Ben took a deep breath. She was coherent and talking. The knot on her head, plus a scraped elbow and knee looked to be the extent of her injuries. He felt she had been lucky. This could have been so much worse.

"I'll be okay. Hand me my purse. It's on the front seat. I have some Kleenex to wipe this cut on my knee."

"I don't see your purse, maybe it fell." Ben leaned past Julie and felt along the floorboards.

"Or it was taken." Julie rolled to a sitting position and again held out her hand for help up. "I wonder if this happens often. I'm surprised the garage isn't better patrolled."

"Yeah, me, too. Guess what I'm going to be looking into on Monday."

Within three minutes, two emergency medical guys pulled up in a golf cart. One took out an ice pack from a Styrofoam chest and instructed her to hold it to the back of her head above her left ear. Then, standing in front of her, he gave instructions and tested her ability to turn her head, and stretch out her arm, and follow a pen with her eyes.

Nodding in satisfaction, he pointed to the quickly

rising welt on the back of her head, and added, "I'd say we're looking at the worst of it. Count yourself lucky. We haven't had any parking lot problems either open-air or here in the garage for over a year now. I hate to see it start up again. Fingers crossed this was just some random hit and won't happen again with proper coverage of the area." The younger of the two offered two Advil and a bottle of water, then both got on the cart and headed back down the entry ramp and around the building.

"You can't tell me that there's no patrol for this lower-level staff parking?" Ben had turned to Roger before putting his arm around Julie and taking over the job of holding the ice pack to her head.

"Well, there's supposed to be." Roger looked uneasy. "This is Sammy Longman's territory but he begged off early tonight. His grandmother's sick and he got a call that he was needed at the house." He looked at the ground, not at Ben directly.

"And he didn't arrange for cover?" Who oversaw this crew? Ben wasn't impressed.

"Not that I heard. Doubt there was anyone free anyway; we had a big crowd tonight. Every able hand was parking cars or retrieving them out there and in here." He turned to Julie. "Looks like your purse and whatever was in that console amounted to the haul. Don't look like they targeted your car; it was just an easy grab 'cause it was open. Sorry you had to get in their way."

"Me, too."

"Don't want to upset you, but I gotta ask was there anything in your purse or the console, maybe under the seat, like guns, ammunition, drugs or excessive amounts of cash in the car that they could have taken? Maybe known was in the car or on your person?"

"In addition to Julie's purse, looks like I'm out a flashlight, a coin purse with about five dollars in change, and a V-1 Radar Detector."

"In addition to credit cards, I had about thirty dollars, some cosmetics, lipstick and blush, and my house keys." Julie added.

"I'm sure I don't have to tell you to change the locks on your house." Roger had leaned against the Rover to write the report. After a couple minutes, he stepped back. "I need to have the two of you read this over and sign, then date here and here." He pointed at the bottom of the page.

"Are you finished with the car? Or will someone check for fingerprints?"

"We'd be wasting our time. They didn't touch the car; the door was already open. Maybe the console would have a print but I'd bet the perp wore gloves. And it probably was just one person. In fact, I'd bet on that, too—one, very careful, gloved, quick, experienced thief. And this wasn't his first rodeo—that's also a sure bet. I don't want to sound callous but by the time we'd get law enforcement to dust for prints—and that means *if* we were able to even talk them into coming out without there being a major loss or injury to your person, we'd be here half the night for nothing."

Ben agreed; he was tired. He wanted to get Julie home. It had been a long evening and he was glad there was one more day in the weekend. He helped Julie into the car, and thanked Roger for his help even though he really thought Roger could have done more. At least the car hadn't been torn up, a smashed window or cut up leather seats. Still the whole thing had left a bad taste in his mouth. A multimillion-dollar casino and hotel and there was this cheap, petty theft attempt that literally had threatened Julie's life.

"You know I'm going to find it difficult to let you out of my sight from now on." He reached for her hand before pulling out of the garage. "It scares me how serious this could have been."

"I appreciate the concern but don't be hard on yourself. This could have happened anywhere—in fact, it does with increasing frequency."

"I still want you to have that knot on your skull checked in the morning."

"Let's see how I feel. I have to admit between the ice and the Advil, I'm coming back to normal pretty quickly."

Chapter 5

Monday morning. He wasn't looking forward to trying to sort through the weekend problems. He'd have to reprimand the Longman kid, follow up on Roger's report, and see what he could do about assigning better coverage to the parking areas—especially during concerts or other popular events. He was probably going to be reminded that he was HR and not hotel management. And he was the new guy on the block—both of those things possibly meant people would dismiss his requests.

Thank God Julie hadn't sustained serious injury. She had stopped by Urgent Care on Sunday and was told she had been lucky—the blow knocked her out but didn't do any permanent damage. A sensitive, sore-to-the-touch, bruised bump poking up through her hair, a scraped elbow and skinned knee—that was it. And even by this morning the bump was decreasing in size and was neatly camouflaged by a strategically placed ponytail.

The first thing he noticed walking down the hall to his office was that the door was open. He never questioned privacy but certainly expected to have it. As he neared the doorway, the man sitting to one side of his desk rose and turned toward him. Oscar Billie, hotel and casino manager, or as Ben noted, CEO. Ben hadn't met the man but had seen his picture in a Who's Who brochure produced to introduce the men, and one woman, behind the running of the Seminole enterprise. Apparently, if Ben remembered correctly, Mr. Billie had been awarded his position by the tribe.

"Dr. Pecos, Oscar Billie here. My apologies for coming on into your office, but I wanted to make sure I caught you before things got busy."

"Not a problem. You were on my calendar to stop by and introduce myself today." Ben shook the hand held out and was struck by the strong grip. Ben fought pulling back and stretching his fingers just to make certain his hand wasn't bruised—this by a man at least six inches shorter and maybe thirty years his senior.

"I'm going to sit, but I'm not going to stay long." Oscar Billie sat and waited while Ben walked around his desk before continuing. "I know I'm just one of many who have been shocked by what happened to your wife Saturday night. The hotel and casino seem to be a magnet for the nefarious. They see this as a monument to easy riches. People attend concerts and gamble because they can afford to. And thieves think the Mercedes, Lexus—yes, a Range Rover—will no doubt contain easy pickings, money, or maybe a firearm. The parking garage is potentially more lucrative than a local Walmart's lot full of Kias. So, I don't see a remedy. This isn't the first time that we've been hit and not the last."

"It's my understanding that the person assigned to the back lot left early, vacated his position and didn't arrange for a backup." Was Mr. Billie even aware that the theft and assault could have been prevented, Ben wondered.

"Ah, Sammy Longman. He's working here because the tribe is giving him a second chance. He was in some trouble as a teen, totaled a car that had been loaned to his family. Actually, the owner claimed it had been stolen but that was never proven. Rez life is hard on some kids—too many rules, too much oversight—too many easy targets to protest, flail against. All in the name of establishing your manhood."

"How old is Sammy?"

"Nineteen. His grandmother, the woman who raised him, is ill. I expect this will be her last season with us. When she summoned Sammy last Saturday night, there wouldn't have been a question but that he had to go. I'm mentioning this because I'd like you to understand the situation. I want to put in a word for going easy on him."

"I want to—"

"No need to decide now. Talk with him, but from the standpoint of being an Indian man yourself. Empathy is what's needed here." Oscar Billie stood, "I won't take up any more of your time. I think our working relationship will be a good one. You certainly were highly recommended by Indian Health Services."

Before Ben could offer an answer or walk him to the door, the Casino manager nodded his good-bye and walked out.

Ben hadn't even sat back down before Andy stuck his head in the door. "Got a minute? I see you're already hobnobbing with the big boss."

"Come on in. I was going to look you up. I need your read on how we can keep what happened the other night from happening again. I'm assuming you've heard?"

"In so many ways the hotel/casino is its own little world. Maybe, small town is a better descriptive. But you know what I mean, everybody knows everybody. Nothing happens in secret."

"I was glad that Mr. Billie stopped by. I had thought there should be some reprimand for Sammy Longman, but the boss would like any wrongdoing overlooked."

"Doesn't surprise me, he would. Sammy's his nephew—been raised by his sister."

"That wasn't mentioned."

"I wouldn't have expected it to. The old man sure protects him. I know you have to talk with Sammy but just be careful. Everything you say will be repeated—if you catch my drift."

Ben nodded. "Any other words of wisdom for a Monday?"

Andy laughed. "Hey, nobody assigned me to be your keeper. But I think the new guy should be given a chance. I'm assuming that Mrs. Pecos is on the mend?"

"Yes, she's doing remarkably well, thanks for asking. "

"Well, this will make her feel all the better." Andy stepped forward and placed a large paper shopping bag on Ben's desk, waited a moment and then with a bit of flourish, emptied the contents onto the blotter. "Purse, billfold, keys—and get this, her money's still there. A crisp twenty, a ten and some change. I found everything next to one of the dumpsters at the back of the lot. I don't know if the guys emptying the bins found the stuff and tossed it on the ground or if the perp just dropped it. Doesn't even look like he or she went through the contents, just dumped and ran. As a rule, they're only looking for money or drugs, so I figure someone scared them off and they didn't want to get caught with anything incriminating. I got a feeling that the stuff out of your car's console is gone for good. It was probably tossed in the bin and the pickup guys didn't see it. I'll keep an eye out though. I still feel real bad that Mrs. Pecos got in their way. Hope this doesn't discourage her from stopping by for a visit now and then."

"Actually, you'll probably be seeing her around here a lot. The legislature is going to take another look at the state's gambling pact, and Julie will be doing some research for the *Herald*."

"I look forward to that. Don't get me wrong, but it'll be nice to see a woman who ain't wearing feathers and sequins and hanging out at the bar."

"I'll make sure Julie gets the message." Ben didn't even try to keep the snideness out of his voice.

"Hey, don't get me in trouble. I'm as red-blooded a male as the next guy, and I've heard that Mrs. Pecos is easy on the eyes. But this is a place of business; nice to see a woman in a suit for a change. Enough jawing for now. Take it easy. Glad everything turned out okay." With that, Andy ducked back out of the doorway and disappeared down the hall.

Ben put the billfold and housekeys back in Julie's purse before dropping it in a desk drawer. Lucky that Andy found everything. He seemed like a good guy, helpful, willing to share his knowledge about the corporation, even if he did have strong feelings about feathers and sequins, and acknowledged that Ben had a hot wife. Had Ben missed a chance to offer a little 'hands off' warning? No, didn't seem like it was needed. Dealing with people inside an organization had its own pressures and possible traps unless you had help. How fast could he learn who was who—the ones not to cross, others to trust? What not to say to the Sammy Longmans, for example. Andy was proving to be helpful.

And speaking of Sammy, he needed to find out when Mr. Longman was due in. A sick grandmother, an emergency, an understaffed parking crew with an overflow problem due to a special event—those were all things outside of a person's control. Depending on the young man's attitude, Ben didn't have to be asked to be lenient. Did Oscar Billie just stop by to size him up? Probably. Maybe the intent was to see if Ben could follow directions, take instruction.

When he called, the assistant to the manager assured Ben that she would ask Sammy to stop by HR at the start of his shift which was three o'clock. But Ben didn't have to wait that long. Within the hour there was a knock on the door.

"Come in." He was beginning to think the job was more face-to-face interaction and less paperwork, which was much more what Ben was used to. He hadn't been thrilled about a desk job so maybe he was going to like what it seemed to be turning into.

"You wanted to see me? I'm Sammy Longman. My boss said you wanted to see me at three, but I came in early to just tell you how sorry I am that your wife got robbed." The kid in the doorway looked all of nineteen, which made him just that, a kid. But there was an earnestness when he made eye contact that instantly made Ben believe him. Pompadour, faux hawk, what did they call the modified mullet hairstyle—dark hair curly and full on the top of his head with sides shaved? He certainly fit the heartthrob mold.

"I understand there were circumstances beyond your control the other night. I think I'd like to meet with your supervisor and make certain that there's a backup list of more than one person who can step in when needed. I realize that might mean needing to hire, but I'll see what your boss thinks."

"Good idea. I've got a friend who's out of school for the summer. Could I send him over?"

"Sure. We've got a full slate of events for the next few months." Parttime might be the best way to go, Ben thought. He'd suggest that to Sammy's boss. "Are you with us just for the summer?"

"Yeah, I'll be a sophomore at Florida International this fall. Is your wife going to be all right?"

"Getting robbed is always an ordeal. She was lucky there were no serious injuries. I appreciate your stopping by—that means a lot. I'll tell her you asked about her."

Chapter 6

What an assignment! How many reporters were able to spend their days in a casino? And not just any casino; this one had three thousand slot machines with names like Buffalo Diamond, Dancing Drums, Little Tom just to name a few. Julie knew that under the circumstances, she could have taken off a couple days but there was truth to getting back on the horse you just fell off of. She didn't want time to overthink the scary parking garage episode. This was her assignment. She needed to get to work, and she had proudly parked the convertible next to Ben's Range Rover on the first level. A little bravado went a long way though, and she was glad to be out of the garage and into the building.

She had passed several buses in front of the casino

unloading what appeared to be full contingents of seniors. A day of slots? Maybe video betting or gaming tables? She couldn't think of a more boring way to spend time. She just wasn't a gambler, never had been. Taking chances wasn't a part of her make-up especially not when it took a part of a hard-earned paycheck. Taking a cruise wasn't on her bucket list either. A whole part of what some saw as the charm of southern Florida was lost on her. But it was best to keep her opinions to herself.

She took a seat in an open entry area and dragged a notebook from her tote bag. A good time to run through the notes she'd taken after the meeting with Ken Usher. Her boss had shared some interesting information. This was probably as good as any place to review what had been said. People around her were enjoying coffee and breakfast pastries, some were simply reading the *Herald*. It seemed an inviting place to relax for a while. She needed to do a quick check of her notes because she was meeting with the administrative assistant to the casino's management. She had a ten o'clock appointment with April Bowlegs. Thank God she loved research; the learning curve for acquainting herself with Native culture in Florida was vertical.

She knew there were six federally recognized Indian tribes in Florida. Even though their populations ranged from a handful, maybe three to four hundred people, to a few thousand, all seemed to have gaming facilities on their land. She was going to need to come up with a composite picture—not of just one group but of many. She expected needs as well as results to differ substantially between recipients. She simply wanted to prove, with concrete examples, how all the tribes had prospered, legitimately, thanks to sponsoring gaming and had not taken undo advantage of any agreement with the US. It was important that voters knew that the Seminole had taken care of themselves and not cheated the general public to do so. There had to be success stories, she just needed to ferret them out.

She unclipped the folded map of Florida from the back of her notebook. Each reservation across the state was highlighted—all six of them. It was more than just a catch-phrase that the Seminole called themselves the 'Unconquered People'. Originally a mere three hundred members of the tribe managed to elude capture by the United States Army in the latter 1800s. That number grew to currently over two thousand, divided among the state's six designated homelands. In addition to Hollywood, there was Big Cypress, Brighton, Immokalee, Ft. Pierce, and Tampa with seven casinos among them. Julie had a feeling that she was going to become very familiar with the state of Florida by the completion of this assignment.

She had gotten far enough along in her research to realize the consequences of building a gaming empire weren't without criticism. Or competition. Hadn't her boss shared that well-established, small gaming businesses were becoming more vocal and were suggesting at the very least, Indian gaming was receiving preferential treatment. She thought of Ben's home, the Pueblo where gaming was first introduced in New Mexico. There was no competition, no casinos owned and operated by non-Natives. The reservations were doing a superb job in supporting their people, providing scholarships and jobs—what a far cry from what seemed to be happening in Florida.

She checked her watch. Five minutes until ten, time to meet up with Ms. Bowlegs. Recently, corporate headquarters for Casinos International had moved from

Orlando to Davie, Florida, about twenty-four miles north of Miami. She was saved some immediate travel, however, because most casinos and hotels had on-site representatives of major departments like human resources, finance, and general management. There was absolutely no doubt that certain personnel were needed close by—this was big business. Advertisements touted modern accommodations with rooms ranging in price from two-hundred to five-hundred dollars a night, award-winning dining, and lively casino gaming. From what she had seen so far, the ads weren't overblown.

Julie had just taken a proffered seat inside the glass-walled vestibule that served more than one office when a woman, somewhere in her fifties, walked across the marble floor and held out her hand.

"Miss Conlin? Or do you use your married name?"

"Thank you for asking. I know it gets confusing but I prefer Conlin."

"Then, Conlin it shall be. I'm April Bowlegs. Come with me." She paused and turned back to Julie. "As you can see, they're not."

"I'm sorry. I don't understand."

"Legs. My legs aren't bowed. Old family name only. Luckily my early schooling was all on the reservation so teasing was non-existent. The name actually carries some clout."

"Yes, I know. I'm assuming that Chief Billie Bowlegs was your grandfather? And Chief Osceola is also somewhere on your ancestral tree?"

"Ah, I'm impressed." The smile was one of genuine surprise. "You've done your homework." April gave Julie a quick pat on the arm, "I appreciate that. Now, let's see how

I can help you."

Her office was stunning and large. Desk, chairs, and tables were all of beautiful, carved mahogany. Indian artifacts were everywhere and not just confined to Seminole interests. The Southwest indigenous people were equally well represented as were Plains Natives. From pottery storytellers to dreamcatchers, the room was a gallery of Native art.

"Breathtaking. I hope you let my husband visit."

"Ah, yes, a Pueblo man. I sat in on his hiring. I'll send him a personal invitation. Now, let me first say how sorry I am that one of your initial impressions of our business was anything but what we wanted it to be. I'm working with Dr. Pecos to offer better security coverage by having more personnel on staff to cover the parking areas—especially on the three to eleven shift. And better training. I think your husband is already working on that one."

"I understand the circumstances were unusual. There are no ill feelings. I'm looking forward to interacting with your staff and enjoying the amenities that the hotel and casino offer. Our dinner Saturday night was exceptional."

"I'm glad you have some pleasant memories of that night. It's too blasé to just pass the incident off as something to be expected in this sort of business. I won't do that. Social media makes certain that every bit of bad publicity becomes magnified. I want to reassure you that we're taking action."

"Speaking of media, I'm here because my paper, the *Herald*, wants background on a headline gracing the papers of competitors outside the state—proclamations like 'Florida Seminole tribe goes to war again with state over gambling income.' I'd like to ask you a few questions."

"Then, let's get comfortable." April motioned to an overstuffed chair and loveseat that flanked a low coffee table. "We've been here before as a tribe; it's not new territory. Greed, jealousy, we may be talking corporate business but that doesn't mean basic human emotions don't come into play. And, as always, there's money to be found supporting anything, true or false, that can be used to stir up trouble."

"I'm assuming you're referencing outside interference, not fellow tribal interests?"

"The nature of the business begs competition, along with scrutiny from more than one side. If it appears that you're too big to fail, there's always those who want to make sure that you do. But yes, the most criticism comes from outside the tribes. For example, our state government decided that allowing people to bet when they are not on Indian lands gives us a monopoly by letting us benefit from online betting as well as sporting events."

"I understand that the legislature says the game compact violates the Indian Gaming Regulation Act. And you think there's been pressure put on lawmakers to make this decision?"

"Of course."

"What is being done? Can the tribes fight this? My paper quoted a spokesperson as saying the Seminole Tribe is reviewing the judge's opinion and considering what its next steps might be."

"Yes, there would seem to be options. Supposedly the door has been left open to other avenues for authorizing online betting for us. The secretary may agree to a new compact between the tribe and the state stating that it can only occur on Indian land. They could even file a notice of appeal and take the issue to the D.C. circuit court of appeals. Another possibility to decide the fate of online betting would be to get it onto the ballot in November."

"Is that the direction that you favor?"

"Too risky. It needs sixty percent voter approval. That might be difficult to get, and opening things up to the public begs millions being spent in advertisement to defeat us. But it looks like it's going to happen. I just know that the opposition would spare nothing to take away a part of what they see as the Seminole's power."

"How strong is the opposition?"

"All but one of the plaintiffs who want to keep the tribe from offering online betting own, live, or work on land close to an Indian owned casino. An additional co-plaintiff is a group that calls itself, No Casinos. It's a non-profit that opposes all expansion of gambling in Florida."

"That seems a little over the top. Does this group have any clout?"

"Yes and no. They have followers, supporters that regularly send them ten or twenty-five dollars a month. So, they've built a war chest. They're not a political group, per se, but operate like one. Actually, it's almost a cult but has the support of more than one state official. It's their tactics that scare me."

"How so?"

"They're good at masterminding situations that will get media attention, paint the casinos as dangerous, a draw for unsavory types that the average citizen doesn't want in his community. What happened to you Saturday night is a perfect example."

"You think that the incident in the parking garage was something more than petty thievery?"

"You'll laugh when I say I'm not a betting person." A wave of her hand took in a series of photographs on the wall behind her depicting various gaming activities offered by the casino. "But I'd put money on the guy making off with a few bucks from you was put up to the job. Thanks to you and your husband for not wanting media coverage. And don't ask me what's next. I don't know but I know it will be something. We're in the 'when and not if' stage."

"I'm not sure I'm comfortable looking over my shoulder. I'm trying to let go of what happened in the parking garage, but it's not easy. I appreciate your sharing with me."

"I wish the environment was different, less contentious, but success brings out the worst in people who don't have what they think should be theirs."

Julie nodded. "I'll be careful. Thank you."

A few more questions, some note-taking and an appointment to meet with the CFO the following morning. A story was forming but she needed some facts—money facts—and he could provide those. She walked back out into the foyer and paused once again to take in the enormity of the place. Glitz and glitter—those two words popped into her head; they were becoming synonymous with casino.

The thunderous noise that became apparent the closer she got to the front of the building didn't register until she'd walked out and then realized there were at least a hundred motorcycles filling the parking lot. Bikers. This was a little late for Florida's infamous Bike Week. And it certainly wasn't October's Bikefest. So, what was the occasion?

"Kinda takes your breath away, don't it?" The man just

outside the door turned to her, offering his hand. "Andy Thunderhawk, I was hoping I'd get the privilege of meeting you one of these days. It is Mrs. Pecos, isn't it?"

"Yes, I'm Julie Conlin, Ben's wife. And thank you for finding and returning my purse."

"My pleasure. Just sorry that you had to go through that." Julie shook his hand before turning back to gaze at the sea of motorcycles.

"Is this some kind of special celebration?"

"You'd think so, but this is just a twice a year get-together. Represents the four major clubs of South Florida. And then there's some hangers-on. See that Fat Boy over there at the end of the first row?"

"Uh, Fat Boy?"

"Sorry, that's a Harley model, popular with a lot of riders. That one belongs to Cal, Caleb Catawnee, the Indian Elvis. He likes to ride with the group if he's down this way when they meet. And there, two bikes over, there's another Fat Boy, older but in primo shape. That one belongs to Bo-Rowdy."

"Is that a person's name?"

"Street name for Beaufort Rowland, leading dentist from Orlando. Guy's got the bucks and the state's prettiest dental hygienist. See there?"

Julie watched a woman in leathers standing next to the dentist's bike take her helmet off and shake her head, releasing voluminous, cascading blond curls. Next, she unzipped the figure-molding jumpsuit revealing short shorts and a midriff-baring top. There wasn't a man among the parked bikes who wasn't watching this show. And Julie wasn't imagining it; the dentist seemed to be enjoying the attention his hygienist was getting. A mock curtsey and a wave to her audience and the show was over.

"Pretty thing and a good rider, too." Andy turned his attention back to Julie. "I know bikers got a bad rep, too rough, too loud—dangerous, even. But half the bikes in front of you are owned by pillars of their communities—doctors, bankers, a church deacon here and there. This is just a fun release for them—dress up, act the fool for a weekend, drive too fast, drink too much—you get the picture. In spite of all that, they're just pussycats."

Julie nodded, but nothing in front of her brought a purring Persian to mind. She was secretly glad that this wasn't Ben's sort of thing. "I'll keep that in mind."

"You know, if you need any help, any questions answered around here, come to me. The boss man decided that I couldn't go wandering around here without a title, so I became the Floor Manager. Just means I walk around a lot and get paid to keep an eye on everything."

"Thanks, Andy, it's always nice to know I have a source. In fact, first question, who's the boss man?"

"Good one. Oscar Billie is top of the heap and has been since this place started up. Different groups have tried to unseat him, but he's had sticking power."

"One more question, I'm meeting tomorrow with the Chief Financial Officer but I'm not sure of a name."

"That'd be Dale Epstein."

"Non-Indian?"

"Yeah, but he seems to know his stuff, brought in a good crew and some new ideas. Just look at that sea of metal on wheels out there in front of you. This place knows how to bring the money in. We're looking at one of Epstein's ideas."

"True, that's a lot of shiny objects."

"That's a lot of chrome. Course you know what they say? Chrome won't get you home but it sure will get you laid." Andy suddenly stepped back and exhaled loudly. "Oh my God, I am so sorry. That was a stupid thing to say. My apologies, no offense meant."

"And none taken." Julie smiled, "I'm sure there's more than a little truth to it."

Julie thanked Andy once again and walked back to the parking garage, taking a deep breath when she entered. Somehow in the light of day, the place looked absolutely tranquil. She passed several workers getting into their cars—must be lunch time. She knew there was a cafeteria for staff but it was probably good to leave the workplace once in awhile. She made it all the way to her car without a shiver and didn't stop once to look behind her. That was progress.

Chapter 7

Airports are fun. When Nathan had shared his views with Zac's mother, she'd admonished him by saying only the young would think that. But she had put the two of them on a plane in Seattle and wished them a good summer, making them promise that next year both would spend their vacation from school in Alaska. Oh, and Nathan had to promise to look after Zac. Nathan promised but thought that was stupid. Zac was just a little over a year younger. The difference wasn't that big—not quite fifteen to his sixteen. But, he guessed, a mom always worried if her child wasn't close by. They both called him Dad. Zac his natural child by birth and Nathan by being adopted when he lost the last of his family on the Navajo reservation in New Mexico. To gain a father, two mothers, and a brother all at once was about the best thing that had ever happened to him. And all that just a little over a year ago.

Most families seemed to have their own weird stories. For example, Raven, Zac's mom, was an Alaskan Native whose college love affair with Ben Pecos produced a baby that she kept Ben from knowing anything about for years. Wasn't it unusual that the father was never involved? So now, Ben's wife, Julie, inherited a stepson and shortly thereafter, him as son number two. He guessed he could wonder about it and never understand it. But it all came down to Nathan being a part of a family. And now he was on his way to Florida. How was that for good luck?

Nathan turned in his seat to look at Zac. How could someone sleep most of the day? But he hadn't missed anything. Travel was boring even if this was only his third flight ever—back and forth to school and now across country. Ben had texted them pictures of their new house with the top floor complete with bunk beds and two TVs. But it was the two surfboards leaning against a bedroom wall with the caption 'anyone interested?' that caught his attention and led to daydreams of fun.

Maybe he was making too much out of what the summer might be, but now all he could think about was sand and sea and surfboarding. Well, he might have to adjust his thinking to just paddle-boarding; he wasn't sure how big the waves were off the coast. He'd never seen the Atlantic Ocean before or even the Gulf. Ben was quick to point out that good surfing might mean a couple hours travel but just swimming in salt water would be closer. And that was okay, too. Anything to be near the water. This last year at school in Washington, he'd gone whale-watching in the Puget Sound. But that was a cold ocean. He couldn't imagine spending much time in it.

They were finally on the last leg of their journey—clear across the United States, Seattle to Miami. Ben texted that he'd monitor their flight schedule and meet them outside, in front of the baggage claim area, forty minutes after they landed, they'd have lunch and then drive back up to Hollywood. Ben had mentioned that he thought he'd found a job for him. A job meant the first money to be saved toward buying a car since he turned sixteen.

Nathan already knew what he wanted. A truck. Almost everyone on the reservation in New Mexico had a truck and where else could you safely carry a surfboard? Plus, he knew how to drive a truck. There weren't a lot of roads among the Navajo hogans, and he'd been allowed to take his grandfather's truck out into the desert once his cousin had taught him the basics. A job was perfect. He had two and a half months to add to his savings.

* * *

Ben hopped out of the Land Rover and opened the back of the SUV the minute he saw them walk out of the airport. Both boys were pulling suitcases. Watching them walk toward him, Ben would swear that Nathan had grown another inch or two in just the last few months. He had to be five eleven. Zac had some catching up to do but he was already five foot eight and Ben didn't doubt that he'd shoot up in another year or so. They were two good-looking kids. Dark hair, long on top, shaved close on the sides, Native features of high cheekbones and strong jawlines. In a rush of feeling, Ben realized how much he cared for his sons. What had started out as a shock was now a family that he couldn't imagine being without.

"Wow, what do you have in here?" Ben had started to hoist Zac's luggage up to the Land Rover's cargo area but instead rested it on the bumper. "This thing is heavy."

"Mom sent Julie some stuff for the house. Native things. There's a bunch of carvings, you know, wooden copies of totems, and a couple of masks."

"Sounds great, Julie will be thrilled." Ben scooted the bag to the back and made room for Nathan's. "Now we've got to figure out what we want to do for lunch. I was thinking about the food court at the casino."

"In the guitar building?" Zac turned to Ben. "Is that where your office is at?"

"Yeah, at the back. I thought you might like a tour of the place. I need to check a couple things, but then I'll be free for the evening."

It was a short twenty minutes until the Seminole Hotel and Casino came into view. And both boys were awestruck. It wasn't like Seattle didn't have the Space Needle, and he knew both boys had seen that; still, their reaction to the guitar-shaped building was priceless.

"Can you go up to the top?" Nathan had opened the window for a better view.

"Pretty close to it."

"It looks real. I mean like a giant or something could play it." Zac had pushed around Nathan from the backseat and was leaning partway out the window. "It looks like it has real strings."

"We're here." Ben pulled into a parking space that now had his name on a plaque attached to the back wall. The lower floor of the parking garage was already filling up, even most staff slots were taken.

"If you guys don't need anything out of your luggage, I'll lock the car." A couple negative shakes of the head and Ben pointed ahead of him. "Right this way, then."

He had locked his office, but there was a note on his desk. So much for security. But it was another command from his boss to stop by when he got in. Couldn't the man learn to text? Oh well, he'd find something for the boys to do and make his appearance in Mr. Billie's office. Ben had notified the HR receptionist that he would be gone for a couple hours after lunch and why. This must be important.

Ben was just about ready to step out into the hallway when he had a better idea than leaving the boys in his office while he was gone. He'd text Andy and see if he had a half hour to show the boys around. Ben would swear that Andy must have been standing outside, he got to his office so fast.

"Hey, my pleasure. I'm the best tour guide they got around here, but if you guys are up to it, I'd like your help. I promised the band that's coming in for tonight's performance that I'd help unload equipment. It's not a lot of heavy lifting, we just gotta push a few carts around—from the parking lot to the stage. You in? I can come up with a couple extra concert tickets for your work."

"Yeah, we're in." Nathan gave Zac a quick look and got a nod. "What band?"

"Well, not sure you've heard of them. Your Dad there is probably a fan—Smashing Pumpkins."

"1988. One of the first bands to mix it all together—pop, rock, goth, psychedelic, you name it." Ben added, "But they made it big." Would an 80's band even be of interest to the boys, Ben wondered, but didn't have to wait for an answer.

"That's Lit! Can we get their autographs?" Both boys were excited.

"I don't see why not. I can usually pull some strings around here." Andy gave the boys an exaggerated wink. "Now, let's get on out there."

Ben almost laughed out loud at how quickly both boys had jumped up and volunteered. This was a whole new experience for them. And they were in for some fun. He left his office unlocked and followed the impromptu work crew out the door.

* * *

Mr. Billie's assistant asked him to wait while her boss finished a call, and Ben was left to catch up on text messages. He knew twenty minutes wasn't that long but he'd rather be with the boys and not twiddling his thumbs. Finally, the door to the man's office opened and a somewhat flustered Mr. Billie waved him in.

"My apologies. I got the message that you were picking up your sons, but I need your reaction to something."

"Andy's taken over my job as tour guide, so I'm in no rush. How can I help?"

"I've had some disturbing news this morning. You may have noticed the motorcycles out front?" Ben nodded. "Well, a couple of riders got through security with boot guns on their person. Even the metal detectors didn't pick the guns up. I'm not saying there was any wrongdoing planned. I honestly think it was an oversight. They get so used to being armed and riding that way, they forget the rules. And we've got some real stringent ones around here, starting with guns."

"You'd have to—booze, gambling, and guns would be a toxic mix especially in today's world of act first, ask questions later. How can I help?"

"Hire up. I'm talking putting on ten more guards. Intersperse them—some in the parking garage and back lot, in addition to the Casino. And I want everyone put through training, the old guys as well as the new hires. I want active shooter training, you know, guy storms a game room, barricades the place, shoots it up, takes hostages— you get the picture. It's all too common today and I don't feel we're prepared."

"I think this is good planning. I'm on it."

"And beefing up security is only a part of our problem." The chairman paused. "I've been reluctant to address this, but we need a top to bottom evaluation. We're understaffed—badly so. A pandemic, fewer students looking for summer jobs, the lure of working from home … I know we're not alone, but most places of business don't cater to crowds of a hundred to five hundred at a time. Our restaurants have struggled; rat droppings were discovered in three kitchens, one of the pools was contaminated—you get the picture. In order to cut corners, we've gotten sloppy, failed to be proactive. All of this made a compelling argument to hire you."

"And I won't disappoint. I enjoy a challenge." Ben was trying to not dwell on 'rat droppings'—that might be more of a challenge than he wanted.

"I'll want progress reports as you proceed. It's not going to be cheap and I answer to the tribe."

"You'll get them. I'll start with adding security and setting up training. I'll check with tribal police and local law enforcement to see what might be offered through government channels. I'll include the FBI and Homeland Security. I know they have training videos, as well as experts in the field. What's the time frame?"

"Yesterday, of course. We'll need to expand housekeeping. I'd like to put a pest control expert on the payroll. This is Florida. Rats and other vermin are part of the landscape—as long as they stay outside. I've been thinking about all this for some time, but we haven't had a separate HR Director to initiate the plans. Now, we do." Chairman Billie stood. "I won't take up any more of your time. I know it sounds like I'm expecting ten-hour days from you, but set up a committee that you can trust and delegate, delegate, delegate. If you have questions, don't hesitate. I'm usually here. I've been accused of spending the night. But it all comes down to being a good neighbor. The tribe has been successful and I intend to see that success continue."

Ben shook the chairman's outstretched hand before heading back to his office. Wow. What a plateful.

Chapter 8

The boys begged to put a pop-up tent on the lanai and sleep outside. Screened in rooms were something new, not something common in either New Mexico or Alaska and even though it was after eleven, the boys didn't seem to mind having to set up their makeshift beds before going to sleep. They were still chattering away when Ben went inside. The evening had been an exciting one. Andy kept his promise and had come up with two passes to the show, and what was maybe the most memorable part of the evening, Zac and Nathan had each been paid one hundred dollars for helping the band's stage manager set up that afternoon—an unexpected windfall and a great start to their summer vacation.

"I have a feeling that the boys won't be getting up with

you in the morning." Julie was setting the timer on the coffee maker for seven.

"I think you're right. I'll come back at lunch and pick them up. I'll introduce them to the guy who's in charge of the valet service, and maybe one or more of the kitchen managers. I worry that they'll be given preferential treatment because of me."

"Maybe in the beginning but I can't imagine either one of them not working hard, proving themselves. I overheard talk of saving up money for a car on the way home. That's incentive for Nathan."

"And Zac?"

"He seemed willing to help Nathan—contribute toward his goal."

"I like the way the two of them get along. Makes me wish I'd had a brother."

"And now you have me. Not exactly the same, but not bad either," Julie laughed.

"Not bad at all now that you mention it." Ben grabbed her around the waist. "I can think of a fun way to end the evening."

* * *

Ben left a note telling Nathan and Zac that he'd pick them up at noon, packed a lunch, kissed Julie good-bye, and took off for the office. It'd been awhile since he'd had a regular work schedule. Nine to five seemed a little structured but he guessed he'd get used to it. The clean-up crews were already at work when he pulled into his parking space. Amazing how much litter there seemed to be, right down to ticket stubs.

First thing on the agenda was an ad. He'd rough out what he wanted to say and then get help in placing the ad. Age limitations, work history, salary, job definition—what was he leaving out? He wanted something showy, attention-getting so maybe a photo of the casino. He'd ask to see other help wanted ads the casino had placed before. He'd already set aside Friday and the following Monday for interviews. He thought he might get the most response from the Sunday *Herald*. But he also wanted to have flyers made. Libraries, the community center, the university—all had bulletin boards for help wanted notices. Online and hard copy would reach the young as well as older population.

The casino did their own printing—they almost had to with all the event publicity they posted almost daily—dining specials, musical events, gaming giveaways. Getting the word out in a timely manner meant success or failure. In the heavily populated surrounding area, local notices probably worked almost as well as newspaper ads. And radio. That was always a good way to get the word out. He'd take his ad copy to the Public Relations department and hope to be inundated with interviewees.

The boys were ready to go at lunchtime, a little sleepy but excited to be talking to people about jobs. Ben wasn't sure what dress code dictated for interviews at a car wash, but he encouraged jeans instead of shorts, and a real shirt instead of a T. And then felt like the out-of-touch parent when he walked with the boys to the car servicing office among two dozen young men and two women wearing shorts and t-shirts.

"Meet me at my office when you're finished." Even early in the afternoon, the wash bay had a line. Just another perk of playing the slots or hitting the tables. You might lose the rent but your car would be clean. In so many ways southern Florida lived by a different set of rules than he was used to. He might be on a reservation, but it didn't feel like it.

He barely had time to pull his chair up to the desk when there was a knock on the door.

"Come in."

The girl who entered was just that, a girl. She looked far too young to be wearing the skimpy one-piece outfit with a short skirt. It wasn't feathers and sequins but it was designed to get attention.

"How can I help you?"

"You're Dr. Pecos?"

"Yes."

"I'll just take a minute of your time." She stepped into the room and pulled the door closed behind her. "I'm Robbi, Robin Aponi. Phillip in PR asked me to run this ad by you and get your thoughts. I'm on my break so I've got a few minutes." Then she walked to the edge of his desk and put a folder in front of him. Paper-clipped to the front was a folded sheet of paper. She pulled the paper out from under the clip and put an index finger to her lips and mouthed, "Don't say anything." She opened the paper and placed it on the desk. It was a hand-written note.

I doubt you've thought about it but I have reason to believe that your office is bugged. I'm not comfortable talking here. Think of some reason to step outside.

Was this a joke? No, her demeanor said otherwise so he simply nodded before adding, "Thanks, Robbi. Basically, the ad looks good, but I'm not crazy about the graphics. I think to get the right attention, the art needs to scream casino, depending on the audience I'm trying to reach. And different areas, not just one. A pitch for kitchen help needs to feature a restaurant, a room in the hotel for housekeeping, the parking lot for the valet station help, and for the call to security officers, I want a panoramic view of both casino and hotel. Can I show you what I mean?"

"Sure."

"Come with me." Ben stood, handed Robbi's note back to her, picked up the folder, and walked ahead of her out his office door, leading the way to the front of the building. He stepped outside and held the door open for her to follow.

"We should be fine here. And I am looking for a really good all-inclusive photo of the valet station and front of the parking garage. Phillip may have something among stock photos. I'm assuming that you will be checking back in with him?"

"Yes, when he found out I was going to talk with you, he asked me to deliver the folder; but just for the cameras' sake, act like you're explaining the shot to me. Maybe point at the valet booth."

Dutifully, Ben did as he was told and ended with an expansive arm wave to take in the parking lot in front of him. "You talk, I'll continue to make notes on the copy in the folder."

"I'll be brief. Several of the women on the three-to-midnight shift have been harassed going to their cars. Maybe, stalked is a better word. No one has been harmed. But I think that's the next step. It has us rattled. And then when we heard what happened to your wife, it seemed like a pattern was forming."

"So, being stalked is something new?"

"Very new. It's never happened before this last week."

"Indian men?"

"Anglo, but it's hard to tell. They all wear baseball caps pulled low and sometimes hoodies. I'd swear that one man has a pony tail."

"What exactly do they do?"

"Mainly walk behind us; duck into doorways if someone comes. They only follow a single girl at a time. Last night, when I got back to my apartment, someone had broken in. Nothing was taken, but a window off the alley was open about six inches. The place had been turned upside down. I didn't find a thing missing. It seemed to be a warning more than anything else—sort of a 'we know where you live' warning. This in addition to being stalked, well, it's scary. Someone is bound to get hurt. Two girls quit just last week."

"As you know, we're advertising for more security officers—as quickly as I can find them. After I've brought some extra hands onboard, I suggest getting an escort to your car and leave in groups as often as you can—at least two of you together at all times. Park your cars close together—do anything to eliminate being by yourself."

Ben pointed at the edge of the parking lot, then pretended to make a note in the file. "That should do it." He handed the folder back to Robbi.

"Thanks for listening to me and taking our concerns seriously. This really has me scared." She took the folder and with a wave went down the steps then turned back. "There's another thing but I don't want to say anything until I know what's going on for sure. I overheard some things—things that are being planned. I'm convinced that we haven't seen the last of the threats and scare tactics."

This time she turned and continued along the sidewalk at the edge of the parking lot.

Between Andy's warning and now Robbi's evidence of scare tactics, Ben was getting a queasy feeling in his gut. But was he overreacting? Was this just corporate life with jealousies and petty grievances coming out in some kind of thug behavior? In a staff population this size, there was bound to be conflict. Did Robbi have a boyfriend who was more than overprotective? And what else did she know? She seemed genuinely frightened. Certainly, the nature of the business with money and booze and betting intertwined didn't help. The word volatile came to mind. Didn't it sort of invite foul play when the stakes literally were so high?

He was almost at his office door before he saw Zac and Nathan. That hadn't taken long. Ben hoped there was good news; then, one look at their faces and those ear-to-ear smiles said it all.

"Good news?" Both boys started to speak at the same time.

"Really good news," Zac offered first.

"We're employed," Nathan followed up. "Both of us in the same place. We were able to take part in some high school summer intern project. We're going to be washing cars and cleaning the bays. We're getting paid fifteen dollars an hour."

"That's great. What are the hours?"

"Nine to three with Monday and Tuesday off, but there's going to be overtime," Nathan said. "We need to pick up badges and come to work in the morning for training and then start Wednesday."

"I'm probably going to be late today. Anyone interested in the video gaming rooms? I'll show you where they are.

Just meet me back here at five."

* * *

"Do you think she knows?"

"Suspects, maybe."

"Better yet, did she tell the doc anything?"

"You're the one who can read lips. What were they talking about outside?"

"Kept turned away from the cameras, I couldn't tell. And it looked like they were discussing something about the grounds. The doc kept pointing at different things--the food truck, around the parking lot—there seemed to be lots of discussion."

"Well, I think we need to go bigger. This petty shit isn't even getting attention. I want a headline tomorrow in every newspaper around here. No Casinos isn't paying us for nothing-burgers."

"You'll get it, boss."

* * *

It was a great evening. Both boys excitedly talked about their respective jobs and then, taking iPads out to the lanai, went to bed early. By eleven all was quiet only to be broken by Ben's cell vibrating on the bedstand at three a.m. Nothing good ever came from calls in the middle of the night. Ben grabbed his phone and walked quickly to the bathroom and closed the door.

"Dr. Pecos?"

"Yes, Andy?"

"Yeah, you're needed over here. We've got a situation."

"What's going on?"

"A girl who works here was found murdered. A fellow worker found the body in the walk-in freezer. Somebody stabbed her, then tried to hide the body."

Ben suddenly didn't have a good feeling. Sixth sense told him he knew the victim. "Murder? Who was it?"

"I don't think you know her. Robin Alponi. She did a lot of step 'n fetch it sort of stuff for the staff, even worked the floor when needed. I don't have to tell you that we've got an upset bunch of women down here. Scared to death and don't want to answer the cop's questions. I got Mr. Billie on his way and he suggested you. Said this is what you're trained to do."

"He's right. I'm on my way."

"I'm going, too." He'd opened the door to see Julie standing in front of him. "I only heard one side, but murder? I think the *Herald* would expect me to check it out."

Chapter 9

When they arrived, Ben showed his badge and was allowed entry into the parking garage. Other than a few cars, the garage was a tomb. But walking back toward the main building, the scene was chaos. Police tape, groups of people some apparently being detained by officers, others milling around seeming to be more curious than involved—all under the harsh lights of the parking lot. Men, everyone armed, with tribal insignia on their shirt sleeves as well as state and county uniformed law enforcement, were part of the mix. The tribe was allowed by law to restrain and arrest non-Indian suspects when believed they were perpetrators of wrongdoing on Indian land. It was a court decision long fought for and put to good use. Staff members that he recognized were huddled together consoling each other, most quiet, others talking animatedly.

Julie stopped just inside the casino's entrance and pointed to a group of four women to her right. They appeared absolutely shellshocked and stood holding hands, one had her arm around the shoulders of the girl next to her. "I'm going to talk with them. They look like they could use comforting."

"Pecos, over here." Ben turned toward the voice. Oscar Billie was standing with two officers.

"Looks like I'm being summoned. I'll catch up with you later. Let me know if you need me for anything."

"I'm just going to listen. They look terribly upset."

"This is shocking for everyone. Thanks for coming with me." Ben squeezed her hand and then waved to Chairman Billie and walked to where he was standing.

Julie took a deep breath. She still wasn't really comfortable at the casino. And she told herself that was stupid. What had happened to her was over and done. An interrupted theft attempt, nothing more, nothing less. Her mantra? Get over it!

The girl closest to her stepped away from the group as she approached. "You're the wife of the new HR Director. Could we talk? I'm Annette Foster. I was Robbi's best friend—the one who was killed."

"Yes, of course. Doesn't look like anyone would bother us over there." Julie pointed to a couch in the foyer in front of several large potted plants. "Shall we? We won't be in anyone's way." Julie walked to the couch and sat down. "Were you both working tonight?"

"Yes, we're backup servers when there's a large crowd. The bikers usually make it an all-nighter; so, this time of year we both count on being busy during our shift." A nervous smoothing of her short skirt, and then, "No one knows this but I found the body first. I was so scared, I just ran. I think it was the bartender getting ice who reported it, or maybe Sammy. He was there, too. Robbi told me she was meeting him at break. I don't think either one saw me."

"I'm sorry. That's beyond shocking."

A nod. "Ms. Pecos, I need to tell you something."

"Of course, I'm listening."

"Last Saturday Robbi and I saw you at the concert. You were wearing a black mini dress. Robbi had a dress exactly like yours. We kidded around that you really had good taste. That black dress was Robbi's favorite. She wore it a lot. When we heard that you had been jumped in the parking garage and beaten; we both thought that the guy mistook you for Robbi. You both have red hair and, well, that dress … it just makes sense, especially now. I think someone was after Robbi, not you."

Julie sat back and held a deep breath before exhaling out her mouth. Mistaken identity?

Was that why there didn't seem to be anything taken, no money or cards from her billfold? But why Robbi?

"Was there a reason Robbi thought that she was the intended victim?"

"Yeah, I guess I can talk now. But other than your husband, please don't tell. I'm not sure it's safe to tell the cops."

"You have my word."

"Robbi had been dating Sammy Longman. He's the chairman's nephew and even though Robbi didn't tell me everything, it seems that she saw some things. I don't know whether it was in his car or at his apartment … anyway, it was stuff that could get her in trouble just for knowing.

Her and a lot of others."

"And you don't know exactly what it was?"

"She wouldn't say. I know there was a lot of money involved, and the reputations of some of the big names, people who run this place. Don't quote me and this is just a guess, but it sounded like doctored books. You know, report one thing to stay legal but fill your own pockets in the meantime."

"You're right, if true, that's dangerous information."

"I'm actually a little surprised. Robbi has always been so careful. She probably got a job at the casino because her grandfather worked here. You know, it was important that she be an exemplary employee, not bring attention to herself. But then, after her grandfather disappeared—"

"Disappeared? When was this?"

"Late spring. He went fishing which wasn't unusual. That was his choice of vacation and it was only going to be a long weekend—Easter break, first of March. His pickup was found about sixty miles south with his fishing gear still in the bed. Only his kayak was missing. The family has advertised but no one seems to have seen him. Unfortunately, this isn't uncommon for him. He was a bit of a shaman and sometimes would take off, not telling anyone where he was going. Sometimes he'd spend a week or two in meditation. But it's been two months now. He's never been gone that long before."

"What's his name?"

"Leonard Holt."

"Holt? Not Aponi? He's her mother's father?"

Annette shook her head. "No, her father's father. I know this gets confusing but Robbi's family was a victim of the Indian Act Naming Policies of the early nineteenth century. Someone decided that in order to assimilate quickly, Anglo sounding names would be a benefit. The family living near a wooded area received the name of Holt. Aponi is a girl's name and means butterfly. Robbi decided to make Aponi her last name—kind of a perverse way to call attention to her heritage. She always said she'd assimilate just fine."

"Does her family live near here?"

"Her father is deceased. It was her grandfather who stepped in and supported his son's family. Robbi used to call him a poster-child Indian. He'd made it big; at least, a lot of people saw it that way. He'd graduated from University of Oklahoma in marketing and finance, maybe thirty years ago, on a government scholarship. He'd worked at the Indian casinos on and off for twenty years, first in Tampa and later here where he was Dale Epstein's righthand. Leonard really smoothed the way for an outsider to join the ranks of an Indian establishment. I don't think our CFO made many decisions without his input."

"That's quite high praise." She paused, then asked, "What was Robbi like?" Julie felt a slight change of subject might be welcome; she didn't want to stray too far from gathering information on Robbi. And talking about the deceased would hopefully lessen the pain, put a happier spin on things. And she got the smile, she'd hoped for.

"Outside of work, she was a wild-child, a prankster, always into things. We all teased her about dating Sammy— he's three years younger. You know, cradle-robbing? But she took it in fun. They were really close. They'd gotten together last summer and stayed in contact over the school year. I think they were starting to make plans, you know, together forever type plans?"

"Was she well-liked by her co-workers?"

"*Loved* by them is more like it. I don't think I've ever seen her mad at someone. Or hear her say a bad word about anyone. She was the sister I never had. I would trust her with anything. She would do anything for you—loan you money, clothes, listen to your problems. She knew I needed money so she talked me into working a double-shift with her tonight. Usually we work three to midnight, but tonight we were on until seven." A pause. "I'm going to miss her so much."

Julie pulled a packet of Kleenex from her purse and offered it to Annette before putting an arm around her shoulders. "I appreciate you telling me this. I know I don't have to tell you to be careful. I'm here if you need to talk. I'll be spending a lot of my work time here at the casino, filling in the blanks on a story for the *Herald* about the casino's success. What I'd like to do now is interview you." Julie opened her billfold and took out her press credentials clipping the badge to the pocket of her denim shirt.

"No, I don't think I could talk about this." Annette pulled away and started to stand.

"Wait. I'm not looking for comments on her death. I want to present a human portrait of Robbi. You knew her. You are in the perfect position to share the heart-warming anecdotes that people will remember. I don't want Robbi to just be a statistic, a dead waitress in a casino. I want people to relate, to think of themselves or their children. Help make her memory a good one. You've already helped me see Robbi and the good things about her."

Annette sat back on the couch. "I can do that. I don't want people to read in something that's not there. She was a hard worker who spent every summer out of school here. You know, she graduated this year—with honors. She worked to pay her own bills and help her family. She was on a full scholarship from her tribe. I'm not a Native but even with the tribe's help, I can see how hard it was for her to work, go to school, and still help those around her. Her major was social studies but she had wanted to go to law school and study tribal law. This was going to be her last free summer for awhile."

"That's exactly the kind of information that I can use." Julie took a small notebook out of her purse. "Let's start with her school work. I'm going to play up a life cut short, promise snuffed out, a loss for indigenous people everywhere. Do you think any of her other friends would like to comment?"

"Probably. We're family here—in the real sense of the word. We care for one another. I think the other servers are still in the dressing room. Do you want to check?"

"Yes, let me just tell my husband where I'm disappearing to. I'll be right back."

* * *

Ben watched Julie and Annette walk toward the elevators and waved back when Julie caught his eye and pointed upstairs. They were probably going to the dressing rooms. He was glad she had come with him. Robbi's friends were going to feel a lot more comfortable sharing with Julie. And that freed him up to hunt down Andy and try to understand what had happened. He found Andy in the hallway at the back of the Beach Club Bar and Grill, standing to one side of the hectic scene playing out at the walk-in cold storage unit. Medical personnel, casino management, someone in uniform taking pictures between shouted instructions by someone who appeared to be the coroner, and cops trying their best to keep order and disperse the crowd already filling the hallway and spilling out of the restaurant; the area was chaos. Andy pulled him aside and motioned toward a side door.

"We'll be out of the way over here. I wish I could tell you what happened. But answers? I don't have any. This is a tough one. That kid was a sweetheart. Didn't have an enemy." Andy kept running his hands through his hair. "Some sick son of a bitch took her out—for no reason as far as I can see. My guess is she interrupted something, somebody saying or doing what they weren't supposed to. Back here in the hallway, nobody saw anything. I don't know what she was doing but I'm assuming that her boss sent her to the walk-in for supplies—pick up something for him before she went on break. A trip she's made hundreds of times. But this time someone was waiting."

"Could she have been set up?"

Andy sighed and shook his head. "I'd doubt it. Well, maybe, but I can't imagine who would do that. The chef left a Michelin Star restaurant in Orlando to come here last year. He's a bit of a prima donna but has a right to be. He's a big draw, been on those TV cooking shows—a real celebrity. Reservations can be a month out—especially for a group. I hadn't heard any rumors of problems with his staff. Robbi had a boyfriend, so it wasn't anything like that."

Suddenly shouting outside the back door drowned out Ben's next question. Andy motioned to Ben to follow him and quickly reached the door with Ben a half-step behind.

"What's going on out here?" Andy yelled above the noise.

No one even turned his way. Two tribal cops, one with

his gun pulled, were cuffing Sammy Longman who had been pushed face first against the side of a law enforcement SUV. Another cop on a radio was standing to the side. While one cop held the car's door open, another not too gently pushed Sammy into the backseat.

Andy walked toward the SUV. "I'm going to repeat myself—what's going on here?"

"Just taking Mr. Longman here in for questioning." The cop who seemed in charge turned toward Andy. "I think we've got a person of interest who can tell us a few things about Ms. Aponi's death."

"Based on what?" Andy's tone had a hint of belligerence, Ben thought. This wasn't going to get Andy any points.

"And who are you?" The cop holstered his gun and stepped away from the SUV.

"Grounds Overseer and Casino Floor Manager for the Seminole Casino and Hotel, Andrew Thunderhawk." Andy held out the lanyard with his corporate badge which contained a photo. "Mr. Longman is an employee of mine—I believe I have a right to know why you are removing him from the premises."

Ben thought for a moment that the cop wasn't going to answer. Then, he said something to the officer now in the SUV's driver seat and the man handed over a plastic zip-lock bag containing a cell phone.

Without opening it, the cop held the bag up. "You want to know grounds? See this? Mr. Longman's phone contains text messages to the deceased setting up a place and time to meet. We believe that Mr. Longman waited for Ms. Aponi in the walk-in cold storage unit having given her an exact time for their meeting which just happens to coincide with the exact time of her murder."

"He was dating Robbi Aponi, for Christ's sake—they were a couple. She was probably on her break. Why wouldn't they meet?" Belligerence was giving way to exasperation, Ben noted. Should he step in?

"And I'm sure you'll agree that often affairs of the heart can lead to unwise choices possibly driven by jealousy of one individual fearing the other has been unfaithful. We've been told by those with first-hand information that Mr. Longman had reason to believe that Ms. Aponi was romantically involved with someone else."

"And just who are these people with 'first-hand information'? Do they have names or have you been listening to vague tales of finger-pointing by those wanting their fifteen minutes of fame?"

"I doubt that, but we'll find out soon enough." With that the cop handed the bagged phone back to the cop driving and walked to the opposite side and got in. Ben and Andy watched the SUV back out and head for the driveway that would take them to the main road back to town.

"I'm assuming that you don't believe the cop's insinuations—that Sammy might have had a reason to harm Robbi."

"No way. I know those kids. It was a great match. He'll be a sophomore this year; she just graduated last month. It had all the ear-markings of turning into something permanent—they'd been a couple for a year."

"Any ideas what might be behind her murder?"

"No, but I'm going to be asking some questions." Andy paused. "I'll keep you in the know. Can I ask the same of you?"

"Absolutely."

"Then I'm going to hang out with the coroner. I'll

check in with you in the morning. Nobody is going to get much sleep tonight. Or I guess I should say what's left of it." Ben watched Andy walk back to the cold storage unit. There didn't seem to be anything else that he could do— might be time to look up Julie and go home.

* * *

All three men leaned forward intently watching the scene play out on the screen in front of them, cops and suspect along with the coroner walking in and out of the walk-in cooler, sirens reverberating through the alleyway below as an adjoining screen showed two more cars of law enforcement joining the group.

"I think we've got a winner there. Papers are going to have a heyday. Young love, jealousy, the taint of lives lived in the glare of neon lights. Just the suggestion of seediness." The man sat back, pushed his chair away from the table and folded his arms over an ample stomach. "Exactly what I was looking for."

"Nice touch, setting up the Longman kid. Kudos to whoever thought of that one. Puts the whole gruesome matter of murder right smack in the chairman's lap. We're going to get some mileage out of this." This man, who had remained standing, turned back to the screen. "The headlines are going to look good. Sure-fire topic of discussion come morning. I'm thinking *GMA* will want some interview time or maybe the *Today Show*. Indians and the Seminole Casino and a few splashy pictures of the guitar? That's guaranteed to get interest. Oh, and before I forget; did our man find anything in the girl's apartment the other night?"

"Not that I've heard. He checked the dressing room here, too. Went through the pockets of her uniforms. Could have been a false tip saying she was on to something." The man changed the screen in front of him to zero-in on the front parking lot and peered closely at the three cop cars and an ambulance now almost impossible to see as they exited the property by a side road.

"All the better. What's that saying? If you're too big to fail, you probably already have … isn't that how it goes? I think we've got enough dirt to get the ball rolling. There's enough info out there now for the public to make up their own minds—is an Indian owned conglomerate really a benefit to this community? Or has this state allowed something dangerous to manifest itself among law-abiding citizens? Given control of large amounts of money to heathens? Just the sort of thing to sway a voter. Thanks to the ASPCA, greyhound racing has been outlawed in Florida. Voters think it's their civic duty to right a wrong."

A third man switched the righthand screen's image back to a panoramic view of the hallway and walk-in cold storage unit. "Let's keep an eye on the investigation. If something turns up, we want to know about it first." All three men nodded; each satisfied with what had turned out to be a successful evening.

Chapter 10

Back at the house, Julie opted for a cup of tea while Ben chose to make coffee. The boys were still asleep. Something to be said for that near-death coma of teenagers; still, they kept their voices just above a whisper, finally moving out to the front porch with their drinks.

"I can't believe what that cop was saying. I rather think Andy has a truer picture of Robbi and Sammy's relationship. Annette's description of the two certainly seems to support Andy. But that still leaves the question of why. What could Robbi have been involved with that got her killed?"

"I think she knew something. And maybe something she'd learned because she was dating Sammy."

"Like what?"

Ben shared his meeting with Robbi including her insistence on secrecy, suspecting his office could be bugged. "Much of what she reported would come under the heading of harassment—stalking, for example. But I didn't get the idea that there was anything life-threatening."

"Robbi's closest friend is convinced that what happened to me was an aborted attempt to harm Robbi. It seems we both have the same black mini dress—and the same color of hair. I believed Annette. It explains a lot—the lack of a true robbery, a thump on the head and nothing more serious for me."

"I don't want to believe that. It scares me."

"I don't think we can ignore it—not after what's happened."

Ben got up and, walking to where she sat, pulled Julie into an embrace. "I won't lose you. I don't know what that's going to take, but I want you out of harm's way. Tell me you're going to be careful."

"I promise." She put both arms around Ben's neck and they just stood there, together, silent, letting their closeness speak for itself.

Finally, Ben stepped back. "I'm dead on my feet. It's five-thirty. I'm going to leave a note for the boys to not disturb us so that we could maybe get another couple hour's rest. I remember Nathan saying a guy from valet parking lives down the block and offered him a ride to the casino whenever he needed it. Hopefully that will work for this morning."

Julie nodded, "Good idea."

* * *

Sleep, it turned out, was an illusion. A shower, a bowl of Corn Chex and Ben decided to just get an early start on the day and maybe be able to take off early. Julie followed suit. She needed to get her notes together and see if she could fill in any gaps for whatever reporter was working on the story. The boys opted to catch a ride with their new friend and not go in at the crack of dawn.

Ben had just stepped through the casino's front door when Andy made eye contact from behind the information desk and mouthed, "Boss." He pointed his index finger against the palm of his opposite hand, indicating Ben's office. And sure enough, his office door was wide open and Ben could see the back of the chairman's head. He'd pulled up a chair in front of Ben's empty desk and was waiting— not too patiently if fingers nervously drumming on the desk's edge were any hint of nerves or lack of patience.

The minute Ben entered, the chairman rose. "Good to see you starting the day on time. The quicker we decide on how to handle last night the better. I want you to call a meeting for all staff at nine. Use the auditorium on the second floor. I want everyone there; we all need to be on the same page. And don't believe that bullshit about Sammy. I want to know who this witness is, this know-all person who sicced the cops on him. It's an out and out lie, but the cops are using it to keep Sammy behind bars."

"I'll get on it. See you at the meeting at nine."

The chairman nodded and left—curt, with barely concealed anger, pulling the office door closed a little too forcefully. Hindsight told Ben he should have offered condolences of some sort. Or maybe assurances, but of what? That he'd find the liar? The one who fingered Sammy as the murderer? But how would he do that? It was just one more unplanned, but time-consuming cog in the wheel. As the new guy on the block, Ben had too many demands on his time as it was. There would be no easing into this job, taking his time to get oriented.

* * *

"It's just not true." Julie sat forward in her chair and made eye contact with her boss. "I've talked with people who knew the two of them. Everyone points to a solid relationship. One with a future."

"Our undercover person says this Robbi was seeing someone else. Older, maybe with the wrong temptations."

"What do you mean by wrong temptations?"

"Money. Big money. The kind that can turn a twenty-one-year-old's head by offering the kind of luxury that would appeal to a working girl. Don't you wonder who bought her that new, silver Corvette? It sure as hell wasn't Sammy Longman on a parking lot security guard's pay. But maybe it wasn't money; maybe she was just tired of wearing next to nothing and getting pinched on the butt. How should I know? That's your job to find out." Suddenly Ken Usher leaned against the back of his chair, tipped his head back, closed his eyes, then shook his head before opening them. "Listen, kiddo, I'm sorry. I didn't mean to come off as some smartass, know-it-all, misogynist. If you want the truth, I'm pissed that suddenly the casino is coming off as less than a stellar member of the community. It couldn't come at a worse time—elections can be swayed by people's perceptions."

"I take it this is the first trouble, so to speak, that there's been?"

"Yeah, more or less. Chairman Billie has always kept a tight rein on things. Oh, there's been the occasional DUI arrest outside the casino, and a couple years back someone threatened a dealer but, overall, it's been an orderly neighbor."

"I'll see if I can find out anything."

"That'd be great. And, Julie, I want you to contribute a positive picture of this Robbi. I want to play down the love-triangle approach. Not sure what the explanation is but maybe mistaken identity? I'll leave that up to you. And discretion? I need to trust you on this. I want to see anything before it becomes print."

"Of course, I'll share. You have my word."

"This is important for the paper. I don't want anything whitewashed, but I want people to feel safe. The casino snagged the Miss Teen USA contest coming up next month by beating out a bid by Orlando. It's big. I don't need to tell you how lucrative that will be for the area—for the entire southern part of the state for that matter. The paper has invested in a lot of backstory—photos, history, lots of interviews. We're even putting a former winner on the payroll just to give us the inside, behind the curtains kind of access that will sell papers and make every teenage princess wannabe yearn for a tiara. And, at least for the next three weeks, I want that to be your priority, too."

"Sounds fun and challenging. I look forward to it."

* * *

Ben had gotten the word out before eight and by eight-thirty, the auditorium was beginning to fill. The meeting would be quick—condolences from Chairman Billie, warnings to be vigilant, a request for information no matter how seemingly trivial. The casino would be closed and this would be an all-personnel required attendance.

Chairman Billie went first, assuring staff that security was being beefed up and that safety took priority. He talked briefly about Robbi and how she had been a valued friend to so many of her fellow workers. She would be missed. He announced a private service to be held at the casino on the following Friday, a celebration of Robbi's life, and all were invited. There was no mention of Sammy Longman. Ben put in a plea for possible summer hires and assured everyone that his door was always open. There was a brief discussion concerning the upcoming pageant with a reminder that a schedule of events had been posted on the casino's website. And then it was everyone back to work.

This time there were two people who had gotten back to his office before he did. He recognized April Bowlegs, Administrative Assistant to Chairman Billie, but the man with her was a new face. Both stood as he walked in, April introduced her companion as Robert Holmes, Executive Director of Miss Teen USA.

"I don't know if anyone told you, but the casino is hosting the Miss Teen USA pageant next month. It's a coup for us—we'll have young women representing the fifty states and District of Columbia with their families staying here at the casino. I've assigned the office just two doors down as Mr. Holmes's headquarters while he's working on preparations."

"Sounds like a great event. I'm sure there will be a lot of interest. Let me know if I can be of help."

"Well, for starters, I'm hoping that your sons will sign up to be escorts. We had a couple cancellations but I'm told that you might be willing to have them volunteer to help us out. It will require a few rehearsals, having a tux made—at the pageant's expense, of course—a brush-up on table manners for the banquets, as well as a few ballroom dance lessons, and a review of the itinerary and how they can best make their contestant feel comfortable. We'll have age-appropriate special events, possibly a group visit to a Marlin's game, for example. Some of the younger girls, the fourteen-year-olds, probably haven't traveled much and they will be living in a somewhat foreign environment for a few days. Their escorts will be young men they can rely on for answers to their questions and help in getting around."

"I'm sure both boys will be thrilled to be involved."

"Good. Have them contact my people as soon as possible. I'll give their names to my organizers. We'll be having a general meeting in the morning and they need to be on their list." Robert Holmes handed Ben his business card. "I'll be bringing quite a crew down. We're headquartered in Chicago, but have learned to set up camp wherever each year's pageant takes place. My assistant is already here. It's important to have your sons make an appointment as soon as they can, to go over what will be expected of them and to set up a fitting for a tux. Time is running out."

The meeting was a short one, but Ben couldn't wait to get the boys' reaction. He picked up his phone and texted the two with an invitation for lunch. Meet him at the food court at eleven.

Chapter 11

"No shit?" Nathan looked incredulous. "I get to take a Miss Teen USA contestant out?"

"Not exactly *out*, more like acting as her guide while she's here. Showing her around, that sort of thing." Ben was trying not to use the term 'escort'—sounded too much like money was going to be exchanged for acts deemed unbefitting of a contestant. My God, did that sound like he was a cast-off of the Victorian era? Even mentioning sex was off limits? Sometimes he wondered if fatherhood would have been easier if he'd raised the boys from infants. Somehow catching up with them as teens had its drawbacks, and left him with too many questions. It was just too easy to do or say the wrong thing. Or worse, give him some kind of old fogey status.

"That's okay, I can do that." Nathan nodded and didn't keep a smile from pulling one corner of his mouth back.

Was Ben reading something into all this or did Nathan look a little smug? Was this an opening to discuss conduct? Do's and don'ts of being casino representatives? Ben turned to look at Zac. A year and a half difference in age seemed to make a difference in level of testosterone, too. Zac had no 'cat that ate the canary' look. More like excited interest.

"Each of you will be assigned to a contestant."

"Can't we pick?" Zac spoke up. "What if they give us someone we don't like?"

"I don't think this is a matter of liking or not liking. This is a job. You're being hired to represent the pageant authorities, the Miss Teen USA corporation, as well as the casino. I think the assignments will be made for you, and I'm sure you'll be courteous and make the most of any situation."

"So, what happens next? Will Zac and I get leave from the car wash? I mean, we just started; are they going to let us do this pageant thing and then just take us back?"

"Yes. If you're not needed by the pageant, you'll work at the car wash but the pageant takes precedence. Actually, it is sort of an honor. You're being trusted to be ambassadors for the Seminole Enterprise." Ben was proud of himself, ambassador was a great word—sounded important, anyway.

"So, what is this going to pay?" Spoken like a kid saving up for a car, Ben thought.

"Don't quote me but I think I heard twenty-five dollars an hour mentioned. And, of course, any entertainment—movies, concerts, dinners—will be paid for by the contest representatives. There's going to be a meeting tomorrow morning. You need to call and make sure you're on their list of attendees. Apparently, they've already made assignments—paired everyone up. Remember, you'll be just two young men out of fifty-one. I know there are some stringent rules—time constraints, that sort of thing. And you'll get a list of must-attend events—a formal dinner and dance, for starters. There's even a suggested dress code. No torn jeans, for example."

"Not even jeans with the knees out?" Nathan seemed to lose a little of his enthusiasm.

"That's my understanding. Nothing too faded, either."

"Where are all the other guys coming from?" Zac asked.

"The *Herald* published an application at the end of the school year. Apparently, the paper forwarded those to the pageant committee. I guess teens from all over the state responded. They had some late cancellations—that's when you were added to the list."

He certainly had both boy's attention. For once, a topic of conversation was of greater interest than the triple-decker, double cheese burgers in front of them. The food court was filling up and it was getting late. The place was popular any time of the day, not just for lunch, but as inviting as it might be to continue the discussion of the pageant, the three of them needed to get back to work.

"Ten o'clock tomorrow in the auditorium. I can't wait to hear how it goes."

* * *

Zac and Nathan signed in at exactly nine forty-five the

next morning and found seats together in the center section of the cavernous room. Nathan wasn't going to let on but he was secretly thrilled with this new assignment. Like how many guys got to hang around with pageant contestants? The guys at school wouldn't believe him. He'd take a lot of selfies. There was a podium and four chairs on the stage in front of him and the entire room quieted as two women and two men walked out.

There was the usual welcome and introductions. One of the men gave a brief history of the pageant. The match-ups had already been done and each escort would receive a manilla envelope with the name and contact information of his "date" along with a schedule of events—times, places and dress code whether they opted for a movie night or a Miami Marlin's baseball game.

Following state mandates no one under the age of twenty-one would be allowed in the gaming areas of the casino without an adult. That rule applied to any establishments serving alcohol. Restaurants closing their bars for the occasion were listed. Most meals would be catered and occur in designated areas—the auditorium, pool-side, and the food court.

Each was encouraged to contact his assigned young woman before the pageant began, sharing appropriate personal information that would make their meeting more comfortable. A woman who introduced herself as the Director of Chaperones—yes there would be adults at each event--put up the pageant's URL and passcode to free email and Wi-fi service via an overhead projector and massive screen at the back of the stage. They were to use pageant supported technology in preference to their own, for security's sake.

The other woman on the stage discussed formal dress. For those needing a tux, there was an alphabetical listing of who, where, and when they were supposed to meet with a seamstress. A men's ready-to-wear in downtown Hollywood had been designated as ground zero for alterations. They were encouraged to get this requirement out of the way quickly as all finished garments had to be ordered and flown in. Only two weeks remained before opening night.

The last pageant representative discussed transportation. No one would be driving his own car. All travel outside the casino would be provided by Uber. If they chose the off-campus game, buses would get them there. The planning was extensive and exacting. Nothing had been left to chance as far as Nathan could see. He wasn't thrilled about someone ordering his life and telling him what to do, but the payoff seemed to be worth it. The presentation ended after a brief Q&A with a montage of past pageants, flitting across the screen with emphasis upon young men squiring beautiful young women to various events.

"What do you think?" Zac followed Nathan out of the auditorium and joined the line waiting to be handed their envelopes.

"I'm kinda glad it's for less than a week." And Nathan wasn't fibbing; he figured that he could survive anything for a short length of time. Both boys took their envelopes outside before opening them.

"Hey, look. My contestant is from Alaska. That's great. Alana Eberly lives in Fairbanks but was born in Anchorage. That makes things easy. I won't have to explain so much about where I live. Where's yours from?"

Nathan pulled a wad of papers from his envelope then

put back all but the top introductory letter. After quickly scanning it, he looked up, "Skyler Thompson is from California."

"Any pictures?" Zac was already leafing through the contents of his envelope looking for a picture of Alana.

"Wow. Look." Nathan pulled out an 8 X 10 glossy, a professional photo that was probably a staple of a press kit—wasn't that what the organizers had called the information in their envelopes? Nathan took a breath and almost forgot to exhale. Long blond hair over one shoulder and piercingly blue eyes under thick black lashes stared back, but it was the quirky smile that seemed caught in those eyes that commanded his attention. "She's beautiful."

"She looks old."

"Seventeen, it says here."

"You don't think she's too old for you?" Zac ducked the playfully thrown punch to his shoulder. "Just saying … that's a year older than you are."

"I think I can handle it. So, let's see this *Alana*."

Zac slipped out the 8 x 10 photo from his envelope. This time dark hair fell from a center part touching both shoulders while curling wisps framed a heart-shaped face. Nathan studied the dark eyes. There was something mischievous about the way she looked out from the photo—like someone used to trouble but also welcoming it. Had her mother looked at a wild animal while she was pregnant? Maybe trickster rabbit? The Navajo would think so. No, there was an honesty in that face and a knowledge of the mysterious. According to Native legend, it was much more likely that a raven had visited her mother before she gave birth. But an Anglo might think she was a Gypsy child.

"She's pretty. I like her and she's my age, fourteen."

Zac carefully slipped the photo back in the envelope. "This is going to be fun."

Suddenly the summer wasn't going to be all work. Nathan had already talked Zac into getting Alana to agree to seeing a Marlin's game. He pulled his phone out to text Skyler; fingers crossed that she liked baseball.

* * *

"You want to know how to spell disaster? M-I-S-S T-E-E-N U-S-A, that's how." Andy had followed Ben into his office but stayed standing obviously agitated. "And look at this. We don't need people suggesting we might fail." He opened the newspaper that he was carrying and folded it to reveal the editorial page.

Pageant having second thoughts? Can Seminole Hotel and Casino pull it off? Assure the safety of contestants?

"Who the hell writes this stuff? Where do they get their information? Half the world is going to be watching us—that's bad enough—but planting negative questions? Setting us up to fail. That's just uncalled for. Gives the community a black eye before we've even had a chance to show what we can do."

Ben picked up the paper and scanned the article. The recent murder was mentioned, as was Julie's supposed parking lot robbery. Now where had that come from? To the best of his knowledge, the incident had been kept under wraps. Those on the inside knew about it but supposedly no one else. But why mention it at all? Wasn't that biting the hand that feeds it? Who stood to gain from casting doubt on the safety provided by the corporation that supported this community?

"Has the casino gone through something like this before? Making the news for all the wrong reasons?"

"Actually, not that I can remember—and I date back ten years. We've enjoyed pretty positive press. I guess I've just chalked up what's happened recently to more people moving into the state and, by the numbers, we're going to have some crime to deal with. We did have that mosh-pit incident about four years ago that sent nine kids to the hospital with relatively minor injuries. Since then, we've made adjustments—pushed seating closer to the stage and put on extra security for music events that are a big draw for teens."

"Which reminds me, I've interviewed five guys that I'm thinking of bringing onboard. Three, at least, have prior training in security, but the other two will need to be brought up to speed quickly."

"Leave it to me. I've already reserved a couple spots in the county training program that we've used before. They'll at least have the basics under their belts by pageant time. I'd like to think that each girl having an escort will keep them safer than having them wander around by themselves."

"I hope you're right." Would either Zac or Nathan be of help in an emergency? Maybe. Ben hoped they wouldn't be tested. There was a certain amount of innocence that seemed missing in young people's lives today. "Oh, Andy, I almost forgot. Where is the service being held for Robbi Aponi? I think it's in this building."

"Yeah, downstairs, first floor in the atrium on Friday. There'll be microphones and people can stop by and share anecdotes. It'll be a short service shared by the local priest and a tribal elder." Andy chuckled, "I bet if Robbi had her druthers, she'd vote to be buried in that brand new

Corvette of hers."

"The black and silver one? The one that was always parked a couple cars down from me in the garage?"

"One and the same. Her granddaddy's gift to her for college graduation this spring. Maybe the last thing he did before just disappearing."

"Correct me if I'm wrong but it would seem to me if someone just disappears, there would be a concentrated effort to find him."

"Yeah, normally you're right. But Leonard Holt was known to take off. Drove his boss, that new guy Epstein, crazy. They'd say he went 'walk about' if he were an Aussie. Old Leonard's in his seventies and every year that I've known him, he's taken some days off to just go meditate in the wilds."

"By himself?"

"As far as I know. He always waited until after tax season. He did taxes for his people free of charge right out of his office here in the casino. Not many people command the respect that he does."

"You sound like you think he'll be back."

"Nothing points to him not coming home. Yeah, he's been gone longer than usual, but there was talk about how this was a pilgrimage, a journey to thank the spirits for a long, productive life. There was talk of him having some health issues, but I don't know anything for sure. I just know Robbi was worried, kept at him to get checked at the Indian Health Service clinic over by Tampa."

"Sounds like he was close to Robbi."

"Her grandparents just about raised her—and did a damn fine job if I do say so. I can't imagine how the old man's gonna take her death. It won't be pretty." Andy looked at his watch. "Damn. Look at the time. I need to get back to work."

"I'll walk you out. I need to check in with Zac and Nathan. This was the morning of the big meeting for pageant staff, I'm curious to get their reaction."

As they reached the end of the hallway, Andy stopped. "Why do I sense that you didn't follow me out here to check on the boys."

"Am I that transparent?" Ben smiled, "You're right. There's something I've been wanting to run by you. Talking about Robbi made me realize I shouldn't put it off any longer."

"OK, how can I help?"

"I'd like you to sweep my office—make sure there are no listening devices planted or cameras for that matter. Robbi refused to even talk with me in the office, said it was bugged. We literally met out at the edge of the parking lot in front. If it is 'live', that would support what you warned me about when we first met—that there are people who would like to see me get into trouble."

"Robbi refusing to talk inside means she had a good reason to suspect that somebody's listening in. And, you're right, it would support an inside intent to catch you at something. Well, this here's your lucky day. I just happen to own a bug detector. I sometimes come back to check on the night shift and tonight's my night for this month. I'll give your office a once over and text you what I find. And if I find something, I suggest you don't mess with it. Leave it in place and just be the wiser because you know where it is. Don't want anyone to know you're on to them, though for the life of me, I don't know who I'd point a finger at."

* * *

The chatter at the dinner table was all about the pageant. Zac and Nathan shared pictures of their assigned contestants and filled Ben and Julie in on what was expected of them, including needing a ride into town for a tux consultation in the morning.

"What's the first big event?" Ben needed to be put on the list to receive a daily schedule.

"There's a dinner and dance in the Pavilion. I think that's the first planned event. We get a couple afternoons and one free choice activity to choose from, too. You know, like swimming, movies, or a Marlin's game." Nathan left the table and brought back his envelope, shuffling through the contents. "Yeah, here's the formal invitation to the dinner/dance." He handed the card to Ben.

"Classy. Gold lettering, embossed outline of the guitar, on an off-white make-believe parchment with its own envelope already addressed to your young lady—this is impressive." Ben handed the invitation to Julie.

"Yeah, Skyler's looking forward to it."

"You've been in touch already?" Julie looked surprised.

"We've texted. I told her I needed to know if she wanted to go to a movie or a Miami Marlin's game—the bus was filling up. That's kinda a fib but I wanted to know if she liked baseball."

"What was the answer?" Ben was actually impressed with Nathan's attention to detail.

"I got a yes, but I think she'd prefer a movie."

"Zac, have you talked with Alana?"

"Sort of. She's going to call me this evening. She's even been to my village. Her mother works for the state, and she's traveled with her mom all over Alaska."

The boys excused themselves after double-dips of

Cookies & Cream and Ben put on a pot of coffee. When he walked back into the dining room, Julie handed him a copy of the *Herald*'s editorial page.

"I saw this earlier. Who knew about you getting accosted in the parking lot? I thought the casino was keeping it under wraps."

"I didn't share with you that the *Herald* has placed someone undercover at the casino. I'm assuming the person is a reporter but that might not be so. I have no idea who it is, but it's obvious that he or she had inside information about my being held up, which they chose to share."

"Bummer. I don't like to think that there isn't a filter on what's reported."

They finished their coffee discussing how the *Herald* was going to highlight the pageant, assigning some twenty reporters to the girls and their chaperones. Finally, Ben felt drained and opted to go to bed early. He knew his body couldn't make up for lost sleep from the night before, but it seemed like it was trying to. When his phone vibrated on the bedstand nearest him at three a.m., he knew who the message was from—and wasn't wrong. The single word, "hot" appeared followed by a screen shot of the fluorescent ceiling light above his desk. He couldn't make out the nickel-sized disc clearly but Andy's drawn-on arrow pointed to the corner of the metal fixture's white plastic shade.

"Damn." He hadn't meant to say it out loud.

"What's wrong?" Julie rolled over.

"Sorry, didn't mean to wake you. Just reacting to something at work. Go back to sleep." Instead of following his own advice, Ben sat on the side of the bed and reached for his shirt.

Chapter 12

He hadn't gotten back to sleep after Andy's text. In fact, he'd gotten up and started a pot of coffee, and now he was standing in front of his office door, key card in hand ready to swipe himself in—but hesitating. Didn't that one word "hot" change everything? Make him some sort of sitting duck? But for what? Why would an Indian Health Service psychologist standing in as a Human Resources Director at a casino need to be watched? Listened to?

If this were a clinical setting, especially one in California, bugging a shrink's office to collect information would render that information unusable under Evidence Code 1014—even if the client was planning a murder. But it didn't appear that anyone was interested in what might be shared by someone else behind closed doors. If he could believe Andy, he was the intended target.

"Busy?"

The young girl in the doorway looked familiar. Ben thought she was the one Julie had consoled the night of Robbi's murder. "No, come in." Should he suggest taking the conversation elsewhere? He'd see what she wanted first. It was going to be damned awkward to have to meet everyone outside.

"I'm Annette. I got to talk with your wife the other night; she is so sweet. I really appreciated her taking the time under such terrible circumstances to offer help. She was so helpful."

"I'm glad she was able to come with me that night. Now, how can I help you?"

"Because I was Robbi's best friend, Chairman Billie has asked that I organize Robbi's celebration of life. I'm putting together a roster of speakers and would like your input—as well as hoping to get you to participate. I'll be honest; I think a Native man would be the best choice to honor a Native woman. You know, it would carry more weight especially if your people have any special sayings for the dead. Maybe like, *vaya con dios*—oh, I guess that's Spanish."

She stood expectantly waiting for him to offer some sacred tidbit of knowledge tailor-made for the event. But, once more, Ben knew he'd have to disappoint. His knowledge of his heritage was sadly lacking, having been raised off the reservation by Anglo parents and only visiting his Pueblo grandmother during the summers.

"Thank you for asking me. I'm flattered. I only knew Robbi casually but was struck by her honesty and dedication to doing what was right. I'd be glad to contribute."

"Oh, thank you so much. I want to have Sammy help with the planning but he's still being held by law enforcement. It's so unfair. There's just no way that he would harm her."

"Maybe Sammy would like to be involved even if he can't be there. I'd be glad to talk with him."

"Would you?" This last was almost a squeal as Annette clapped her hands. "I think you're just as wonderful as your wife. Could I give you an outline as to how I'm looking at the event? You know, a theme, speakers and such—Sammy might have other ideas of what Robbi might have wanted. For example, the casino florist is donating baskets of white carnations to be placed around the dais. Would there be other decorations that Robbi might like? That's another thing, I can't forget to involve maintenance; we're going to need at least two hand-held mics and help with setting everything up."

"This is a lot of work."

"I can't imagine not doing it. And I think it's something we all need, a way to say goodbye. Anyway, thanks for your help. I'll keep in touch." With that, Annette waved from the door as she continued out into the hallway.

Ben waved back. Well, that conversation was harmless enough. If someone was checking up on whether or not he was doing his job, this meeting would prove his involvement. He checked the time. Still early. He had no idea if the jail had visiting hours but he'd call them. He could get there by ten. Speaking with Sammy Longman took priority, didn't it? He couldn't help but think that the kid was being wrongly detained. And maybe he could shed light on whatever Robbi knew that might have gotten her killed. It was worth a try and at the very least it might be important to assure Sammy that he hadn't been forgotten.

* * *

The local jail wasn't set up for visitors—no two-way phones behind plexiglass. An officer thought Ben would be able to use one of the interrogation rooms but he'd have to run it by the sheriff. Ben waited after passing on a cup of what looked like last weekend's coffee. Finally, a woman at an information desk motioned him over and pointed down the hall to her right.

"Last door on your left, and I need to have you leave your phone with me along with any other recording devices."

Ben pulled his phone out of a jacket pocket and laid it on her desk before walking down the hallway. The room was empty and he pulled out a chair and sat with his back to the two-way glass partition directly behind him. Everything was metal—easy to clean and disinfect. A plastic bottle of water and two Solo cups on the table were the only decorations in the room.

When an officer opened the door for Sammy to enter, Ben was shocked at his appearance. He wouldn't miss it by far if he thought Sammy had spent time crying. Red-rimmed eyes and a nose raw from wiping were giveaways. This was a kid who was struggling with grief. Ben held out his hand and shook the cold hand he was offered.

"Thanks for coming." Sammy took a chair opposite Ben and poured himself a cup of water. "Want some?"

"I'll pass."

"At least it looks clean." Sammy drank whatever was in his cup and poured more. "Don't ask me how I am. I shouldn't be here; I hope you agree."

"I do. And I want to help you get out of here." That was the truth. All his intuition was screaming 'wrong man'. "Tell me about what they think they have that implicates you."

"Next to nothing. Nothing truthful, that is. I'd texted Robbi to meet me at the cooler at three. I didn't say inside; I used the word 'at.' That means in front of; any idiot knows that. It was her shift break so we weren't doing anything wrong. Doc Pecos, we were engaged to be married. We were going to wait until after I graduated, three years. In the meantime, Robbi would have finished her Juris Doctor. Her grandfather was helping us out. We had a really good life planned."

Ben nodded and waited while Sammy swiped at tears with the back of his hand. "So, what is this evidence that the sheriff's department thinks it has?"

"They say the time of the meeting proves that I set her up. I could disprove that but someone, and they won't tell me who, says they saw me exit the cooler with blood on my clothes. That I almost ran into them while trying to run from the scene. Doc, that's a lie—at least that last part. That never happened. The door to the cold storage unit was unlocked like it always was. I was early. It was about two forty-five when I got there. When I looked in the door, I saw someone slumped over on the floor at the back. The minute I stepped inside, I knew it was Robbi. I turned her over, and felt for a pulse; there wasn't any. Yes, then I ran back outside yelling for security. Two guards came around the corner, and I asked them to call for help. I went back inside the cooler. I had blood on my hands and clothing, but I had nothing to hide. I tried to resuscitate her but my guess was she had been killed some thirty minutes or maybe even more before I found her. The point is I never left the scene."

"That seems pretty flimsy to hold you on. And the fact that you stayed, that you didn't try to leave should prove your innocence. Aren't there cameras to prove that? The ones in the hallway?"

Sammy sighed. "Yeah, camera footage would be conclusive if there was any. The power to the back hallway was out. No cameras, no lights. And, this unknown informant apparently added that he or she heard two voices from inside the cooler—supposedly the door was propped open—and they recognized my voice. Can you believe that the door to a cooling unit was open? That never happened. Robbi and I were supposed to be having a fight, and then they heard sounds of a scuffle and Robbi begging for her life. They even went so far as to say I was yelling at her because I'd caught her with another man. That's absurd."

"Once this person has come forward, given a deposition under oath—"

"But it's still he said/she said or he said/he said."

"I haven't heard that a weapon has been found. Aren't they looking for a knife?"

"Yeah, again if there was footage of the walk-in, it would prove that I never left, never took the murder weapon away from the scene, never handled a knife of any kind."

"Cameras or not, I want to believe that this person can be proved wrong."

"Not if they've been bought and told what to say."

"Bought?"

"Yeah, you haven't been around long enough to

know that casino money doesn't all come from tables and machines. There's a lot of it that changes hands for other reasons. A casino is a ready-made place for laundering. And I'm not talking about tribal leaders. There are others, outsiders, who try to use this place. Who do you think wants to break up what they call the Seminole monopoly? There are those who can't stand the fact that the Seminole have been so successful—helped the community, and helped the tribe."

"Am I wrong when I say this sounds like the rumors that have always circulated in Vegas? I guess actually been proved that mafia money is involved."

"My uncle says it just goes with the territory. He's a good man but it's sometimes impossible to dislodge the criminal element. Sometimes you don't even know who the bad guys are."

"Speaking of Chairman Billie, I haven't talked with him but I imagine that he's working toward your release."

"I hope so. But sometimes I'm not sure he doesn't find it easier to just ignore, look the other way, hope things will right themselves. I know he believes in my innocence."

"And you're his nephew."

Sammy shrugged. "I'm counting on that meaning something. Uncle Oscar was always there when I was growing up after my dad took off. I can't even let myself think that he'd abandon me now."

"Before I go, I want you to tell me anything that you think Robbi might want included in her celebration of life ceremony."

"Only one thing, and I've given this some thought. I want to have her car detailed—the Corvette. She loved that car. Bring it into the foyer for the ceremony. It will be like having Robbi there."

"I'll run it by maintenance."

"And I'll pay extra to have it detailed. Your boys could do that. I'll have my uncle pay them. He should have the key. I don't think he's had it moved."

"The car was still in the parking garage as of this morning. Shouldn't be a problem to detail it. And if they can't bring it inside, it could be parked at the door."

"Doc, there's one more thing. It's important that you and your boys clean the car. This is between us. I think there might be something hidden in Robbi's car."

"Such as?"

"I don't know. I do know that she was keeping something for her grandfather. Something he'd asked her to be very careful about. I got the idea that it was a journal or a notebook of some kind. I think it has information that would be dangerous if it got out. Somebody trashed her apartment the night before she was killed. There were other break-ins in the building that night, but I think someone was looking for something in particular in her place. There were pillows cut open, frozen food tossed out of the fridge; someone doing a normal grab and run wouldn't take the extra time."

"She told me. Was the break-in reported?"

"Yeah, but it was lumped in with the other burglaries. Cops didn't see anything special, and Robbi didn't want to say too much. Anyway, tell the boys to go over every inch of the Corvette, and if they find anything, they need to give it to you and not tell anyone."

Ben hesitated. Did he want to involve the boys in some kind of cloak and dagger deal that would put them in danger? Maybe he could get around it somehow, even work with them and not have to tell them he was looking for something. He knew the boys would be thrilled over the extra money and if the chairman asked, the wash bay at the back of the parking lot could probably be at their disposable. It would be private and out of the way of the valets parking vehicles. Ben said his good-byes, thanked Sammy for the great idea about staging the car at Robbi's service, and promised to work toward getting him out of there.

* * *

"This car is fire." Nathan was slowly walking around the Corvette, stopping to get a good look at it from the rear and then the front. "How fast do you think it can go?"

"Rumor has it that a hundred and ninety-four is top-out." Ben was secretly glad that the boys weren't driving ... yet. Speed and testosterone—not a good mix especially when the hormone was in a teen body. And he didn't have long to wait before Nathan would want a car. Wasn't he already eligible for a learner's permit? Ben needed to check the license laws in Florida.

"Now, Nathan wants a sports car and not a truck." Zac said it to tease and got a curt answer.

"Wouldn't you?"

"C'mon guys, we need to get to work. Zac, what about a long-handled brush?" Zac pointed to one leaning against the side of the wash-bay. "Did you remember the wash products and sponges?"

Both boys nodded and pointed to a cabinet along the wall. It looked like everything was there. Finally, they were ready. They divided up duties with the Zac and Nathan wielding the two hoses after Ben applied a coating of road tar and grease remover to the undercoating before giving the body a once over with liquid soap. He used this time to check the exterior.

Ben just wished he knew what he was looking for. On the outside he patted down wheel wells, headlight rims, washer blades, license holder—any crevice that might hold something hidden. On the inside he checked the console, glove box, instrument panel, floor mats, door pockets— Ben used the excuse of applying leather cleaner to get access and not arouse the boys' suspicion. But there was nothing, not one thing out of place, or suspicious. It was a dead end. Of course, it might be a different story if he could rack the car and go over the undercarriage. But to think Robbi had crawled around under the car to hide something was just too farfetched. If she had something to hide there was no reason to think that she wouldn't have simply kept it inside the car or a place within easy reach.

At the end of two hours, the boys returned to work washing patron's cars, and Ben rolled the Corvette into position at the front of the casino. It looked grand with all of its black and silver elegance shining in the sunlight. Ben knew Robbi's friends would be pleased. He'd talk with Annette about placing some tributes outside, cards and flowers around the car with maybe some signage to explain why it was there. Sammy was right. It was the perfect touch. It made Robbi's presence felt.

* * *

"So, you're saying he didn't find anything?"

"Here, I'll run it again. Look for yourself." The man in

front of the screen didn't turn to look at the man standing behind him, he just pushed a couple keys and slid his chair to one side. All three watched Ben go over the outside and then the inside of the Corvette. "I'd say he was pretty thorough."

"What's your honest opinion, are we wasting our time?" The man who seemed to be in charge pulled a chair out from a table along the opposite wall and sat down. "Overreacting, maybe? But let me point out that nothing's a waste of time if we're possibly saving our necks. We've got a good thing going here. No one suspects us. We've all got jobs to do and we're under the radar. We need to keep it that way." The other two men in the room nodded.

"We're relying on our informant telling the truth, but we know the computer codes were compromised. It's not much of a stretch to think old Leonard had helped himself to some pretty privy information. I know you couldn't keep an eye on him all the time. What's your best bet? Is the old coot going to show back up one of these days?"

"Wouldn't we have heard something by now? Some threat, a demand for money with something being ransomed? The old 'I know something that people would be interested in' ploy. Instead of banging our heads against the wall not knowing, I'd say we should have just put an end to him when we had the chance. But I think we're safe. My guess is he was a meal for the sharks. He's never been gone this long ... 'course, he declared he'd retired, but I think something happened on his fishing trip."

"With any luck, you're right. Still, as close as he was to that granddaughter and the fact that he was seen handing her a package—"

"But we didn't find anything, tossed her apartment

pretty good for nothing. And just in case she knew something and could talk, that's also been taken care of. Might be easier to just get rid of that psychologist. He seems to be the only one snooping around."

"I've got some ideas there."

"Care to share?"

"Let's just say those boys of his might get into some real trouble during the pageant. The kind of stuff that'll make dear ol' dad have to resign and move on out of here. You know, save face and protect the reputation of one of his sons."

Chapter 13

Robert Holmes, Executive Director of Miss Teen USA Incorporated, moved into an office exactly two doors down from Ben's. He was setting up a week early to "get things in order" as he put it and he seemed to think that Ben's time was at his disposal. Ben knew he had to put a stop to the constant interruptions—where was this? Who was in charge of that? Could he have his meals delivered to his office? Why hadn't he been assigned his own space in the parking garage? How could he get his hotel room changed to a suite? On and on. Ben wasn't above locking his office door and hanging a Do Not Disturb sign from the door handle, but it wasn't overly helpful. Ben swore the man watched his office and was primed to jump into action the minute Ben entered the hall. Now, he only met Julie for lunch off the grounds and spent more time than needed on the floor with the gamblers.

His best excuse for disappearing a few hours during the day was helping Annette prepare Robbi's celebration of life—the perfect reason to work outside his office. After he'd brought the Corvette around to the front of the casino, he'd helped put up the posts and string the ropes that would hopefully keep an inquisitive crowd away from the car—if they stopped to read the 'do not enter' signs. Tributes of flowers, cards, stuffed animals, even empty bottles of what was supposed to have been her favorite brew were stacked some four feet deep completely forming a circular skirt around the automobile. It was colorful and eye-catching.

On Friday the service started promptly at eleven. An Indian elder from the Immokalee reservation shared several letters that had been written to Robbi by her friends and tribal brothers and sisters, letters thanking her for her friendship and for being in their lives. Someone had told Ben that Sammy had cut his hair. This was another Native tradition to signify a major life change and to honor the time spent with a loved one. Ben acknowledged that most North American indigenous people considered their hair a source of strength and power. It was a special tribute all its own to cut it, alter one's appearance and literally signal stepping away from the past to embrace a new beginning.

Ben knew that Robbi had been buried in a grave or To-hop-ki, the Seminole word for "fort" on the neighboring reservation. Her feet were no doubt positioned to the east and a blanket was carefully wrapped around her body. Palmetto leaves were placed over this bundle and the grave site tightly sealed by a covering of logs. Ben had heard that in the old days, all of the belongings of the deceased were thrown into the swamp. He didn't think that custom was followed anymore as he had seen Annette handing out pieces of clothing and other of Robbi's belongings to her friends at the ceremony.

So many of the old ways had given way to modernization. He wondered if the fires that were customarily lighted at the top and bottom of the grave site were kept burning for four days before being allowed to go out. Did people still visit the site during those four days and wave lighted torches in the air to scare away night birds, the evil Ta-lak-i-clak-o? It was even rumored that the Seminoles of Florida had buried their dead in hollow trees once upon a time; the bodies placed in a standing position. Maybe an upright burial was only rumor. He was pretty certain that this type of natural casket wasn't used anymore.

At exactly twelve, staff members wheeled out several tables offering a light lunch of sandwiches, chips, and soft drinks. People congregated in groups or rearranged the chairs set up for the service in varying sized circles and enjoyed lunch together. Ben wished Sammy could have been there. He needed to follow up with Chairman Billie and see what was being done to get the young man released. Had a tribal lawyer been assigned? Ben would have to believe that this detail had been taken care of, but he'd make sure.

Ben surveyed the room. Had two hundred people attended the ceremony? The foyer was packed. Ben was surprised that he knew a great many of the people around him. In the short time he'd been at the casino, he had been impressed at the strong feeling of community. Yet, there were people he didn't know. With friends interacting with friends, the three men in dark suits who stood apart from everyone caught his attention. When Andy walked by, Ben asked him who they were.

"Auditors. Chairman Billie told them to come on down and get something to eat." Andy started to walk away, "Oh, before I forget. That Holmes guy from the pageant is looking for you."

"I'm hiding." And Ben wasn't altogether lying; he was using every pretext to stay away from his office.

"Good idea." Andy grinned, "That one's a pain in the ass. He had me go to each of the rooms assigned to the contestants and flush the toilets. Seems like wherever they had a pageant recently, three toilets overflowed. And he wouldn't trust staff, nope it had to be me 'cause as he said, I had a title. Yeah, that made a difference somehow. I'm gonna get cards printed, Chief Toilet-Flusher at your service."

Ben laughed. There was no doubt that the guy was rubbing everyone the wrong way. "We need to keep him busy. Maybe after the girls arrive, he'll have enough to do without hounding us."

"Hey, ain't that your missus?" Andy pointed toward the entrance.

Ben quickly looked over his shoulder. "Yeah, I was hoping she'd get here before all the food was gone. I'll catch up with you later."

Julie had stopped to speak with Annette, but motioned Ben to join them. "I hear the celebration of life was a success. It looks like the food was pretty popular, too."

"Let's go get a plate before it disappears." Ben said hello to Annette before taking Julie's hand and stepping toward the nearest table. "Prime rib sliders with horseradish sauce.

My favorites. Let's have lunch in my office."

Ben put a finger to his lips as they walked past Robert Holmes's door, but it sounded like the man was busy with a phone call. Ben shut his office door behind them and walked to his desk.

"Never crossed my mind that this roll of paper towels would come in so handy." Ben retrieved the roll from a desk drawer, put folded sheets under sweating soda cans at the edge of his desk, and single layers as plate mats. "Oops, almost forgot napkins." Ben tore off two more single sheets and handed one to Julie.

They hadn't had even two bites of their sandwiches when the pageant director stuck his head in the door.

"Just the person I'm supposed to meet. Ms. Pecos, isn't it?"

"I use my maiden name. I'm Julie Conlin."

"Oh, who cares about names. The Julie I'm looking for works for the *Herald*."

"You've found her." Julie turned in her chair before reaching in her purse, pulling out a card and handing it to him.

"I need to see you about publicity. I've been talking with your boss, and Ken wants us to work closely together to get our young ladies some press. I need the names of any photographers who will be assigned to the pageant."

"I don't know if assignments have been made yet, but I'll be glad to check and get back."

"Perfect. Perhaps we could set up a meeting for the morning? I want to share my staging ideas—things that have worked in the past to show the girls at their very best. Ten is free on my calendar. May I put you down?" He had pulled his phone from his shirt pocket and was poised to add the meeting.

"Ten should work. I'll call when I get back to the office if there's a conflict."

"Good, then. I'd say we're all set." He turned to Ben. "I'm also going to need to speak with housekeeping. The pageant will need lockers and changing rooms here at the casino. Is there someone I can contact in housekeeping?"

"You might want to double-check this with the chairman, but I'm guessing that Florence Hornsby is the person you want."

"Thank you both." With that he turned and was quickly out the door.

Chapter 14

Excitement was building. It seemed like everyone was talking about some aspect of the pageant—what they would wear as chaperones and serving people, what activities had been planned, the extra staff that would be needed, not to mention food. What did teenage girls eat, anyway? Julie was going to work early and coming home late. Ben decided that the only good thing was she was spending a minimum of half days at the casino, setting up interview times and places, and organizing photo shoots. That meant lunches together and sharing his office.

Robert Holmes had apparently taken the last available office that would allow him to establish the pageant's control center within the casino. Ben soon learned the cost of having his office at the back of the building and not on the first and second floors with other administrators. Being this close to the pageant's work area, Ben's office suddenly got crowded with dress racks, an extra desk and filing cabinet, and FedEx delivered boxes of who knew what. Regular staff had been moved to other quarters and lockers at the far end of the hallway opposite Ben's office had been cleared for use by the contestants. Storage areas had miraculously turned into dressing rooms with walls of floor to ceiling mirrors; a large conference room had been equipped with swiveling barber-type chairs for makeup artists to do their magic; and lastly, parked just outside the back door was an entire fleet of golf carts to move contestants between the hotel, the casino, and amenities on the grounds such as the swimming pools and the golf course.

The scope of the planning for the pageant was mind-boggling, actually awe-inspiring. People had full-time jobs, year 'round, from local contests to the national level, to ensure its success. A career pageant-planner? Interesting career choice but obviously a great number of people had chosen it. Ben knew this wasn't the first pageant to be held at the casino, but there was an entire regiment of pageant aficionados who were new to the scene and were now busying themselves with becoming familiar with protocol. Ben couldn't even name all the categories that seemed to have one to five people listed as contacts. At least the increased activity kept Mr. Holmes busy and out of Ben's way.

Ben did learn that according to Chairman Billie, the witness who swore to seeing Sammy Longman in the walk-in cooler at the time of Robbi's murder and supposedly heard them talking was sticking to their story. No one seemed to know who this informant was—even Chairman Billie was in the dark. Was it even someone from the casino, a worker? Maybe a guest now long gone? Or maybe the actual murderer? The person had certainly seemed to be convincing. As far as Ben could tell, law enforcement wasn't looking further than Sammy for someone to blame.

Overall, the pageant was turning out to be a big distraction. Robbi was becoming yesterday's news, much to Ben's frustration. Her death was not some random act. But even *his* attention would be diverted for the next week and a half. He had been volunteered to chaperone several events and had ordered the customary tux. He doubted this casino staple was listed in the fine print of his contract, but it was a necessary requirement. He'd probably wear it more than once.

Mr. Holmes had even dropped off a copy of the Contestant Handbook. Pages and pages of do's and don'ts. Everything the girls needed to know. Things like what activities to plan and how to make the most of free time, how to organize schedules, pack formal wear, helpful tips for being successful, as in how to act during an interview, general pageant etiquette, who pays what and when. The list seemed endless. In addition to an initial fee at registration of $300, a sponsorship fee of $1500 completed what was paid up front. All other fees were paid by sponsors—hotel rooms, food, transportation, special costumes. And each girl was tasked with finding a cadre of these supporters. The handbook even had sample phone dialogue, as well as sample letters to be used for securing monetary help from her community. Had they left out anything? Ben couldn't think of one addition; the handbook was that complete. Only teens between the ages of thirteen to eighteen were eligible. It would be interesting to meet the girls that Zac and Nathan had been assigned to escort. The boys were talking about nothing else.

Five days out and the colorful bunting, the hundreds of yards of dyed and printed cloth, was being artfully draped above entrances, combined with messages of welcome from the governor of Florida, past pageant winners, and celebrities. But it was the photographs that commanded attention. What looked to be a complete history of Miss Teen USA in pictures was everywhere. Photographs suspended, photographs attached to walls, on easels, taped to windows and doors—there was no missing the upcoming event—and all of it was building a palpable current of excitement.

"You know there's going to be a quiz on this." Andy had stuck his head in the door and waved a copy of the pageant handbook his way. "Did you read this shit? Kinda glad I'm male. This involves some hard work."

"And some luck."

"Yeah, that, too. I bet your boys are thrilled. Do they know which contestants they'll be squiring around?"

"Zac will be escorting Miss Alaska, and Nathan is with Miss California."

Andy quickly leafed through the manual in his hand. "Have you seen their pictures? Look at the publicity photos at the back of the handbook. Those two are cuties. I wouldn't mind being a teenager for a week."

"I could pass. I don't remember those years as my best. Took a lot of work to just stay out of trouble."

"I know what you mean, buddy. Well, gotta get back out on my beat. See ya." With that, Andy stepped into the hallway and closed Ben's door only to have it open and

Julie step in.

"I feel like I should take a number just to see you. Mr. Holmes was in line before me but was called away."

"Thank God! He has a tough time taking no for an answer. I dodged responsibility for one of the dressing rooms being locked. A member of the staff told me Florence Hornsby had taken up hiding from him. Members of her crew were to send coded messages if they saw him coming her way."

"I believe that. I only stopped by to say that I need to beg off from having lunch. Seems like it's the best time to meet with Annette."

"Probably just as well. There's another all-hands meeting with pageant staff at eleven-thirty. That's going to tie me up for at least an hour and a half."

"See you for dinner? At six?"

"With any luck, I'll text if I'm going to be late."

* * *

"If my boss sees me out here, I'm dead meat. He says it's like advertising for a competitor." Annette stood in the line forming in front of the food truck offering tacos. "But between you and me? These are the best—get the shrimp in crispy corn shells. In fact, why don't you stake out one of the picnic tables along the side of the truck. No use two of us standing here. I'll get our lunch and meet you."

Annette wasn't wrong. Julie loved the tacos. "I swear these rival Garcia's in New Mexico. They're great. I'm glad you could meet for lunch."

"I knew you'd love them. Don't move. I'm going to get another container of salsa. That stuff is so good.

They make it fresh right here on the truck." Julie watched Annette walk to the truck and come back with extras for each of them. Conversation was put on hold until the last of the tacos disappeared.

Julie sat back and sipped her soda. "I've been wanting to ask you about Sammy Longman."

"He's still in jail."

"I know, but I'm wondering about the person who reported that the two of them were fighting. Did you hear anything that night?"

"No. Absolutely not."

"Have the police contacted you? Taken a statement? If you were really the first one on the scene, your testimony would be invaluable." Julie sensed she'd struck a nerve somehow. Annette avoided her eyes and looked away as she shook her head. "Maybe you should volunteer, call the police, tell them what you know."

"I don't know. I don't want to get involved. The cops seem so certain. It's not like I have proof. I thought I knew how Robbi and Sammy felt about each other but if Sammy's guilty …"

"But if he isn't?" Julie waited but Annette only shrugged and looked at her watch.

"Listen, I need to be getting back inside. I'll give some thought to doing something about Sammy. Honest, I promise I will."

"Let me know. I'd hate to think someone innocent is sitting in a cell and maybe the real murderer is free."

Julie cleared their trash and carried it to one of the bins at the end of the row of picnic tables. Something was so weird about Annette's reaction. Frankly, she was shocked that Annette hadn't come forward before. People just didn't feel comfortable getting involved. Or maybe Annette had been threatened? Could that be it? Ridiculous. Julie was letting her imagination run away with her.

Back to business. She pulled her phone out of her purse and scrolled through her calendar. Her schedule was packed; in fact, she'd have to hurry to make her next appointment on time. April Bowlegs had requested they meet to discuss some staging ideas that the administrative assistant thought would make great photo-shots for the paper and show the casino to its best advantage. Then it was off to pick up three tuxedos before the shop closed at four.

Chapter 15

The day finally arrived. Ben watched from the front entry as two Greyhound buses pulled into the parking lot followed by an entourage of cars and one eighteen-wheeler. The girls got off first.

Separated as he was by a couple hundred feet, he could still hear the laughter and feel the excitement. As per contest rules for their initial meeting, Nathan and Zac had dressed casually that morning, jeans and tucked in button-down shirts—no t-shirts, cut-offs or anything that would suggest see-through. That meant no mesh body-builder, body-hugging outfits. The look was all-American, clean-cut, and scrubbed clean. Fresh hair-cuts, even manicures were in abundance as the line of escorts and contestants made their way past Ben and into the building. Ben was impressed. As for the contestants, there were no short-shorts, not a bare midriff in sight, and nothing strapless showing uncovered shoulders.

The first event, held in the casino's amphitheater, was a welcoming—an introduction of pageant personnel, and overview of the upcoming seven days. Packets were handed out with room key-cards, and meal tickets. Each contestant was also introduced to her escort. Ben watched from the back as Zac and Nathan met their young women. At the end of an hour, the couples and chaperones left by a side entrance to have lunch in one of the many private dining rooms on the second floor. Judging from the animated conversations, Zac and Nathan were both enjoying getting to know their new acquaintances. He was impressed as both boys slowed to let the girls walk ahead of them and then held the door open as they entered the hallway. Manners. So far, so good. He was sure he'd hear all about their day at dinner. Time now to get some work done.

* * *

"Come in, come in." Ben hesitated at the yelled command, then stepped into the chairman's office. The man was on the phone, which he suddenly slammed down and got up from behind his desk. "They're not listening. I can't get through to anyone down there."

"What's going on? Can I help?" Ben had never seen the chairman so agitated. His hands were shaking and his face was red—right up to the roots of his hair.

"My nephew is getting a raw deal. I can't believe I've been so foolish, but I expected reason to prevail. No one would believe that Sammy could do such a thing. But, you know what? I've just been told that he's being moved off the list from 'someone of interest' to being fully charged with the murder of Robbi Aponi. Fully charged, can you believe that? The kid is barely twenty; Robbi was his fiancée. They had life plans." The chairman sank down into an overstuffed chair and tightly grasped the arms, closing his eyes and leaning his head back. "What am I going to do? My sister is beside herself; all she does is cry. She thinks I'm a miracle worker and here I am sitting here doing nothing. I let the craziness of this workplace take up my time and attention." This time his voice trailed off into a whisper.

Ben sat down on the leather couch facing the chairman. "There's got to be something that can be done. Do you know who the witness is? They're not going to be holding him if the witness isn't credible."

"I've asked but nobody's talking. And I've been told to let go of the matter—not to rock the boat while the pageant is going on. I guess they have a point there. I know it wasn't up very long, but it was a good idea to clear out that memorial in the front. Not very good press to keep reminding everyone that the murder of a young woman took place here recently."

"Who's discouraging it?"

"Pageant sponsors, for one, and our fiscal officer, Epstein, who keeps an eye on the numbers. He's hoping the pageant gives us a bump in attendance. It's the start of our busiest season and we should have picked up by now."

"I think gas prices and inflation are maybe bigger causes."

"I'd like to think it's economics and not the fact that someone was murdered—not to mention your wife getting mugged in the parking garage."

"Let me see what I can do." Ben had no idea what that

might be but he'd ask Julie. Did the paper have an in with law enforcement? It wasn't out of the question to think that they could have. But maybe not on the reservation. Still, someone had to know the name of the star witness. He gave the chairman a quick report of the day so far—the arrival of the contestants and the opening presentation—and a reminder that the chairman was due to speak at breakfast in the morning.

* * *

Julie was actually looking forward to the meeting with April Bowlegs. It would help her plan her feature stories around a particular place and time. She just needed to know where and when each photo shoot would be. She knew about the first one and had already approached the grounds crew to make sure the area around the cascading waterfall and pool was not only clean but devoid of people. Robert Holmes would provide the list of young women taking part. The original idea was to change out up to six girls at a time using at least half of the roster of contestants in this setting. It had seemed simple enough.

But there were particulars. Was the shoot being sponsored by a company? For example, did a manufacturer of swimsuits or beach wear need to take center stage? At least be prominently mentioned in signage, as well as her article? Should the girls be doing something? Would a water volleyball game film better than static, prearranged poses? And would everything be taped, in addition to still photos? Julie realized that there was a lot that she didn't know and all were questions for Ms. Bowlegs. The assistant's door was open but Julie still knocked.

"Come in. You're just in time. Look who I've snagged here." Ms. Bowlegs had a distinct Cheshire Cat smile as she stood behind a conference table and pointed to a man sitting with his back to the door.

"Ken? I didn't know you were coming by today." Julie was surprised but wasn't sure why. It wasn't like she kept tabs on her boss.

"I called with some of the same questions that you've already voiced and got invited to sit in." Ken pulled up another chair to the table. "Easier to look at maps of the grounds and make logistically correct decisions." Two maps covered over half of the conference table. Numbers under or on each entry indicating a building, parking lot, or road could be cross-referenced to a photo in a stack at the table's edge.

April handed Ken and Julie several photos. "These areas really show the casino off nicely. I think our water elements are exceptional. Look at the cascading falls that spill into an enormous pool just below Marky's Caviar Lounge. Gorgeous, isn't it? That would make a perfect setting."

Ken took the photo she handed him and agreed. "But I also like Julie's idea of showing the girls at play—a water volleyball game, maybe just a swim-day with some of them diving and floating around one of the smaller pools."

"I agree with Julie, but don't overlook the gardens. That might be a nice backdrop for formalwear. And golf or tennis—we have both available. Might be nice to include escorts in some of the shoots. I just need to know times so that I can have the area cleared of other participants and dedicated to your needs." April was busy taking notes. "I should have had our general grounds manager join us today, but I'll copy him with our ideas. And don't forget Friday night is an optional Marlin's game. We have several VIP boxes earmarked for contestants and their dates."

"I'd forgotten the baseball game. Julie, contact a photographer, start with Alex; he'll probably jump at a chance to see a game—in fact, let's plan on Alex going into Miami that evening." Julie nodded and put the date in her phone. By the end of the meeting six possible photo event areas had been chosen. Good ones, Julie thought, ones that would advertise the casino and show that it had more to offer than just gaming tables.

Ken held the office door open for her on the way out. "Have time for coffee? I can probably play hooky a little longer; the paper will do just fine without me for another hour. I remember they have a food court around here somewhere."

"On the second floor. Coffee sounds great."

They found a table toward the back and Ken added a Danish to his coffee order. The place was quiet in the late afternoon.

"I've been wanting to get your ideas about something." Julie put a second creamer in her cup.

"Shoot. What's up?"

"I'm concerned about Sammy Longman. Supposedly, a witness has come forward with damaging information, and Sammy has now been charged with the murder of Robbi Aponi. Only, I don't think he did it. The so-called witness is either mistaken or for some reason is trying to set him up."

"But you don't know that, do you? Who is this witness?"

"That's a part of the problem. No one seems to have a name, or not one that they're sharing. Do we have an 'in' at the county jail? Someone who has given the *Herald* tips in the past? Someone who has access to the case's paperwork?"

"No name pops up. I read the initial police report. It alleged Mr. Longman became enraged after finding Miss Aponi was having an affair—seeing someone else, at least. Sounded like a cut-and-dried reaction out of jealousy. He set up a meeting at their break and confronted her. Their argument has been documented by this witness."

"I realize that's the story that's been given out. Only, I don't believe it. If there was a witness to anything, it was the murderer himself."

"That's a pretty strong statement. What makes you think that?"

"Robbi was already in danger. She knew something. Her friends think that her grandfather might have shared something with her before he left."

"What sort of thing would he have shared?"

"I don't know. He was an accountant for the casino before he retired. It wasn't as though he didn't have access to the inner workings of the business."

Ken finished his Danish and pushed the plate to the center of the table and leaned forward. "Listen, I don't like the sound of this. I not only want you to put this on the back burner for awhile and give a hundred percent of your energy to the pageant; I really want you to forget playing Nancy Drew all together. Leave it up to the lawyers. If there's been some misinformation given, let them uncover it. Don't put yourself in danger."

Nancy Drew? That rankled, but Julie guessed her boss was just trying to look out for her. And, she guessed, that was kind of sweet. Of course, being told not to do something by anyone really bothered her. Maybe it was just saying that she was wrong about something that made her want to prove that she wasn't. She could multi-task—give attention to the pageant but also do a little snooping into Sammy's situation. So, she thanked Ken and nodded her acceptance of his orders.

Chapter 16

She had to share a room. There would be a total of four aspiring Miss Teen USA contestants—two sixteen-year-olds, a fourteen-year-old and her, the oldest at seventeen. The girls represented the states of Alaska, Illinois, and Tennessee; and, of course, she was from California. It seemed the pageant directors had assigned younger girls to rooms with older ones. Probably a good idea, but she didn't see 'taking someone under her wing' as the director had recommended. She knew plenty of fourteen-year-olds who might resent that.

Luckily the room was large and they could each have their space. Unfortunately, it had been set up with double bunk beds, a terrible reminder of that bad week at Girl Scout camp when she was eleven and hadn't seen the tarantula until she'd crawled into the upper bunk and pulled the sheet back. Falling to the floor from that height had broken her arm. Could you have PTSD from some asshole kid putting a spider in your bed? She dibs the bottom bunk.

Sharing a room wasn't so bad in itself, but one of the girls who had moved in had already borrowed a blouse without asking. Her favorite blouse. And there wasn't room on the bathroom counter to leave her makeup out. But maybe that wasn't so bad. If she left it out, it probably would get borrowed, too. Bitch, bitch, bitch. She could hear her mother's voice, "Smile at everyone, be sweet, you never know who's watching. Someone from Hollywood might be looking for talent." She had to remind her mother that Hollywood in this case was in Florida, not California. And she doubted anyone from there would be looking.

Shouldn't she be thrilled to even be here? Chasing a crown. No, chasing a scholarship, a way out—a guaranteed debt-free start to a new life, and at a college of her choice. Even runners-up walked away with some pretty cool prizes. It was worth a little inconvenience, including borrowed blouses and memories of tarantulas.

She was more concerned about being paired up with this Nathan kid. A year younger, from New Mexico, a Navajo who had grown up on a reservation—she knew nothing about indigenous people. He seemed nice, quiet, and he was cute … really cute. It was hard to talk at lunch with everyone sitting around them but there was a pool party at three. Maybe they could talk then.

Bikinis were a no-no but her one-piece had more cut-outs than material, a gold shimmering lamé. And she looked good. Her blond hair almost matched the gold color of her suit. She'd spent extra time on her hair, a single, fat braid down her back that, even wet, would look freshly plaited. And the finishing touch was a run-proof, water-proof mascara for her lashes. No fake, alien-looking, fluffy eye-coverings for her. If she did have to admit it, her eyes were her strongest attribute. At least, she always got tons of compliments. Eye liner helped along with a really sparingly applied lightly tinted base and just the whisper of a pink blush. A last check in the mirror and the face staring back looked great—if she did say so herself. She grinned. She could allow herself a little bit of ego to show. She grabbed lotion, sunglasses, beach towel, a cover-up, baseball cap—and packed her bag. She was ready to go.

Oops, she almost forgot. She had one stop to make before going outside. Each girl had been assigned a locker in the lower-level hallway. She needed to check the combination lock and leave whatever clothing she might want to change into after swimming hanging inside. There was a poolside cookout planned for six. Shorts were acceptable along with "appropriate" tops—whatever that meant. But she was going to add a denim shirt, white denim shorts and white sneakers. Casual but the white against her tan would look good. She pulled the clothing out of a drawer, tossed them on top of the beach bag and headed out the door.

She had locker number 14 which was close to the end of the first row of like-metal boxes flush with the wall and reminded her of gym class at school. It opened easily and was actually roomy, not so deep but tall. There was even a rod affixed close to the top of the three-foot high enclosure and modified hangers. She carefully shook out the denim shirt, slipped it on a hanger and buttoned the top button. When she replaced the hanger, it was bumping the back wall and needed to be turned outward. She ran her hand up the inside wall to push her blouse forward when she knocked something to the floor of the locker.

A flash-drive. Odd. It had scotch tape crisscrossed over it, like someone had stuck it on the locker's back wall. Who would do that if they weren't trying to hide something. Well, it wasn't her business. She should turn it in, but to whom? She didn't have time to worry about that now. She dropped the drive into the pocket of her beach bag.

* * *

The pool area was unlike anything she'd ever seen before. There was even sand that had been brought in to simulate a beachside experience with cabanas, a pool bar and grill, and loads of beach umbrellas and lounge chairs. The total water area was over four acres and could accommodate water activities including canoeing and paddleboarding according to the guide closest to her. Apparently, guided tours were an hourly occurrence. And she hadn't even counted how many waterfalls and swaying palms there were, all brightly lighted with strings of tiny, sparkling incandescent bulbs. It was magical and overwhelmingly immense.

The escorts met the girls at the entrance to the pool area and walked them to individual small round tables with their names on an embossed card prominently displayed in the middle. Each setting also had two lounge chairs and umbrellas.

Nathan had obviously scouted out where they would be sitting beforehand and quickly led Skyler to the second row on the near side of the pool. "Here we are. Small table, number nineteen—all ours." He smiled. "Not a bad seat, almost front row. At least we're close to the water." He placed Skyler's beach tote on a chair.

Skyler almost felt underdressed. Slipping off her coverup, she was showing as much skin as was possible without bending the contest rules, but Nathan was wearing a long sleeve t-shirt over his swim trunks. Odd. It was stifling hot for that kind of extra layer. He had waved over one of the waiters who had started working the crowd and ordered a couple Cokes.

"Anything else?"

Skyler shook her head. "I'm thinking I'd like to swim and then maybe just get some sun. And you?"

"Swimming sounds great."

Skyler folded her terrycloth coverup, then reached in her tote and pulled out a spray can of sunscreen. Stepping to the side, she sprayed her shoulders. "Want some?" Nathan shook his head. He was just standing there waiting on her. It appeared obvious that he wasn't removing his shirt. "Are you going in like that?" She pointed to the shirt. Nathan shrugged. "Are you allergic to the sun, or just shy." She said this last with a teasing smile, but Nathan quickly looked away and seemed upset. "Hey, I was just trying to be funny." She reached out to touch his arm. She needed to do something reassuring, but he pulled away and then just as quickly turned back to face her. Making eye contact and not flinching, he slowly began rolling the fabric of the t-shirt upward until he was standing in front of her bare-chested, the shirt in his hand.

And she caught her breath. She had never seen such scarring. Bumps of folded skin at the edges of his chest, pencil-thin lines of skin that doubled back, forming rounded tunnels from one side of his rib cage to the other looking like it had been pulled off the bone and wadded up, left to heal in knotted protrusions. "Nathan ..." she stopped. She didn't know what to say. What could she say? Had he been in some terrible accident?

The awkward moment was interrupted by the waiter placing two cups of ice and two cans of Coke on the table. With an "enjoy" called back over his shoulder, he moved onto the next table.

"Want to sit for a minute?" Nathan popped the top off of his drink, poured half a can into a cup, pulled out a chair and sat.

"Sure." She put her tote on the ground and sat down. Would he tell her what had happened to him? She honestly hoped so. As of that moment, she was feeling terrible for upsetting him and goading him to take off his shirt. They were off to a terrible start. And he seemed like a really nice guy.

Nathan took a couple long swallows before setting his soda to the side and relaxing against the back of his chair. "This is going to sound like some kind of history lesson, but I want to share it with you."

"I want to hear," Skyler assured him.

"A couple summers ago I was honored by being invited to take part in a Sun Dance ceremony held on the Lakota reservation in South Dakota. It's a ritual of pain and sacrifice but it prepares the person for manhood. The ceremony involves piercing. Bone skewers are forced through the skin—threaded actually like big needles." He pointed to the insertion points. Skyler didn't realize she had placed a hand over her mouth until he stopped to ask her if he should continue.

"Please, go on." She placed both of her hands on the

table in front of her and willed herself not to overreact.

"There are five scars on each side of my chest." Nathan pointed to each. "Rawhide is tied to the end of the bone skewers, here and here," again, he placed an index finger at each point before continuing. "Then these rawhide ropes are attached to a central pole. Tethered in this way, I danced until the skewers pulled through the skin. Some dances—especially those ceremonies in the Midwest—don't use a pole but tie participants to huge buffalo skulls that are then dragged around over rocky areas and uneven earth. Some ceremonies call for the elevation of the dancers—they actually dangle from the pole, their feet not touching the ground."

Skyler didn't realize she was holding her breath until she let it whoosh out in a sort of gasping sound. "I don't know what to say."

Nathan put his hand over hers. "I'm sorry to upset you." He slipped his hand away and sat back. "Really, I don't have to tell you all this."

"No, please, I want to know. It's just that it's different, that's all. There's a part of me that's fascinated."

"It is fascinating. The average person has no idea about most Native ceremonies and there's a lot I'm leaving out. For example, the use of eagle feathers for healing and how the hollow bone of the eagle's wing becomes a whistle calling out to the participants. The eagle is revered because it can fly close to the sun and it's courageous, swift, and always the strongest of birds. For some tribes, it's the buffalo that is the theme of the dance. There would not have been life without this animal on the plains. Everything came from the buffalo—food, clothing, housing, children's toys, even fly swatters."

She almost laughed, then realized that he was serious. "Fly swatters? You're kidding?"

"Not kidding. My people invented fly swatters." This time he grinned.

Had she been forgiven? Why did she think that the fly swatter was a modern invention? Was 'invention' even the right word? Couldn't you just roll up something and hit the buggers? Did something have to be designed? Of course, indigenous people suffered with the pests, too; perhaps, they *had* designed some tool. She wondered if they had also invented something to get rid of ticks and fleas.

"I can't even imagine how painful that must have been." She pointed in the general direction of his chest. It was still difficult to look at it.

"No shit. So, shirt or no shirt?" Nathan stood and picked up his t-shirt from the back of his chair and held it in front of him.

"No t-shirt, if you're comfortable that way. I want you to be comfortable."

He grinned. "Thanks."

"And Nathan, thank you for explaining."

"You're welcome, but no more history lessons."

He took her by the hand and headed for the water. She sneaked a sideways look at some of the other girls and their escorts. There was a lot of horsing around—pushing and shoving, splashing water, even dunking each other, and belly-flopping off the diving boards. She couldn't help but smile as she looked at Nathan. He seemed light-years older and far more interesting than what she was seeing. She'd lucked out.

Nathan was a good swimmer. Something he attributed to stock ponds and natural springs on the reservation. And he made her laugh. He said he still felt overdressed because when swimming, clothing was optional on the Rez as a child. They swam and then just relaxed out in the sun on the lounge chairs. It was comfortable. She could be quiet with Nathan, not talk, just enjoy the sun.

They went into the pool one last time before needing to dress for the cookout. It was already after five and the cookout started at six. Nathan's dry clothing was in his dad's office. She'd get her things out of the locker, change in the nearby contestant's lounge and meet him there. Again, he took her hand and walked her back into the main building. The guy was sweet, really sweet. He turned to smile and wave before disappearing down the hall.

The lockers and lounge were in the opposite direction but not that far away. As she turned the corner to walk down the long row of lockers toward number 14, she stopped. Not only was her locker open, there was a girl going through the pockets of her shorts. What the—?

"Hey, excuse me. Do you want to check my beach bag, too?"

Skyler didn't try to keep the sarcasm out of her voice. And it got the result she wanted—her shorts were quickly stuffed back into the locker and the girl whirled around to meet her, instantly looking contrite and stammering, "Oh my God, you're using this locker?"

"Well, yeah. 'Using' might not be the best word. I was *assigned* this locker. Why do you ask?"

"I'm so sorry. I know what this looks like. How about a truce? Please accept my apologies. My name is Annette. This used to be my best friend's locker. She died recently and the casino asked me to gather up her things and return them to her family. The floor manager guy gave me the combination. He must not have realized that these had already been given out. I work here by the way. You're a contestant? I've seen your picture in the publicity stills. Welcome."

"Thanks." Skyler waited expecting Annette to walk away.

"I can only imagine how messy this locker was when you opened it. Robbi wasn't known for her housekeeping skills. I bet you found all sorts of things." Annette turned to peer inside the metal box.

"Nope. So clean it looked new."

"Wow. I can't imagine. Makes me think I have the wrong locker." She laughed nervously. "You didn't find any papers? Like classroom stuff?"

"Nothing." Skyler was getting impatient, but more importantly she was now really wondering about the flash drive in her bag. Someone must have thought that this Robbi had information or something that would have been of value to them. Blackmail came to mind; at least, something that was worthwhile.

Annette locked eyes and lowered her voice. "You know, Robbi was murdered."

"Here? In the casino?" Skyler hoped Annette hadn't noticed the slight, involuntary shiver that made her catch her breath.

"Actually, just down the hall, in a cold storage unit behind a restaurant." Annette was watching her closely.

"I hope they caught the murderer."

"They have someone but it might not be the right someone. I mean, like everyone needs to be careful. You with me? Places like this attract trouble."

Skyler didn't give her a yea or nay or in any way

acknowledge what places like this might do. She simply gave a slight shrug. "Well, I need to get changed." Skyler reached past Annette and removed her clothing and shoes, put her beach bag in the locker, and closed the door.

"It was nice meeting you." Annette offered.

Skyler just nodded and watched Annette walk away. Then once she was certain Annette was out of sight, Skyler quickly reopened the locker, retrieved the flash drive from her beach bag and tucked it into the pocket of the shorts she was soon to change into. Better to keep it with her so she wouldn't worry about finding that someone else had gone through her things and have it disappear. It still didn't solve the problem of having something that didn't belong to her.

And the murder of the supposed owner? A much more serious situation—something with consequences, maybe. She had to give it to someone. Wasn't Nathan's father the Human Resources Director at the casino? He would know what to do and hopefully be an impartial recipient. That was it. Settled. She would hand off the drive to Nathan.

* * *

"We need to step up our game—again. This pussy-footing around is getting us nowhere. I would have thought the Aponi murder would have gotten more coverage, but thanks to the pageant it's been almost overlooked. What's our man saying? Is he ready with Plan B? We need to get that Pecos guy out of here. I'm not convinced that he's stopped looking for whatever it was that he thinks Robbi had. And we sure as hell haven't uncovered anything ourselves." The man held the phone in place between his cheek and shoulder freeing his hands to type. "Listen, I know you think you've got things under control, but I'm not so sure. We cover our bases and don't take chances. Questions?"

He paused, listening to the answer on the other end of the line. "Well, it better be foolproof. You think the person he hired can be trusted?" Another pause, "The money's been paid? Okay, then, stay on top of this. If we're implicated in any way, it's your neck, too. Got that?" He slipped the phone back into his pocket and closed the laptop. He didn't feel like working. If there was one thing in life he hated more than anything else, it was when everything depended upon 'wait and see' and he had absolutely no control over the outcome.

Chapter 17

This was going to be the first time that they'd gotten to spend any length of time together, and Zac was nervous. He'd talked Alana into going to a baseball game and then felt guilty. Skyler had passed on the baseball game and talked Nathan into the movie being shown in the casino auditorium. Would Alana rather have gone to it? Maybe she was just being a good sport and would hate baseball. They'd had a choice between baseball or a Disney movie and she'd let him choose. Had she secretly hoped he would want to see a movie? Now it was too late to change their minds. He hoped he wasn't off to a bad start.

"I'd rather see Tampa Bay, you know, the Rays; but the Marlins are a lot closer." The Rays were second in their league and had been doing really well. He'd like to talk more about his heroes, but Zac could tell that Alana wasn't that interested. Was she just being polite? But, at least, she had agreed to go. It would be up to him to make the evening interesting. Whatever that would mean. "Dinner is on the bus before we take off for Miami. We're supposed to meet in the parking lot to board by five-thirty."

"I guess there's a dress code?" Alana pulled out a brochure from her bag. "There's a rule for everything." She leafed through the booklet. "Yeah, here it is—off campus rules. No shorts, and no denim, and no skin showing such as midriff, décolleté, and back."

"Damn. My belly button's way cool." Zac said it completely deadpan without even the hint of a smile.

Alana frowned, then burst into laughter. "That's funny."

Whew! He'd made her laugh. Maybe this wasn't going to be so bad after all. "We better get going."

Alana put the brochure back in her bag. "But no shorts? It's so hot down here. I hate the humidity."

"It's not the tundra." Zac liked the idea that he could talk about Alaska and she understood. He'd shared a little about his village, about how it was being moved because of rising seawater. She had even visited Moose Flats and seemed to know it fairly well. And she wanted to go to the University of Alaska in Anchorage like he did. On the really positive side, she liked soccer.

* * *

Dinner was sandwiches in boxes handed out on the bus—a choice of roast beef, chicken, Bar-B-Q pulled pork, or a veggie avocado and Swiss cheese on rye. Chips, a piece of fruit, chocolate mousse, or a wild cherry empanada rounded out the menu. He opted for the Bar-B-Q, and it was actually pretty good. The buses remained parked until leftovers and litter had been deposited in plastic bags held by casino staff who walked up and down the aisles before depositing the refuse in bins at the edge of the parking lot. Finally, they were on their way.

The Marlins' new ballpark was exactly thirteen miles away but, depending on traffic, could take up to a half hour to get there. Zac had read about it and wasn't disappointed in its size or design. Located on seventeen acres, the stadium could hold up to thirty-seven thousand fans. Wow. That seemed like a lot of people, but there were music events held there, too. Wasn't Elton John scheduled?

It was super modern looking and had a retractable roof. That's why it wasn't uncomfortable inside. There were four parking garages, Zac counted them as their bus rolled to a stop in one of six asphalt covered lots outside the arena.

Four VIP boxes had been designated as Miss Teen USA seating and each had a bar, several TV screens that captured various views of the field, in addition to two wait-people to serve soft drinks, and snacks. Plus, every box was air-conditioned. Before the game, several players visited the boxes, handing out autographed baseballs. Alana whispered that he could have hers too if he wanted. Like yeah, did she even have to ask?

It was a good game. The Marlins were hosting the Dodgers and the game was tied for several innings before the Marlins pulled away with a walk-off homer in the ninth. It was a big win for the home team, and to celebrate there was a show of fireworks. Finally, they boarded the buses for the ride back to the casino.

"What'd you think? Would you go to another game?" Zac was curious. Alana had spent most of the evening texting.

"Yeah, no. Well, maybe." She smiled, then leaned back against the seat. Before they reached the hotel, her eyes were closed, and her head rested on his shoulder.

* * *

Both buses pulled up in front of the casino to let their passengers off at the main entrance. It was already ten-thirty at night but the place was swarming with people. In any other business, this would be considered a morning rush to work. Most of those contestants who had chosen not to go to the baseball game had seen the movie and were now going to the pool or having a late dinner in one of the restaurants.

"Hungry?" Zac realized his stomach was growling.

"Sort of. I've been thinking about pizza."

"The food court's open until 11. If we hurry, they'd probably still serve us."

Not only was it open, having extended its hours until midnight, the Friday special was pizza—a choice of deep dish, thin, or stuffed crust. They had to wait on a table but not for long. One along the floor-to-ceiling windows opened up in under ten minutes. They both agreed on sausage, mozzarella, one half black olive, the other half mushroom and settled back to people-watch the pool below.

"So, tell me what you have to do to win?" Zac was honestly curious. "I mean, are there like categories that you have to get a perfect score in? People hold up cards and you try to get all tens?" He was trying to be funny throwing in an Olympic reference, but he was interested in what she had to do.

"Sorry, nothing as exciting as the Olympics. There are

three categories: fitness, evening dress, and the interview. Each is one-third of the total points. There isn't a swimsuit competition. The judges want to see that you portray a healthy lifestyle. Unless you tell, no one will ever know that I'm eating pizza tonight." She said it with a totally straight face, but her eyes were laughing.

"Hey, I didn't see a thing." This was said just as the waiter plopped the extra-large three-topping pizza down in the center of the table. "Actually, this looks pretty healthy to me." He was already pulling a slice of the pie from the mushroom side and putting it on a plate. "What about the evening gown? How is that judged?"

"On poise, stage presence, confidence."

"Not on what you're wearing?"

"Only sort of. They want to see that you have a sense of style, even a sense of elegance. You have to rock something current, and tasteful. They want to know that you are aware of what looks good on *you*. I mean you can't wear something from your mom's closet."

"So, the interviews are the hardest?"

"Could be for some. You have to be able to talk."

"Do you know the topics beforehand?"

"No, but in general they could be questions about your family, or school, or future plans. Do you have hobbies? Are you involved in your community? That sort of thing. I organized a group of student tutors from middle schools in Anchorage and Fairbanks to help those displaced in sea coast communities because of environmental issues—like Moose Flats. A lot of schools were closed when communities were moved or consolidated. Students lost learning time; it was easy to fall behind. We travel on weekends and hold classes in churches or school gymnasiums, and help students get back to their appropriate grade levels. I want to talk about that."

"Wow. I'm impressed. You're going to do great." And Zac meant it. Alana was smart, really pretty and already working to help others. The judges would be impressed, just like he was.

The talk turned to his school in Bellingham and what it was going to be like for Alana starting high school in Anchorage. She admitted to being a little nervous, mostly because she didn't know what to expect. He reassured her and allowed as how he felt the same. Soccer, however, had given him a head-start on getting to know some upper classmen. And he'd been pretty much accepted as a jock.

But then, so had she. Alana had moved from a position of center-midfielder to goalkeeper last year. Her success had even gotten her a trip to state finals as an alternate. Zac assured her that her success on the field would give her an 'in'—she didn't have anything to worry about. High school would be a no-brainer.

They continued to talk until all but one slice of pizza had disappeared. Zac was already giving some sort of follow-up visits serious thought. Going to school in Bellingham, Washington, during the year Zac often met his mother in Anchorage for a weekend. It wasn't farfetched to think he would be able to see Alana again. He wasn't going to mention it tonight, but would before she left.

"Now I'm really tired." Alana couldn't quite stifle a yawn. "I have to meet the makeup people tomorrow morning."

"Let's go. I'll walk you to your room."

There were three hotels: the Guitar Hotel with 638 rooms, the Oasis Tower offering another 168 guest rooms with exclusive swim-up suites, and the actual hotel itself with 469 luxury accommodations—every lodging choice from single rooms to suites had unbelievable panoramic views. At least that's what the publicity brochures said. And from what Zac had seen from the size of the buildings, it wasn't a lie.

All the contestants were housed in the Guitar Hotel which made walking Alana to her room a matter of choosing the right elevator.

The crowds had thinned other than the literal hordes still swarming around the foyer. Zac couldn't help but think he was on another planet. Women in evening dresses, men in suits, scantily clad waitresses stepping off the elevator. It was overly bright and made his eyes hurt the minute he came in from outside. Lights in the parking lot were nothing compared to the blinking lights, colored lights, spot lights—all the flash and sparkle with floor-to-ceiling color inside. And the place was loud. Most of the crowd was heading upstairs to gamble. But for the life of him, Zac couldn't see the fun in standing around all night or slouching on bar stools trying to win money. It didn't even look inviting.

"I have no idea what time it is." Alana stood in front of the panel of buttons beside the elevator and pulled her phone out of her purse. "Oh no, I just blew curfew. It's a little past one."

"Are you going to get in trouble?"

"I don't know. I can prove that we were at the restaurant. I don't see anyone from the pageant, I mean, like hall patrol."

"Maybe, you can sneak in and nobody will know." Zac appeared to be right when they exited the elevator on the twelfth floor and made it to her room without anyone stopping them. In fact, they passed exactly three people in the hallway, all older.

"I think I mentioned that I have makeup and hair in the morning, then interviews. I have no idea where I'll be at lunchtime. How about meeting me at the pool at four?"

"Ok. And Alana, thanks for going to the game tonight."

"I liked it ... sort of." She grinned.

"If you cross your fingers, lies don't count."

"You're sure?" She laughed, opened the door to her room and disappeared.

* * *

"He just saw his date to her door. He'll be walking back to the elevators in three minutes, tops. Everything ready?"

"Got it covered, boss. We're ready to go."

"This has got to be perfect. No fuck-ups."

"Hey, have a little trust. We know what we're doing."

"I hope so. We've got a lot riding on this."

"Easy now. Just sit back and wait for my call."

* * *

Zac reached the elevators, but this time he had to wait. He paused, pushed the down button twice and then leaned against the wall. Must be others who were just getting back to their rooms. This could take a while. So much for a curfew. It would be tough to police fifty-one contestants. He slid to the floor and tipped his head back to rest and waited before pressing the down button again. He'd about decided to find a staircase when he heard the almost silent whir of the car coming his way from above. When the elevator stopped and the door slid open, there was already a passenger inside.

"Hi." The girl standing by the control panel nodded but kept her eyes lowered and didn't return his greeting. She was wearing shorts, really short shorts with a dirty, torn shirt over a strapless top. Her hair was a mess, half in and half out of a ponytail clasp at the top of her head. And she seemed agitated, hands shaking, stepping back against the wall of the elevator after he got in.

Zac was trying not to stare and didn't notice what floor button she'd pressed so wasn't surprised when the car smoothly and gently settled into a stop two floors later. And then what happened next would play over and over in his mind for days to come. Before the door could open, she pressed the close button and using the wall as leverage, she hopped up both feet against the wall, then kicked off to tackle him, pushing him backwards.

A foot snaked between his legs catching him by the ankle and jerking a leg out from under him sending him to the floor to land on top of her. Where had she learned to do that? Was she some kind of Jiu Jitsu wrestler? He pulled back, trying to roll off but couldn't. Her hands were everywhere and two well-muscled legs wrapped around his back were pinning him to her. What the fuck? Why was she unzipping his fly? Was she drunk? How did you fight a woman? Could he hit her?

Suddenly a hand with razor sharp fingernails raked across his cheek then tore open his shirt. He could feel blood dripping onto his bare chest. What was she stuffing under his shirt? He squirmed to one side, freed a hand

and pulled out the wispy silk triangle of cloth, ripped on one side. Panties. Now the nails cut diagonally across his shoulder and her screams reached an ear-shattering pitch just as the elevator door opened. She suddenly kicked out from underneath him, shoving him sideways, hitting at him, yelling, calling him names—"bastard, filth, rapist ..."

Two uniformed security guards grabbed him, dragged him out of the elevator and slammed him up against the wall. "I'll teach your red-ass some manners." The fist grazed Zac's cheek and caused his head to bounce against the elevator's control panel.

"Wait. Stop. You don't know ..." Zac couldn't think straight. What was happening? What did they think he'd done? "I didn't do anything." He'd dropped the panties when they jerked him upright, but they'd seen them in his hand. Did they think he'd ... oh, shit, what did they think he'd done?

"I know what I saw with my own eyes you piece of shit." The guard jerked him forward and body slammed him back against the panel, then turned him face-first into the wall, pulled out cuffs, and slapped them on his wrists, arms behind his back.

"Hey, take it easy. He'll get what's coming to him. We just have to take him in, not kill him." The taller of the two guards put a restraining hand on the man holding Zac. "What we gotta do is get that poor girl some help. Are the EMTs on the way?" He turned toward the youngest of the three guards.

The kid nodded. "Any minute now. They've been called."

"No. Don't take me to the clinic. I need to report this. Look what he did to me. Don't let him get away with this."

Zac looked sideways as the second guard half-carried the girl through the elevator door. She slumped against him, almost falling twice. Her clothes were torn, a blouse hardly covering anything, one breast peeking out from what must have been some kind of tube top before it was ripped halfway to her navel. But the bruises ... Zac sucked in his breath. The insides of her thighs were red with patches of blue. Dried blood—his? hers?—had glued a strand of hair to her face. Her lip was bleeding; she'd lost a shoe and her shorts were unbuttoned and torn— hanging onto her body by one leg. And no panties, the black thong with a busted strap was already in an envelope. Evidence? And, if so, of what? A white, bare cheek flashed out at him with every step she took. Zac sucked in his breath. He wasn't an idiot. He was going to be slammed in jail for rape. But he didn't do it. Would they believe that he was the one attacked?

There was absolutely no doubt that she had been attacked. It just wasn't by him. But who did it? And where? Had she been knocked unconscious, maybe only coming to in the elevator when he entered and thought he was her attacker? No, he remembered clearly that she attacked him. She had been waiting on him or maybe just for any male that she could blame for something that had happened somewhere else.

Those bruises on her inner thigh hadn't been put there by him. But now what? How did he prove he'd done nothing wrong? It was going to be his word against hers. His cheek was stinging from the hit by the guard. Would he be hit again? He knew he wasn't safe with these men in uniform. Nobody wanted to listen to him.

"Hey, gimme something to cover her up. This girl deserves some decency from us. Somebody get a blanket."

This last guard yelled over his shoulder as he still had an arm around the girl to keep her from falling.

By now a crowd had gathered. Zac counted almost twenty people staring at them. And camera flashes. Where did photographers come from? Of course, during the pageant week, they were everywhere always primed to catch that bestselling pic of whatever they could peddle to some hot teen mag. But this? Where would these pictures end up? Evidence? And not for his side. Zac had watched enough TV to know that he shouldn't say any more. Just shut up and find some way to contact his dad.

"Let me through, move to one side ... now." Andy Thunderhawk was ushering two emergency medical technicians toward the group of people tightly pressed around the so-called victim who was still leaning on the older of the original guards. At least she had a blanket wrapped snugly around her and had put on her missing shoe. Her head was still down and she was sobbing softly. Two cops moved to her side and whispered something and helped her walk with them to the lounge area with the medical techs close behind.

Was this all an act? It was a good one. Torn clothing, blood, bruises ... Zac knew it looked pretty convincing. He needed to get someone who was on his side. Wait. Wasn't that the floor manager guy? He'd be able to call his father.

"Andy?" Zac yelled hoping Andy would hear above the buzz of noise from the crowd.

Andy turned to look at him, and in that moment, Zac was sorry he'd called out to him. Andy just looked disgusted and kept shaking his head, but he walked closer to stand about four feet away. "I don't want to tell you how disappointed I am in you. You're disgusting. You beat the shit out of that poor girl and scared her to death, I'm sure. Anybody ever teach you to keep that thing in your pants?" Andy gestured toward Zac's crotch.

"Call my dad." Zac could feel his anger rising. He didn't have to take this. He was innocent, only no one seemed to care. No one would listen to him. The guard standing nearest him who had been talking on a two-way, pulled Zac out away from the wall and pushed him in front of him.

"Start walking. We're going to find a nice hole for this scum to crawl into."

It was apparent that Zac was being pushed toward the back door. Now came getting locked up. He was probably in for a ride to the county police station—if that's where they took people in situations like this. There was something mentioned about his being from out of state and only visiting the area. Would he get a chance to talk then? He only hoped that Andy would call his father.

He could hear the girl yelling as they walked past the open door of the lounge. She was demanding to be taken to the police station, too—demanding that someone take her statement. She was still yelling that Zac needed to be locked up; he threatened her life, tried to rape her … Zac stopped listening. Why was she doing this?

* * *

His phone was vibrating. Ben picked it up off of the nightstand and checked the number. The casino—at two twenty in the morning? What the hell?

"Hello?"

"Thought I better be the one to tell you that that piece of shit, half-breed son of yours is on his way to jail."

"Andy? What are you saying? Jail? What's going on?"

"I'll bet you this wasn't his first time. I'd put money on the fact you've had to save his ass before, cover up some mess, maybe more than one."

"You're not making sense. I have no idea what you're talking about."

"I'm sure we'll find out soon enough how much you know. Good luck with this. That kid won't get out of detention until he's eighty." Click.

Ben stood holding his phone. Not one word of all that made the least bit of sense. And Andy? He sounded genuinely angry. No hail and hearty, good 'ol boy banter. Hadn't he called this guy his friend?

"What's going on? Who was on the phone?" Julie propped herself up on one elbow.

Ben shared what he'd heard. "I'm going to take a run over to the jail—quicker to just go there and not wait for someone to pick up the phone and then try to track down what's happening."

"Wait. I'm coming, too."

"Hey, babe, this may not be anything at all. I don't want you to miss sleep over some false alarm."

"If there's even a smidgen of truth to the fact that Zac might be in trouble, I don't want to be left here. I could go to the casino while you stop by the jail and see if anyone knows anything. I'll take my car. We know Zac took his date to the ballgame. Do we know that he didn't come home?"

"I'm checking on the way out."

Inching the boys' bedroom door open, he could plainly see that Zac's bed hadn't been slept in. Damn. He'd been hoping to literally put all this to rest quickly. Looked like that wasn't going to happen. Nathan was fast asleep. He'd leave a note in the kitchen to let him know why he would wake up to an empty house.

* * *

Pockets emptied, frisked, ID cards for him and Zac that proved their Native heritage and their relationship, handed to the desk sergeant, a brief history of his employment that involved the casino; then, a cop escorted him back to an interrogation room.

"What are they holding him for?"

"You don't know?" The cop seemed surprised. "Sexual assault, attempted rape."

Ben stifled a laugh. Was the cop kidding? "Ridiculous. There's no way. That's my son; I know him. Who was the victim?"

"That's something you'll find out. I'm not at liberty to say. The kid's a minor. That's why you'll be with him. I'll be right outside the door if you need anything."

Ben thanked him and started to enter the room just as a guard was leading Zac down the hallway from the opposite direction. Zac looked terrible. His clothes were torn, buttons missing from his shirt, his cheek was swollen and his left eye was black and blue. It looked like blood on his shirt and Ben could see long scratches across his cheek. What had happened?

"Dad ... I ..."

"It's OK, son, I'm here to find out what all this is about." Ben quickly hugged Zac, then stepped to one side as Zac and the man ushering him forward entered the room in front of Ben.

The man in jeans and a t-shirt, probably a detective, pulled a chair out from the table for Zac and then moved to sit opposite him. Ben took a seat at the end of the table and waited while the detective opened a folder.

"Name and then age, address and place of work if you are currently employed." Ben heard Zac comply. "How long have you been in this area? Your relationship to Dr. Benson Pecos?" Again, straightforward questions and quick answers. Now it was his turn, Ben verified the question of parentage, shared Zac's home Alaskan address and added his school address in Bellingham. He also verified Zac's age. After a brief admonition for Ben to speak only when spoken to, and for Zac to tell the truth, the detective was ready to begin.

"I want you to tell me exactly what happened this evening. Start with your night as an escort. I understand that you attended the Marlin's game? I need to know the particulars—give me names of who you were with, where exactly you went before the game, after the game … and maybe most importantly, give me times. For example, when did you take your date back to her room?"

Zac sat staring down at the table until the detective prompted him. "You can go slow. Just don't leave anything out."

Zac nodded and began. "I'm an escort for the Miss Teen USA pageant." He described dinner in boxes on the bus, going to the game, pizza, and finally a goodnight in front of his date's room door in the Guitar Hotel—a complete step-by-step overview—with Zac carefully accounting for everything they did.

"And what time was it when you got back from the game?"

Zac paused, "I guess it was about ten-thirty. We were both hungry."

"We? Doesn't this young lady have a name?"

"Yeah, sorry. I was assigned to Alana Eberly from Alaska. After we got back from the Marlin's game, we had pizza in the food court. We didn't watch the time and it was after one when I walked her to the door of her room."

"And where was that exactly?"

"Twelfth floor."

"Did you go in?"

"No, that's not allowed. I walked back to the elevators to go downstairs and catch a ride home. They have Ubers lined up outside for those of us who live in town."

"Had you been drinking?"

"I'm fourteen."

"I'll repeat, had you been drinking or taking drugs? Were you in any way impaired?"

Zac slowly shook his head.

"I didn't hear that. Keep in mind I cannot record a nod." He pointed to the recorder at the edge of the table.

"No."

"Did you go anywhere else before arriving at the elevators?"

"There wasn't any place else to go."

"Ok, now I want you to tell me exactly what happened. Was the elevator at your floor when you got there?"

"No, I had to wait, I guess about five minutes. Maybe more."

Ben leaned forward placing his forearms on the table. He didn't want to miss any of this. And he needed a clear view of Zac—his expressions, in addition to his tone of voice and answers.

"What did you notice, if anything, when the elevator door opened?"

"A girl."

"Was she coming forward to leave?"

"No, she was leaning against the side wall."

"Did you speak to her?"

"I said hi but she didn't say anything."

"What happened next?"

Zac related how the girl jumped onto him using the wall as leverage, tripped him and pinned him to the floor.

"Whoa, stop right there. You're a good-sized kid, you want to rethink what you just said? A girl that weighs maybe a hundred or so pounds jumps you? Holds you down? Should I remind you that you were caught holding her panties?"

That did it. Ben knocked over his chair pushing back from the table and standing up. The noise caused the guard standing in the hallway to open the door. Ben stopped the questioning and demanded that the session end until his son had a lawyer. Everything Zac had shared so far screamed setup. A nasty, well-planned set up. But why? Was Zac the intended victim? It made no sense, but Ben was pissed as hell. He hated people who took advantage of kids. If Zac said the girl jumped him, then, that's exactly what happened. And a lawyer? Where did he get one of those in the middle of the night?

"Let me talk to my son."

"No can do, sorry." The detective motioned the guard to stand back. "Whatever's said is done with me in the room."

Suddenly a man appeared in the doorway. "I'll talk with the father. Escort Dr. Pecos to my office, and I'll have the young man here taken to a holding area." The man giving the orders seemed to be in command of the situation. "Dr. Pecos, I'm Chief of Police, Raymond Patrick. I'll be with you in a moment."

"Don't worry, we'll get to the bottom of this. I promise." Ben hoped those weren't just empty words, but he thought Zac looked relieved as he quickly hugged his son and followed the guard out the door.

Ben didn't have long to wait before Chief Patrick walked into his office. "Glad I caught you. I'd like you to have the full account of what happened from our side before you involve a lawyer."

"I appreciate that. As I'm sure you can imagine, this is a shock."

"I have a sixteen-year-old son. The teen years aren't easy—for parents or child."

"I remember."

"This is what the girl alleges took place. We took her statement earlier. In fact, she insisted that we bring her in. She refused to go to the clinic. Seemed to think that wasn't needed." He handed Ben a folder. "Here, use my work table. Some of these are cell phone shots, but they're fairly clear. You might want to match up photos with text. I'll give you a few minutes. I'm going to get a cup of coffee, anything for you?"

Ben thanked him but shook his head. The folder in front of him was the only thing he could think about. He picked up the first page, separated the attached photos, spread them out, and started to read. Sickening. And it got worse. Torn clothing, shorts pulled down, panties ripped from her body ... a photo of Zac tossing the panties onto the floor outside the elevator. Ben sat back. The description was one of a full-out assault, a frenzied attack on this girl's body, bruises left by knees forced between thighs, breasts roughly grabbed … and her report? Graphic and angry. She wanted revenge for being accosted. Yet, why was Ben not comfortable with what he was reading? He had photos in front of him to back up her words … still, something was off. Ben leaned forward and took a deep breath. What was he missing? Maybe if he reread.

He hadn't heard the chief come into the room. "Questions?" The chief walked to his desk and sat down.

"Yeah, a lot. For example, what about cameras? My figuring says all this was supposed to have happened between ten and twelve minutes—with at least five of those minutes Zac spent waiting for the elevator in the hallway by himself. I didn't read anything about cameras … video tape proving the assault didn't happen as she reported— either inside or outside of the elevator."

"Exactly. Now you understand why we're talking. Very conveniently the circuit to that part of the hotel was out of commission. The breaker box is in a mechanical closet that opens onto the back parking lot. Unfortunately, yesterday a backhoe that was being used to tear up and redistribute soil from an extended planting bed in preparation for new landscaping, backed into the closet. Electricians patched some of the wiring together—what was deemed needed for safety lighting—but cameras will be out for another week."

"Convenient is the right word for it."

"Certainly leaves a lot of unanswered questions." The chief took a sip of his coffee. "I suppose the main question is why? Or maybe *who* would find a need to set up a fourteen-year-old boy? Any ideas?"

"None that I can think of at the moment. What do we know about the girl?"

"A local, works as a spa attendant on the first floor. She's currently doing double duty, having been hired by the pageant folks to support their staff. It's in the notes somewhere but I seem to remember that she's helping mornings with hair and make-up. As for particulars, I've written the stats down. Let me take a look." He picked up the top page from the folder. "Here we go. She's twenty-one, been working at the hotel since high school mostly in housekeeping, nothing out of the ordinary, no priors of any kind. Good work record, very few days missed from work in two years. Does the name, Brianna Walters mean anything? Ever hear your boy mention her?"

"No. My sons haven't been here long, not quite three weeks. Not sure they've met very many people their age. I was pleased that they were asked to be escorts for the contestants. I thought it would be a chance to make friends, even get to know what the area has to offer. Zac was thrilled to get to go to a Marlins game."

"No interest in girls?"

"Not yet. At least nothing serious that I know of. I have that to look forward to. As long as we're trying to figure out the *why* to all this, do you think I'm going to get hit up for money? Since my son's telling the truth that would be the only thing that makes sense. A nice tidy sum to make all this go away, some sort of a payment to drop the charges?"

"That's my best guess—assuming your boy's innocent. Now, whether this is something that Miss Walters thought of, or she's being put up to it, I can only hope we'll find out before more damage is done." The chief paused, "I think that's a good kid back there. I believe him. The time frame, the lack of cameras, his having just completed escorting a young lady to a baseball game … it's not the portrait of a rapist lying in wait outside an elevator to ravage a young woman that he couldn't have known was already in the elevator car." He gestured toward the hallway. "I have the names of a couple lawyers that you might want to talk with. Both have had experience with young adults. I can vouch for either one. And I'd bet one would be available to talk right now. Let me have Zac brought back to the interrogation room. A guard will have to be present but you can have some time with your son and hopefully, at least on the phone, converse with a lawyer."

"Thank you. I'm out of my depth here. I really appreciate your help."

"I hope I've been helpful. Dr. Pecos, stay in touch." The chief stood and offered his hand, "I want to think that this will have a happy ending."

Ben pulled out his phone and texted Julie. She'd be on her way to the casino and he needed to share what had happened and that, just maybe, they had a supporter in the chief. He didn't want her to worry.

* * *

Julie pulled into Ben's parking slot in the casino's garage and hurried to the front entrance. It wasn't even four a.m. and the place was crazy-busy. She had seen two police cars in the back and two cops in the front foyer. The rest of the floor looked like business as usual. So far, so good. She'd worried that there had been some kind of general alarm with a crowd of people seeing Zac in cuffs. If there had been a crowd, the cops had done a good job of dispersing it. She couldn't really see anything out of what would be considered normal for a casino.

Maybe she should just grab a cup of coffee and wait for Ben. Then, she read his text. Oh my God. There was no way that Zac could be guilty. Rape? The accusation was just unfounded. There was no way that girl was telling the truth.

"Annette." She hadn't meant to yell out the girl's name, but just as the main elevator doors had opened, she had walked out. "Wait up. I need to talk." Who better to know what had taken place than Annette who had been here all night. Julie had taken a step in her direction when Annette whirled to face her.

"I just bet you do. Probably want to talk about that sleaze stepson of yours who tried to rape my best friend. I hope he never gets out of jail. He doesn't deserve to be free." She turned, then yelled over her shoulder, "Don't bother me again." With this, Annette hurried into the nearest restaurant and disappeared.

Wow. Julie couldn't be more in shock if Annette had slapped her. And best friend? Certainly seemed that Annette had her share—in addition to Robbi. To be fair, maybe Julie couldn't expect anything different. There was something to be said for one friend supporting another. But it was tough for Julie to process the anger. She hadn't been expecting it.

"That husband of yours around?"

Julie had no idea how long Andy had been standing behind her, but she was glad that she hadn't jumped. "No, not yet, he's still at the police station."

"Figures. But just a word to the wise: It's a little late to practice any good parenting skills. Kids don't get in trouble if they've had a proper upbringing."

"Andy, I think—"

"Personally? I don't care what you think. What happened tonight was unthinkable. That pervert gave us all a black eye. All those young girls running around here? They've got to be scared to death about now. And I don't blame them."

"I don't think you've heard the whole story." Julie could feel the anger rising. How dare he draw such conclusions?

"Oh? Really? Let me tell you something. I don't need to *hear* anything. I *saw* what happened with my own eyes. The cops had to drag him off of her. He had her panties. I *saw* him throw her panties down. I *saw* her injuries. Don't give me some 'poor misunderstood kid' crap; I was there."

"I don't have to listen to this. I'm disappointed that you seem intent on misdirecting your anger and concern. Frankly, I expected better from you. Do you need to talk with my husband?"

"Not I. Assistant Bowlegs wants him in her office the minute he shows up." With that, Andy walked past her.

Julie pulled her phone out and texted Ben. If he hadn't planned on coming into work, he needed to reconsider with Ms. Bowlegs looking for him. She promised breakfast and said she'd wait in his office. She started to put her phone back into her purse.

"You know, you wouldn't be my choice for this story."

The man was close enough that she felt his breath. She needed to pay attention to her surroundings. "My god, you scared me." Julie took a couple deep breaths before turning toward her boss. What was Ken Usher doing here at the crack of dawn? "Mind if I ask a snoopy question?

What are you doing here?"

"Got a call that there was a little excitement earlier. Sorry, I don't mean to make light of what happened; it's serious, really serious and is going to get the casino a whole bunch of bad publicity. Damn. I can't think of a worse time for this to happen—right in the middle of the Miss Teen USA pageant. Absolutely rotten timing. And I'm sorry that you're involved."

"You know, you're the third person who has drawn and quartered my stepson before a trial. Isn't there more than a little possibility that he's innocent?"

"Hey, no need to go all mama bear on me. I hope for your family's sake that there's some explanation. But, as of right now, things don't look good. And I don't want to get called out for prejudicial reporting—you're off the story."

"Right. See you at the office. I'll be in by eight." She stepped away and turned toward the hallway leading to Ben's office. Julie knew if she said more, her job might be in jeopardy. Everyone seemed to have his mind made up—Zac was guilty of a heinous crime and deserved severe punishment. And that was just something she knew was a lie. But how to prove it?

Chapter 18

I want you out of here just as quickly as you can clean out your office. Do you know what this says about you? Your son is some sort of perverted, sex fiend—just how did you raise this young man? Our children grow up in our image. But more than that. Your son is a Native, the recipient of warrior blood. He should be a proud young man ready to step into the shoes of the leaders of his tribe. But in jail? For an act of atrocity against a woman? For shame. And you the father. No one around here is going to trust you. I don't trust you anymore."

Ben sat in front of April Bowleg's desk and waited for her rant to be over. He had no proof of Zac's wrongdoing being a lie, only his word with nothing to back it up. And, yeah, Ben was more than a little partial. Believing with all his heart and soul that Zac was innocent wasn't good enough. They would be meeting with the lawyer in the afternoon after their phone conversation earlier. The lawyer had seemed hopeful that time would be a key factor in proving Zac's innocence. Maybe there would be answers then. But leave his job? That seemed a little over the top. And difficult to do, seeing that he really was an employee of Indian Health Service and basically on loan. He'd call his supervisor. And hope that April Bowlegs would cool off. Though that seemed highly unlikely anytime soon.

He was just beginning to think he was free to go when Oscar Billie walked in.

"Sorry to keep you waiting."

"I just told Dr. Pecos our decision to let him go." Ms. Bowlegs sat down at her desk.

"I'm certain that you see our logic? There's no way that we—the tribe and corporation—can condone this behavior. Not by you or a member of your family. This is a huge personal scar on your ability to work here—to represent and help people in our hire. We run a tight ship. That's how we remain an accepted part of the community. We contribute to worthy causes, bring first class entertainment in, provide job opportunities for a couple hundred citizens—we do not endanger lives. About all we have left to do in order to salvage our good name now is get you and your family out of our casino. Show everyone that we can act decisively and move quickly."

"And if what you've been told isn't true? What if the story of sexual assault was fabricated?" Ben struggled to keep anger out of his voice.

Oscar Billie laughed sarcastically, not hiding a sneer as he faced Ben. "Just who are you trying to convince?

Sounds like you don't even believe it could be a lie yourself. Trusted individuals saw what happened. Miss Walters has a sterling reputation. She's worked here since high school. What reason would she have to lie?"

"I imagine we're going to find out. I don't rule out money playing a part in all this."

"Really? So, a respected Indian psychologist is planting seeds of doubt. Twisting a story to save the ass of his misbehaving son. And I use the word 'misbehaving' only because I can't bring myself to even discuss the heinous crime of accosting a helpless woman. I don't understand how you can discount witnesses. Doctor Pecos, people *saw* your son's actions. There's no mistaking what was observed by a number of people. I'm giving you the customary thirty-day notice to terminate your position here at the casino, but I'm counting on you to act expeditiously. You know, on second thought, might I suggest a carefully written letter of resignation? Offering apologies to all that you and your son have disappointed?"

"You'll have my answer by tomorrow morning." Ben turned and walked out of April Bowleg's office.

* * *

Alana was tired. The knock on the hotel door at four a.m. was too much. And Zac? Accused of attempted rape? Ridiculous. At first, she had thought it was a joke, and had laughed and said so; but the cop got testy and told her she better behave. Behave? How old was she? Five? He was treating her that way.

He kept pushing her to say that Zac had scared her, too. She refused, of course, and then later she did the math.

How could Zac have done all they were accusing him of by walking back to the elevators and riding down three floors? Didn't the cop say the *incident* took place on the elevator between floors twelve and nine? At or about one fifteen that morning. Less than ten, maybe at most fifteen minutes, for everything the cop described? Something didn't make sense. He couldn't have known there was anyone in the elevator, let alone a single woman. There was certainly no way that the incident could have been premeditated. After a night of baseball and pizza, he walks her to her room and then ten minutes later jumps someone in the elevator? No. Did not happen.

Should she try to call him? Oh, wait, the cop said that he was being held ... whatever that meant. Jail, she guessed or some kind of detention because he was a kid. And her day was packed. She had makeup and hair at nine immediately after breakfast, then a coaching class on speaking, and after lunch the interviews began. Maybe Zac would reach out to her. Surely, he could prove that he hadn't done what they were accusing him of. He was a sweet kid; she liked him a lot—baseball and all.

She grabbed a bagel and a small carton of orange juice. There were no sit-down breakfasts or lunches, only tables filled with anything anyone could want—at breakfast there was even an omelet bar. Alana took her food outdoors by the pool and kept her eye on the time. She had a half hour before she needed to show up for makeup.

* * *

The makeup area was set up in a large conference room. Twenty-five barber chairs were partially concealed behind curtains hanging on circular rods that could be pulled around to conceal each chair's occupant. In addition, these cubicles had a four-foot by four-foot mirror hanging on the wall. Open chests with slide out trays held brushes, Q-tips, tissue, and pots of color—color for lips, cheeks, as well as, eyes. Alana had been assigned to chair six and took a seat. She was five minutes early and had to wait ten minutes before a young woman stepped behind the curtain and introduced herself as Brianna.

The girl had been texting and put her phone down on the edge of the cabinet next to Alana before shaking out a nylon barber cape and draping it around Alana's neck. She'd just clipped it in place when the cubicle curtain was pushed aside and a rather stern-faced older woman whispered something and, excusing herself, Brianna followed the woman out of the room.

No reasons for needing to be called away, just a quick "I'll be right back." Oh well, maybe Alana could catch up with Zac. She'd text him. She'd placed her purse on top of the cabinet and reached to drag it closer. And that's when she saw the screen of Brianna's phone. She didn't mean to be a snoop. Not really. But there it was.

Brianna was pissed because she hadn't been paid the five thousand dollars that she'd been promised. Alana scrolled up a screen.

I was supposed to have it this morning.
You'll get it.
All five?
Every penny.
What's going to happen to that kid?
He's in jail.
I know that but when he gets out.

Not going to be anytime soon.
What if he comes after me?
That wuss? No way. He's 14.
But he's got friends, parents …
You worry too much. I told you we'd take care of everything.

Alana grabbed her phone and took pictures, barely touching the phone lying in front of her and not moving it. With an index finger, she carefully scrolled back two screens, snapped photos, moved forward one screen, until she'd captured the entire conversation. Most of the dialogue was this Brianna whining—they couldn't have set the assault up without her, she was the one who told them how she could make it look real—foolproof. And they better not try to cheat her out of what they promised. Remember, she could name names. That seemed stupid to Alana and more than a little dangerous. Who was she threatening?

The initials at the top of the page were of no help unless she knew of someone matching TD with the name Bossman. Nope, didn't mean a thing, but she didn't expect it to; she'd met so few people at the casino. What she did know was how important this newfound information was. They were talking about Zac, and didn't this completely exonerate him?

Right now, things didn't look good. Everyone was talking about what had happened and not once did she hear anyone stand up for Zac, excuse or explain his part in all this. No, it was up to her. She had to do something; at least, show what she'd just captured on her phone to someone—and the quicker, the better.

She put her phone back in her purse. And waited. When was Brianna coming back? She needed to make a move, show someone what she'd copied. She didn't think she'd heard the name of his supposed victim but she was assuming it was Brianna and she knew that what was on that phone proved the assault had been a setup. Someone, maybe this person with the initials TD, was paying this Brianna five thousand dollars.

She needed to be careful, talk to the right people. But who could help? His father? Yes, but wouldn't it be better to go to the police? Not leave any room for suspicion of a family member trying to produce evidence to clear a son's name? Think. What had she learned from watching police shows on TV? She was beginning not to trust anyone. But she had to act.

She got up and took the cape off. Still no Brianna or any other staff member coming her way. She'd do her own makeup; this was more important. She left the conference room and walked out to the foyer, looked up the number to the police station, and dialed. She introduced herself and asked for the Chief of Police. Wasn't that the person in charge of a station? Or was it called a precinct? When the grand total of her experience was a few TV shows, she could make mistakes. Not good. She needed to sound older than fourteen.

"He's not in, Miss Eberly." The receptionist was cordial, but not very helpful. Maybe if she told her why she was calling.

"I have information about the supposed attempted rape at the casino last night. I think he will be very interested. I think my information will prove that Zac Pecos was set up."

The receptionist paused. "Let me have you speak to Detective—"

"No. I need to speak to the chief." This was serious

enough to go right to the top. No second or third parties to maybe lose the information or not take it seriously, or worse, put off meeting with this Brianna and evaluating the evidence. It had to be someone who could release Zac right away. And to her way of thinking, that would be the chief.

"May I put you on hold? I'll text the chief and let him know you want to speak to him."

The elevator music came on, and Alana leaned against the wall of the casino's entry. She was doing the right thing. Intuition told her that her information was dynamite. She just hoped it wouldn't take long to locate the chief and that he'd be interested.

"May he reach you at this number?" The woman came back on the line. That was impressive. Alana had waited barely three minutes.

"Yes, this is my cell."

"He'll call you within five minutes. And Miss Eberly? Thank you for reporting what you know about this unfortunate situation. That's really good citizenship."

Alana was still standing in the foyer holding her phone when the Star Wars theme blasted out telling her she had a call.

"Hello?"

"Miss Eberly?"

"Yes."

"This is Chief Patrick. If you turn to your left and look over by the restaurant, I think you'll see me."

Alana laughed. There was a man in uniform waving from that exact spot. She waved back, dropped her phone into her purse and walked toward him.

"This turned out to be convenient. Let's find someplace

comfortable to talk. There's a table and a couple chairs over there. Doesn't look like we'd be disturbed." He pointed to a corner well out of the traffic of people coming in and out of the front entrance. He ordered a couple bottles of water from a passing waiter and then sat facing her across a low table. "Now, how can I help? I understand that you know the young man we're holding?"

"He's the escort assigned to me during the pageant. I was with him last night. We went to a Marlins game."

"Lucky you. I'd like to be able to cheer the home team on in person."

"Well, yeah, I'm not into baseball … not really. But we had a good time. Chief, there's no way that Zac Pecos could have done any of what that woman is saying he did. He's nice, considerate, cares a lot about how he treats people."

"I believe what you're saying. I got that impression when I met him. But the receptionist said you have information that might clear him?"

Alana nodded. "It'd be easier if I sent you screen shots of what I have."

"Text them to this number." He handed her a card and pointed out his cell. "What am I going to be looking at?"

"I guess it all depends on whether the girl who is blaming Zac Pecos for attempted rape is named Brianna."

"She is."

"Then you have copies of three pages of text messages between this Brianna and some unidentified person discussing what happened last night—what appears to be a promised payment but is still owing for the incident."

The chief pulled up his text messages. "Got them." He read through the texts, looked up and then back at his phone again. "Tell me exactly how you got these."

Alana explained being a part of the pageant and meeting Brianna for makeup, only to have her called away leaving her phone on a cabinet top in plain view.

"This turns the entire investigation three hundred and sixty degrees. We're starting over and may not even have an incident to investigate, at least not as a felony. I gotta say that this supports what my intuition has been screaming— the kid is innocent. You're a life saver; do you know that? Quick thinking and making the right decisions. You saw something and acted—you ever think of becoming a detective?" He was kidding but Alana was flattered.

"What will happen now?"

"For starters, we'll reinterview Miss Walker. I need to get ahold of her and set up a time for her to come down to the station. I should probably do that now. Which way is that makeup area?" He paused, "You know, it'd be helpful if you could point her out to me. Do you have the time to come with me?"

"Sure. And Zac? What will happen to him now?"

"If everything goes the way it's pointing, he'll be free by the end of the day."

"That's great. Follow me." With Alana going first, they walked back down the hallway to the conference room now full of teens and makeup artists.

"So, there you are." Brianna was standing outside the curtained cubicle that had been Alana's and was literally tapping her foot. "I can't believe that you just took off. You know my time is worth something. You've managed to waste about a half hour of it so far. And who are you?" Brianna appeared to just realize that the chief was with Alana.

"Chief Raymond Patrick, local police. We need to

revisit your testimony. I'd like you to accompany me to the station."

"Now?" Brianna sighed, "I have a job to do. I work here. I would have thought your guys asked enough questions this morning. You have my statement."

"Some new evidence has surfaced."

"How can there be new evidence? It happened last night, over ten hours ago. There were witnesses, photos of my injuries, I met with your people at the station and gave a complete report … what can possibly be new?"

"I understand that you're waiting on a payment of five thousand dollars for your part in the—what should I call it? Maybe 'scheme' to frame an innocent kid with the type of crime that could ruin his life. I don't know the *why* and that's where I'd like your help."

"I don't know what you're talking about. Five thousand dollars? I've never heard of any five thousand dollars." Alana watched as all of the color drained from Brianna's face. Her makeup seemed to be sticking to an ashen background that made the rosy highlights along her cheekbones to appear as blood-red streaks.

"Your phone records say otherwise."

"My phone records?" Brianna suddenly reached past Alana and grabbed her purse from the edge of the cabinet, knocking the ceramic tip jar to the tile floor. The shattering glass scattered shards and money as Brianna backed away, then turned and ran. But not before she'd yelled, "I have a lawyer. Talk to my lawyer."

The chief turned to Alana. "I'll get my guys on it. They'll be able to pick her up." The chief pulled his two-way off his belt. "After I get the word out, I'll see if Zac's father is in. He needs to hear the news and you probably need to finish up here. I'll keep in touch. And, Alana, again, let me say thank you for some quick thinking and taking action. That kid owes you, big time."

* * *

"Hey, calm down, no worries."

"Oh yeah? Cops are trying to find her. Why the fuck didn't you pay the 5K up front? She's going to buckle. She won't stand up to strong-arm tactics used by the cops. She'll be naming names and singing like a canary."

"First of all, she's with me. Nobody's going to find her."

"How do you mean that?"

"That's for me to know and you to find out."

* * *

"He's free to come home? I can just go pick him up?" Ben shook his head in disbelief. "That's the best news I've had in what seems like a long time." Ben motioned for the chief to take a seat. "Thank you."

Julie moved to hug Ben. "Yes, thank you, Chief Patrick. That's wonderful."

"Don't thank me, thank Miss Alaska. She might not like baseball, but she'd make a hell of a detective." He filled Ben and Julie in on what had taken place, ending with showing them the screen shots Alana had provided. "I think it's safe to say that we put a scare in one Brianna Walker. We just need to know who put her up to implicating your son in that bit of elevator theater last night."

"I think that's the big question, why ... what would anyone have to gain by the attack on Zac? Though I've been given my walking papers this morning for being a bad parent and setting a despicable example as a human resources authority."

"Really?" Julie looked shocked.

"Yeah, I was called into Ms. Bowleg's office and she and Oscar Billie gave me thirty-days' notice to be gone."

"Have you even been here a month?" Chief Patrick leaned forward frowning. "That seems a little over the top, even in reaction to what had happened if it had been for real."

Ben shrugged. "I think whoever decided to hire a Native changed his or her mind. For whatever reason, I don't think I fit in. I'm not perceived as a team player."

"I'm not political but with the statewide elections coming up and Indian gaming being on the ballot, there just seem to be a number of incidents recently that have called unfavorable attention to the casino and its overseers. There's been a push to more equitably represent all gaming interests across the state and not have a monopoly held by the reservation." The chief paused. "That takes a big investment. We're not playing with amateurs here, and not poor ones. I guess I'm trying to say, be careful. I don't think we've seen the last of these incidents."

"Unfortunately, I think you're right." Ben wondered how his bosses would react when they found out that Zac had been framed. Would everything be swept under the rug? Everything they said to him just be forgotten, as if it didn't happen?

It was going to be interesting to find out.

"I think Miss Walters will be able to bust this wide open. I'm assuming my guys will be able to pick her up quickly, and we can sit down and get the straight scoop."

Chapter 19

Dinner at home. The day ended up a whirlwind of activity with the most important thing being picking up Zac at the station that afternoon after all charges had been dropped. She and Ben both opted to take off some time and just be together with the boys. It was only after it was all over that Julie realized how upset she'd been, and she knew the ordeal had crushed Ben.

If things hadn't come around so quickly, Ben would have had to share what was happening with Zac's mother. Raven would have come unglued. And probably shown up on their doorstep within forty-eight hours. That wouldn't have been pretty. No, they had dodged a bullet. Blending families was never easy, but being new at it caused Ben to blame himself if anything went wrong. She hoped that with more experience, fatherhood would become easier—but no one ever said the teen years were easy.

The two extra-large pizzas on the dining room table looked like they had been attacked by wolves and a sixty-four-ounce plastic bottle of soda was already empty. As always, she told herself that they could make up for all the carbs by eating extra veggies tomorrow. But wasn't that what she always told herself?

If Ben worried about fatherhood, didn't she worry about step-mothering? None of it was a given. And no teen came with a set of directions written on his back. She continued to carry plates to the kitchen. She'd opted for KP duty while the guys decided on a movie. From her vantage point, it looked like a *Spider Man* episode had won out.

"Hey, you're missing out on the good part," Ben called from the living room. "I can pause it and wait for you."

"No, I need to get laundry out of the dryer. You can catch me up later."

"Are you in if we decide to pop some corn?"

"Definitely." She laughed. Hadn't they just finished dinner not so long ago? She wasn't going to protest. There was something relaxing … comforting even, about having the family together.

She grabbed a laundry basket and headed downstairs. It was nice to have a utility room in the garage. Anything to keep extra heat out of the house during the summer. Days could be in the high nineties and the heat index substantially higher. She even put off doing laundry until the evening. She pushed the door open and was met with a blast of hot air. At least the dryer had completed its cycle and the temperature of the room helped her decide to do the folding upstairs.

She placed the overly large plastic laundry basket under the dryer's glass door. It was mostly work clothes—shorts and t-shirts for the boys, short-sleeved, button-down Henleys for Ben, navy slacks, and three of her favorite sleeveless, cotton dresses plus an assortment of underwear. She pulled the warm clothing out of the machine into the basket. Oops, someone's jockey shorts were hugging the back of the dryer. She almost had to stand on her head to reach the back, but as she snagged the errant undies, she heard the clatter of something metallic banging against the metal drum.

Reaching in, she pulled out what appeared to be a flash drive—a very warm one. Apparently, it had been in someone's pocket and had received a washing along with a trip in the dryer. That probably didn't bode well for any info that might have been on it. It had to be Ben's. She could only hope that it hadn't held important information. She emptied the laundry basket on the bed in the guest bedroom and walked back out to the kitchen where the sound and scent of popping corn had Ben and his sons' full attention.

"Hate to interrupt, but does this belong to anyone here?"

"Oh, shit." Nathan leaned over the counter to take the flash drive from her. "That's mine. Well, not exactly mine but it was given to me for safe keeping. Guess I flunked that—it's been washed and dried?" He looked at Julie who nodded.

"Where'd it come from?" Ben was curious; some sixth sense was warning him that he just might want to know its contents.

"Skyler found it." Nathan went on to share how she'd

found it taped to the back wall of the locker she'd been assigned—a locker that had originally belonged to a woman who was killed. He added that Skyler had surprised another girl who was going through her things in the locker looking for something, but Skyler had already taken the flash drive out. She suspected that the flash drive might be important. "Do you think anything can be saved?"

"I can soon find out." Ben's laptop was in the home office he shared with Julie; he didn't hold out hope that the drive would still be viable, but fingers crossed. Was this what everyone thought Robbi had? Some proof of wrongdoing? Something that people would kill over?

"Can I come?" Nathan had followed him into the hallway.

"You know sometimes people are only safe because they don't know anything. If there's incriminating info on the drive, then it might put a target on your back if people thought you knew what it contained."

"So, what about you?"

"I don't worry about me—I'd worry about you."

"That's an answer?"

"Maybe not a good one, but it's true. Better to have just one person with one target than two people with two."

Nathan sort of smiled. "OK. Thanks, I think." He walked back toward the kitchen.

Ben closed the door to the office behind him, opened his Mac and pressed 'on.' He wasn't allowing himself to even think about what he would do if there *was* incriminating information. First things, first—he needed to find something before worrying about the next step. He slipped the drive into a USB port and waited.

The name of the drive came up in the menu column—

The Noose. That was ominous enough. And the index to the files popped up, five in all with titles: Black Money, Spread Sheets, Where the Bodies are Buried, State Legislators, and simply X. Ben sat forward. Here came the big test.

He opened the first file. It was a video, not in the best of condition—because of its recent bath or how it was originally filmed? Maybe the gray, blurriness was how it was captured. All Ben could make out in two frames was Andy Thunderhawk standing over a suitcase full of stacks of money, before closing the case, picking it up by the handles, and disappearing off-screen. Then the tape went blank. Not one other file opened.

Ben sat back. Andy? Of course, he worked for a casino where lots of money changed hands. But was it moved around in large suitcases? What happened to Brink's uniformed men in armored trucks? No, Ben doubted that large sums of money entered or left the casino in suitcases. But that would probably be Andy's excuse if confronted; he was only accepting a bank deposit.

At the moment it just looked like he was trying out for a bad Al Pacino film, sneaking around with maybe a hundred thousand or two in tow. But the list of file names? They all sounded like once upon a time they had held seriously incriminating evidence—involving money as payoffs? To state officials? Maybe even murders? But wasn't Ben allowing his imagination to run away with what was usually his sound, logical thinking?

So, what now? He couldn't ignore what was in front of him. Wasn't this what Robbi was killed over? And maybe her grandfather, too? It was exactly seven; he doubted that Chief Patrick was still in the office but he could leave a voice mail and ask him to set aside a half hour to see him in the morning. He picked up his phone and dialed the chief's direct line.

"Chief Patrick here."

"This is Ben Pecos. I can't believe I caught you at the office this late."

"Just leaving—my hand was on the door knob. What can I help you with?"

Ben offered a quick overview and reiterated that he didn't have a lot of evidence, but it might be worth taking a look at. Too many suspect situations seemed to be linked to the flash drive.

"If you have a few minutes in the morning, I could stop by on my way to work."

"I've got a better idea. I was toying with the idea of coming by your house on my way home tonight. I was out when you picked up Zac, and I wanted to wish him well and commend his actions in the midst of a pretty upsetting situation. He handled himself like someone far beyond his years."

"That would be terrific. I would appreciate you sharing that with him. I'm a firm believer that teens need to know when they've impressed us."

"I agree. See you in about fifteen."

* * *

"This is a movie night; 'fraid I can't offer too much in the way of food unless you like popcorn." Julie had answered the door and invited the chief in.

The chief laughed. "One of my favorites but I have dinner waiting. I would like to talk with Zac for a minute if I'm not going to be interrupting a good part." He motioned toward the TV screen.

"They'll survive." Ben offered from the doorway.

"I just wanted to tell Zac that under extreme duress, not once did he strike back or in any way even say something inappropriate. I've reviewed what was caught on the cop's body camera and the man has been placed on leave. We will investigate further but for the time being he's off the street. He was completely out of line. You were adult in all your actions. I appreciate that and I wanted you to know that exemplary conduct is recognized and applauded by local law enforcement."

"Thank you." Zac stepped forward and shook the chief's hand. "I appreciate you telling me."

Ben beamed. The kid really impressed him. Raven had done a good job of raising Zac. It wouldn't hurt to tell her that. "Follow me and I'll share what we've found."

The chief watched the segment three times, before asking Ben for the flash drive and then just sitting back, shaking his head. "I don't have to say what a shame it was to lose the majority of what was on the drive. I'll have the techs look at it but it's very likely wiped. I personally think calling the contents 'The Noose' says it all. But it's like we have this teaser. We suspect but really have no proof. By the way, I hope I don't have to tell you not to trust Mr. Thunderhawk."

"That one shocks me. It was Andy who warned me about being set up to fail when I started the job, then he swept my office and found a listening device—was all that done just so I wouldn't suspect him of any wrongdoing?"

"It worked, didn't it? I'm not trying to speak for Andy but it's reasonable to say he knew how to appear to be one of the good guys. You know, I've been thinking. We need to be smart about this. Tell you what I'd like you to do. Turn the drive into Andy." The chief handed the drive back to Ben. "If he's in cahoots, he'll give it to his boss, or bosses. And that could give everyone a sense of security— but buy us time to do some digging."

Chapter 20

She was back on the pageant story with just two more days—the formal dance tonight and the final judging and crowning tomorrow. Even her boss had stopped by her desk to say how happy he was that the set-up to ensnare Zac had been uncovered before any more damage had been done to anyone's reputation.

Julie thought he seemed especially pleased that the casino walked away without a black eye. It could have wrecked their bottom line according to Ken. And, she supposed he was right. What promoters of beauty pageants would feel comfortable bringing in young women if a rape had occurred? The murder of Robbi Aponi had been relegated to a back page and the story was still circulating that Sammy Longman had reacted out of anger to a girlfriend who had cheated on him. Bail had been refused by a local magistrate.

She pulled into the parking spot next to Ben's and got her briefcase out of the trunk. Walking toward the casino, she waved to Zac and Nathan in the wash-bay. A look of normalcy. She wouldn't take that for granted ever again. All would have been lost if Zac's pageant date hadn't spoken up when she saw something suspect. She knew both boys were going to escort their contestants to the ball and she thought Zac was planning something special for Alana—a thank you for her quick thinking. They were so cute together. Had Julie ever been that young?

The morning was going to be devoted to interviews. Two of the girls were national level gymnasts and were training for the upcoming Olympics. A third was being scouted by a national women's soccer team. So much talent in addition to good looks and brains. It was comforting to see the emphasis upon the well-rounded girl—scholarship, community activism, talent, athleticism—it gave the pageant meaning. And it gave the *Herald* some wholesome, down-to-earth stories to share of young women achieving their goals.

Julie couldn't imagine a project that she'd rather be chronicling. Lots of young girls would be watching Sunday's finale and imagining themselves accepting top honors. It felt good to support the event.

"Ms. Conlin, Julie? Can we talk?" Annette was standing just inside the main entrance. Had she been waiting on her? Julie thought so; it certainly looked like it. "You have every right to be pissed at me. I was so rude yesterday. Please accept my apology."

"All right." Julie was a little reluctant to let something interrupt her otherwise uneventful morning, but that curiosity and cats thing got her every time. Had the truth of Brianna's fabrication of the incident come out?

"I thought we could go back out to the food trucks. They have tables in the shade."

"Sounds good." Julie turned and followed Annette back out the door.

Julie dumped purse, laptop bag, and briefcase on a nearby table and walked to the truck's window to order a latte.

"This is on me."

"You don't have to."

"But I want to. I was so wrong about what happened."

"Then, thank you." Julie picked up her coffee and walked back to the table, threw a leg over the bench seat and waited for Annette.

"I suppose I should first tell you that I'm Brianna's roommate. We've roomed together for two years, so I know her, or at least, I thought I did. I didn't think she would ever pull the type of stunt that she did. I can't believe she would set up some kid for money. I heard that she was demanding five thousand dollars from you and your husband. I do know that her grandmother is really sick, but to ruin a kid's life ... well, there's no excuse, nothing that would make that okay. I'm so glad she came to her senses and went down to the station and confessed. I mean, that took some guts. I'm sure you're relieved." Annette was looking at her, waiting for a comment.

Julie could only hope that the shock she felt wasn't registering on her face. Confess? Go to the police on her own? The last she heard, the police were still looking for Brianna and hadn't found her. Someone was spinning a story that was absolutely untrue. Why? But didn't she know the answer to that? It was easy to see that whoever set her up, the one paying the 5K would need to cover their ass.

"Very relieved. Chief Patrick stopped by just last night to commend Zac for how he handled himself. I assume Brianna won't be punished?"

Julie knew that, when found, Brianna wouldn't be held only because Zac didn't want to press charges. And she and Ben agreed not wanting to put him through anything that he would be uncomfortable with. It was a malicious setup, but a felony?

It was the real culprits who were the ones who needed to face punishment of some kind for using, actually bribing, someone to do their dirty work. It was the chief's intention that when they found her, Brianna wouldn't be held. He shared that releasing her might lead them to whomever was behind the incident. Julie hoped that was true.

"No punishment, but she's taking some time off. I imagine she'll spend some time with her grandmother in Jersey. But to be honest, I would have expected her to pack more clothes. She just sort of walked out the door."

"She's gone? Have you talked with her since she left?"

"I've texted but no reply. She was driving and will probably get in touch when she gets to her grandmother's. I even left a message for the boyfriend so maybe he'll get back."

"Local guy?"

"Well, yeah." Annette looked away. "You know, I really need to get back inside. I just wanted to apologize."

"Does he have a name?" Why was she asking, other than suddenly something was a little fishy. She sensed Annette wished she could take the reference to a boyfriend back.

"Look, I really don't gossip. But you should know who I mean. I'm sure everyone at your workplace talks about it."

"I'm afraid I'm not in the office that much." She was running an inventory of office personnel through her mind. Yeah, there could be a person of interest at the *Herald*. There were a couple of cute reporters about Brianna's age … maybe one of those.

"Your boss, for God's sake. And you didn't hear it here."

"He's twice her age … and he's married." Julie had just blurted it out. And what a stupid thing to say. When did age or marital status make a difference in an affair? And it made Julie sound frumpy and out-of-touch.

"Are you that naïve? Some people don't let wedding vows get in the way. And isn't it fun in your forties, to act like you're twenty? Listen, I'm out of here." With that, Annette hurriedly tossed her coffee cup in the nearest trash can, waved and fairly trotted across the lot, up the steps and into the casino.

Julie picked up her phone to call Ben. He needed to know the latest twist. And she needed to just sit there and finish her coffee and think about this new information. Her boss. She was smart enough to realize that the knowing could get her into real trouble.

Was he involved in any of this? Could he be the one Brianna was texting when Alana copied the phone screen? The one who had promised to pay her the five thousand? But why would Ken Usher want to set up Zac? That made no sense. Wasn't he the one worried about bad press for the casino?

* * *

Ben was already in his office when he got Julie's text. That was a new twist—Brianna confessed to staging the assault to ask *him* for 5K to not press charges implicating his son in a supposed rape attempt? He wasn't sure the chief was up-to-date on this latest explanation for what happened; so, Ben left him a message.

Someone was pulling the strings in all this and made the answer to *why* all the more intriguing. Following Chief Patrick's suggestion, he needed to get the flash drive to Andy. It would be interesting to see what story was circulating in his part of the casino. Ben had barely stepped into the hallway when Andy rushed around the corner toward him.

"Hey, buddy, just the person I need to talk to. Gotta minute?"

"Sure, what's up?" Really—after all the insults, Ben was still a "bud."

"Can we sit for a minute?" Andy was pointing at Ben's office.

"Not a problem." Ben held the door open. Andy walked past him and sat at the small conference table.

"Look, I don't know where to even start, but I'm gonna beg you to forgive me. I was way out of line the other day and blamed your son when he was totally innocent. I never liked that girl—didn't trust her, if you want to know the truth. And to try to set you and your wife up to pay some ungodly price so that she could dismiss charges ... well, she should be strung up. You and your wife were too kind to refuse to press charges—way too kind. I hope she appreciates that. She's damned lucky her life wasn't ruined."

"Thank you for the apology. All is forgiven. I understand her grandmother is ill. Who knows what stress will lead people to do."

"Yeah, she's taking off some time to go be with her grandma. I think that's what she needs. The pageant was putting a lot of pressure on her. Things should be better when she gets back. But I'm not real sure she'll have a job waiting for her. The powers-who-be around here expect, to say the least, that everyone be above the law and not call attention to themselves unless it's to pay tribute to the casino."

"Hey, before I forget ... I've got something that I think you'll know what to do with." Ben walked to his desk, opened the middle drawer and picked up the flash drive. "The contestant that my older son has been escorting found this in the locker she was assigned. Just like a kid, he stuck it in his pants pocket and it took a turn through the wash. But I don't feel comfortable just throwing it away."

Andy held out his hand. "What's on it?"

"I have no idea. Like I said, after being washed and dried, I'm sure it's fried. I don't think we're talking porn here, more like some kid's schoolwork."

"I'll take care of it." Andy pushed back from the table and stood up. "Not a problem. Thanks for getting it to me. Now, I better run."

Was it Ben's imagination or was Andy practically licking his lips in anticipation? This must be what Robbi was suspected of having, the thing that got her killed. The poor man couldn't wait to leave. Probably meant some extra brownie points for coming up with it.

* * *

"It went through a wash?"

"Kid stuck it in his pocket and forgot about it. I'd say

we dodged a big one here. It's gotta be what Robbi was supposed to have. It was found in her old locker."

"Old man Holt just about got away with tripping us up. You know he thought he had us this time." The man chuckled, held the drive in his hand before handing it to the third man sitting in front of a computer. "Let's check this out before we destroy it."

Under Location in the menu, the drive's name popped up, The Noose. "Well, there's a little humor for you. And look at these other file names. Must have been some good stuff in them."

"Open them up."

"I tried. You'll only get a couple screens from the first file. Nothing else is viable. See? Half way decent pic of our pal Andy with a suitcase full of money though, but that's it."

"I think we're resting easy tonight. Finding that drive is just about as good as it gets." A series of high-fives punctuated their supposed good luck.

Chapter 21

The tux made him look at least sixteen. Zac turned first to his right and then to his left in front of the full-length mirror in his bedroom. Shoes polished to a shine, a fresh haircut, even a manicure, though he could only imagine how that would make him the laughing stock of his class at school. He could understand clean nails but soaking his hands in little bowls of solvent, well, that was way too much. But he was ready for the ball.

This gala was the highlight of the five-day pageant events and was always held the night before the final selection of the girl who would wear the Miss Teen USA crown. There was a lot of excitement. He could almost feel it. Families were allowed in for the final two days and to attend the final judging. If he'd thought the casino and hotel were crowded before, it was wall to wall people now—parents swimming, gambling, waiting in line at the restaurants, sightseeing in the area, many of those who had driven in from surrounding states wanted their cars washed and detailed. Tips were good. But he was just relieved to be back at work.

Even though it had only been a couple days since the Brianna fiasco, once word circulated that Brianna had confessed the attack was all staged, people came out of the woodwork to congratulate him. Congratulations for being a victim? How did that make sense? And how quickly people believed the lie that she had taken responsibility for setting him up so that she could demand money from his parents.

Brianna had gone to the police station that night to report an attempted rape, to point a finger at *him*, get *him* locked up ... ruin his life. And someone had put her up to it. That was the real truth. The chief had requested that this real story be kept under wraps, as he put it. He told Zac and his dad that this approach, lie though it was, would keep from scaring off the scheme's real criminals. And make them feel safe while the police followed every lead.

Where would he be now if Alana hadn't seen the text that proved Brianna's story false? And then acted quickly to involve the police? He owed Alana and he knew exactly what he wanted to give her—something that she would treasure, but understand its meaning. He'd called his mother and asked Raven to buy a Haida Indian bracelet with a hummingbird design. He had saved his tips and would send her money for it. The one he had seen in the Native market in Anchorage was a slim, sterling silver band with an engraved hummingbird whose long bill curved around the half circle, and had one single, small, round, moon stone for an eye. His mom agreed to over-night it to him quickly.

Would Alana understand why he'd chosen the hummingbird? He thought so. Many Alaskan schools, even elementary, encouraged a knowledge of Native symbols. And the hummingbird represented intelligence and beauty. They were also respected as fierce defenders of their territory doing whatever it took to safeguard their belongings. But most of all, they represented good luck. Could there be a better symbol for Alana? Zac thought not. He would give it to her at the pageant finale tomorrow.

He took one last, long look in the mirror, and with a slight smile, nodded appreciatively. He looked good even if the dickie-thing, or whatever it was called, scraped his neck. What a stupid piece of material. He was glad he wouldn't be wearing anything like it again any time soon. Luckily his tux-wearing days were numbered. Thank God junior and senior prom were a few years away.

* * *

All the chairs had been removed in the main auditorium and a dais set up for the band. Along the entire north wall tables for four and six people filled the area. Each white-clothed table had a small glass vase of flowers in various bright colors in the middle, and a ribbon commemorating the event that stretched across the width and draped to the floor. Baskets of flowers flanked the stage and the entry. The auditorium had morphed into a beautiful ballroom, Nathan decided.

He and Zac had picked up Alana and Skyler at their room. Corsages were suggested, but optional. Both girls requested floral hair ornaments and Zac and Nathan had had their requests delivered to the girls' room. Skyler's hair was divided and the top half was caught up in a fresh flower barrette at the crown with her long blond hair flowing out beneath to reach her shoulders. Alana tucked a huge, deep purple Cattleya orchid behind one ear, her dark hair twisted into a messy bun with tendrils framing her face. Stunning. Ben and Julie were asked to be chaperones and kiddingly promised Nathan and Zac that they wouldn't embarrass them.

Each couple was introduced as they entered the ballroom and camera flashes exploded. Their table was close to the band, number eleven out of over fifty. That had been a lucky draw. He vaguely wondered how they had been assigned. Dressy affairs might not be his favorite thing, but Nathan was enjoying it so far. The band was local, but good. They played a couple opening numbers that featured a better than average vocalist. He leaned back and put his arm across the back of Skyler's chair.

"I'm really, really glad that you were cleared of any wrongdoing with that mess in the elevator." Skyler looked at Zac. "That was so unfair, and to lie like that. I heard that she was going to try to get money from your parents."

Zac nodded. "I think that was the goal."

"Apparently, she confessed to having set up the whole thing. What will happen to her? She'll be punished, won't she?" Skyler asked.

"Not if we don't press charges. She's left to visit her grandmother up north." Then, Zac added, "I don't think she'll be back."

Alana quickly agreed. "I wouldn't show up here again. I mean if she's smart, she'll just keep on going."

The conversation quickly turned to the pageant. Both girls shared their interview topics and seemed pleased with their responses. Nathan thought both were relieved that part of the pageant was over. The music was loud and any talking was a challenge. Nathan asked Skyler to dance and the two stayed on the floor, moving up to stand closer to the stage. Nathan liked to dance but wondered about Zac. There had been a couple school dances last year but he couldn't even remember Zac going. Then he saw them on the floor, and Zac was doing okay.

Nathan felt responsible in a way that he hadn't kept Zac out of trouble. He should have insisted that he and Skyler go to the ball game, too. But never in a million years could he have guessed that his kid brother would be assaulted in an elevator. No way. It still seemed too bizarre.

* * *

Ben was enjoying his new family obligation—chaperoning. Not something he'd seen in his immediate future, but it was growing on him. Even Julie had jumped right in. He looked over at the vibrant, red-haired woman singing along with the band. There wasn't one contestant who could hold a candle to her—not one teenager who could compete with the 30-something who was his wife. And, yeah, he was prejudiced. He grinned and winked as she looked his way.

He wondered, if he mentioned that the band seemed a little loud would that date him? He imagined that it would give the boys a chuckle. They looked so grown up—was it the tuxedos? He watched both boys interact with their dates. The pairings had worked perfectly. They seemed at ease and having a good time. He'd slipped his phone into a back pocket of his dress slacks and had forgotten about it until it vibrated. A message from the chief: meet him in the foyer during intermission. That felt a little ominous. Was there new information?

Within ten minutes Ben walked into the entry and waved to the chief who stepped away from a group of officers and came his way.

"Glad you could join me. We're on security detail tonight, but I didn't want to give anyone more to gossip about by showing up at your table. And I don't know whether you can help; I'm grasping at straws. Brianna Walters has eluded us. Simply disappeared overnight. At this point my guess is that she didn't leave town and is somewhere close by. Have you heard anything?"

"Only the story that you heard about visiting her grandmother. Doesn't she live in New Jersey?"

The chief nodded. "Apparently, she had planned on driving up there—even called her grandmother as to when to expect her. The grandmother is pretty upset, but swears that Brianna never left town. Brianna hasn't called her grandmother either to explain any change of plans. I don't like it. She rooms with Annette—not sure of her last name, Foster, I think. Annette is convinced that she took off. Apparently, she was in the room when Brianna packed a bag. She saw Brianna carry her purse, car keys, sunglasses, and a couple ball caps out the door. Ready to hit the road. Her parking space behind the apartment is empty. She drove a Chevy Traverse—those aren't cheap and aren't small. It didn't just evaporate. I guess I'm telling you all this as just a heads up. If you hear of anything, see anything ... heck, I don't know what it might be ... but if it's information about Brianna, give me a call. Anything would be helpful. I know you guys aren't pressing charges, but we still have 'causing a disturbance, and lying to officials with malicious intent' hanging over her head. That has to be resolved."

"Sure, no problem. I'll check with the boys, too."

"Thanks." Two officers had walked up and the chief excused himself, turning back to add, "I'll keep you informed."

"I'd appreciate that." Ben paused by the door to the ballroom. He wished his sixth sense wasn't just about screaming that something was wrong, very wrong. The text message on Brianna's phone clearly indicated that someone was behind the incident. Who could say that person hadn't tried to silence her? It made sense that she was a liability—a big one. Made all the bigger if the mastermind was well connected.

Chapter 22

Ben was just pulling into the driveway, having waited to pick up the boys after each had walked his date to her room, and his phone rang. It was one-thirty in the morning. Julie had folded up her jacket and placed it between the seat and the passenger-side window, resting her head against it with her eyes closed. Even the boys had been subdued. A few comments on the band and the dance in general before each had lapsed into silence. The truth was they were all worn out. The week had been a crazy one. He checked caller ID—the chief. Before he answered, Ben knew it wasn't good news.

"Can you hold for a minute? Let me pull into the garage." Ben pushed the automatic garage door opener, parked inside and sat in the car while everyone else went into the house.

"What's going on?"

"First, my apologies for calling so late. Brianna has been found."

Ben heard the intake of breath on the other end of the line and simply waited. He didn't dare to hope that it was good news.

"I know it won't come as a surprise that we found her body at the bottom of a twelve foot deep holding pond about five miles from the casino. Looks like a tire completely separated from the rim, front passenger side. The Traverse went off the road, struck a tree and entered the water. I won't know all the facts until after the autopsy but she has quite a pronounced head wound. Whether it's pre- or post-accident remains to be determined. We'll know something later in the week. I should add that the body was found in the back seat. This could simply mean that she was conscious after entering the water and was attempting to exit the vehicle. But it's suspect. As I said, I won't know until we've had a team go over everything. At the moment, for all intent and purposes, I'm treating this as a homicide."

Ben leaned his head back against the headrest, thanked the chief for filling him in, hung up and then just sat there. What was going on? Two young women dead, a young man in jail who shouldn't be there, his own son the recipient of a plot to ruin Zac's reputation and maybe force Ben to leave his employment at the casino. What was he missing? Was there some connection between the incidents?

* * *

Sunday wasn't a usual workday, but the finale and crowning of Miss Teen USA made it one. Ben was up early and fixed breakfast. He needed to be at work by eight. There was no doubt that a fourteen- and sixteen-year-old fared better on six hours sleep than two adults. He felt drugged, and Julie shared that she didn't feel much better. Even a ham and green pepper quiche wasn't met with much enthusiasm.

The boys were already grousing about having to wear a tux two days in a row. The girls would be in evening dress and their escorts would be accompanying them to and from the stage. The final night was all glitz and glamour. In some ways, Ben would miss the pageant and its entourage. What he wouldn't miss was having to stand in line at every restaurant and having to eat dinner at four in the afternoon because that timeframe offered the only available seating. If he was working late and needed to eat in-house, he learned to skip lunch. Even the food trucks filled the parking lot, with lines waiting to place orders at almost every hour during the day. Snacks and cold drinks were good any time.

Something else he wouldn't miss was the ubiquitous Robert Holmes, the pageant's ever present executive director, and it would be nice to not have barber chairs in the conference rooms. It was amazing how pageant crews had swept in, altered areas to meet their needs, and no doubt, would restore things to normal in the same amount of record time. He reminded himself to be prepared to spend Monday in his office and out of everyone's way.

He was Julie's date for Sunday evening. But before that, she had a full day of work ahead of her. She would be interviewing the contestants prior to the crowning for a jitters and glitter piece for the paper—a hopes and aspirations special—something thoughtful and inspiring. Then at the end, after interviewing the winners, she was planning on a segue to what memories they would leave with, their reactions to the setting, and then how they could use their experiences at Miss Teen USA and apply those to their everyday lives.

Ben knew she had gotten up at six to work on her notes. Everyone ate quickly and went back to their rooms to dress. He cleared the table and stacked dishes in the dishwasher. Finally, everyone was ready to leave. But ten minutes before eight, FedEx pulled into the driveway. Zac's gift for Alana had arrived.

It was perfect. The bracelet sparkled in sterling silver that was the backdrop for the hummingbird, a Haida carving traced in black with a pearl-white, moonstone eye. Julie offered to wrap it; she just happened to have a gift sack and tissue in her closet. Did he need a card? She had that, too.

Zac sat down and wrote a quick note—more like a half dozen words that pretty much just said thank you and good luck for the evening, Ben noticed. But he applauded Zac's quick thinking and choice of gift. He was going to be a lucky catch for someone, someday.

Ben and Julie took separate cars. There was simply no knowing how late Julie would be after the end-of-ceremony interviews. The boys carried their tuxes in suit bags and placed shoes and clothing for the evening in the trunk of Julie's car. It would save time running back and forth to the house later. This promised to be a big day.

* * *

"You're making me look bad." Nathan glanced at Zac as they walked toward the carwash bay.

"Huh?"

"You know, coming up with a gift for Alana."

"It's just a thank you. She got me out of a lot of trouble."

"I could give Skyler this." Nathan dug in his pocket and pulled out a key chain. "What do you think?" Attached to the chain was a silver charm of the Zia sun symbol about the size of a quarter with a rounded turquoise stone in the center.

"Hey, that's perfect."

"Seriously? The Zia symbol would remind her of me, or New Mexico, that is. The symbol's on the state's flag."

"Yeah, I mean it. She'll like it."

"I just have to find an envelope somewhere."

"Try dad's office. You've got time; it's not nine yet." No one expected them at the carwash before ten.

* * *

If Ben thought the last week was busy, today made the lead-up time to the pageant finale look slow in comparison. Everyone was rushing—stage hands with set pieces, tables, chairs, bleachers, backdrop curtains to be raised or lowered from rods above the stage, baskets of flowers, microphones, lights hanging from the ceiling and on poles—Ben made a promise to himself that he'd stay out of the way and get some work done in the office. Then, his phone rang.

"Help me."

"Who is this?"

"Come to your car in the garage. Don't say anything to

anyone." Click.

What was that all about? Did he believe that someone was in trouble? Yes. That was the problem. The voice wasn't kidding; the person sounded one half-step from hysterics—breathing quickly, whispering--a woman's voice from what he could tell. Ben stood up, slipped his phone into his pocket and walked toward the door.

"Hey, just the guy I want to see. Going somewhere?" Andy stood in the doorway.

"Left my briefcase in the car. I'm just on my way to get it."

"That'll work. We can multitask, talk while we walk." Andy stood to one side and let Ben step into the hallway. "I've had some complaints about that Robert Holmes. He's driving everyone nuts. He's demanding people bend over backwards to please him. Double-checking everyone's work, making a couple stagehands redo the curtain-hanging. Do you think I should talk with him—suggest he tone it down a notch? Or should that come from Chairman Billie? Or even you. This sounds like an HR problem to me."

"I think you're right. Let me handle it. I can always meet with him in the chairman's office. That might be best—a show of clout by way of visual background might be helpful."

"Thanks. Knew I could count on you." With that, Andy offered a mock salute and took off toward the casino's main floor.

One problem solved; now, if Ben could just make it out of the building without another interruption. But that wasn't to be. Before he could reach the front door, he heard his name. Julie. What was he going to say? Use the briefcase excuse? She'd know he was lying.

"Sorry to bother you, but one of the chefs hasn't shown up. I was asked to hunt you up because you'd know who to call and everyone else is too busy to leave the kitchen."

"Thanks for the vote of confidence but check with April Bowlegs. She keeps tabs on hires and replacements, as in temporary staff. I bet they have food service people on standby for events like this."

"Of course, great advice. I'm on my way." Julie abruptly turned and headed toward the elevators. "Love you." A blown kiss and she was gone. And Ben had reached the front door.

As he entered the parking garage, the eerie stillness was in sharp contrast to the people-packed, noisy, casino. He'd never seen the garage as full of cars as it was today. He started down the first row, but saw nothing out of place. He could see the back of the Land Rover but no one was near it—at least, not that he could see. He opened the hatchback but nothing was out of place. The boys had loaded the pup tent, hoping to go camping sometime during the week; their days off were coming up. A pup tent and two bedrolls pretty much filled the back. He shut the door and moved to the side. He had barely opened the passenger-side door when a voice ordered him to beware of cameras.

"They're watching. Don't even act like you hear me." A flap of the blanket haphazardly thrown across the seat moved and Ben could see Annette's eyes and nose and a strand of hair in a shade of red that would leave her unrecognizable for the cameras. Looked like she'd taken some serious precautions. "I mean it. It's dangerous." Ben did as he was told and feigned looking for his briefcase, closing the back door and opening the front passenger-side door. "Good. I need you to take me to somewhere safe. I'll explain as we go. Just get in and drive out of here. Leave a message that you need to pick up something at your house."

Ben did as he was told. He called and left a message at the front desk saying he would be back within an hour or so, and with that, he backed out of his space and headed off the casino's campus.

"I'm not getting up. I need you to take me to a safe place. Somewhere away from here—a long way away. I'll figure out what to do then. And make sure we're not being followed."

"Am I allowed to talk?"

"As long as no one pulls up alongside and sees you talking. Can you pretend singing along to the radio?"

Was she serious? "Is all this necessary?"

"Yes, a thousand times yes. I don't want to end up like Brianna. And that could happen. I'm not being melodramatic. My life is in danger."

"Why?"

"Because I know too much. And … I played along for awhile. Okay, I'll be honest. I took money to say I heard Sammy Longman and Robbi fighting. I also said there was someone else in her life. I mean they believed me because I had been her roommate. I said I saw Sammy leave the cooler with a bloody knife in his hand after the yelling stopped. I'm the one who put him in jail."

Ben was shocked but didn't say anything; it would be best to just play along. "And that's exactly what happened to Brianna—wasn't she offered money to set up Zac? Only she wasn't paid and when she complained, that got her killed? Sorry, don't know if I was supposed to share that."

"Yeah, it's okay. I know they killed her. They had to; they couldn't let her live."

"Who are *they*?"

"Sorry, can't share and I can only guess." There was a pause, then, "Are you paying attention? Are we being followed?"

"I'm watching; no one is following us." Ben was driving with one eye on the rearview mirror. There were no cars or other vehicles that were even suspect. No one was even behind him. Most cars were passing him—speed limit be damned. "I'm going to pull over at the next gas station and get a Coke. That should tell me if anyone is tailing us. By the way, where are we going?"

"Your house?"

"Nope. I won't endanger my family." Cruel? No, smart and careful. Julie and the boys came first. "Why not just go to the police?"

"You're kidding. You haven't figured that one out yet?"

"What are you talking about?"

"Never mind. But you can't tell anyone about what you're doing right now. Got that? No one. Especially not the police. It was the cops who went along with the rape story."

"But why is all this happening? It doesn't make sense."

"It does if you want a stake in the casino. If getting rid of the Indians—you'll excuse me—breaking up their monopoly and giving more opportunities to non-Indians by giving present ownership a black eye, it makes total sense. And a project worth billions. Yeah, that's right, billions. And it's going to be voted on. It's been added to the upcoming ballot. If it looks like indigenous people can't offer a safe environment for locals to play, then it might be time to divide up the spoils. I hope this doesn't shock you, but Florida has its share of racists, too. And let me just say, there are way too many people standing around with their hands out. Money makes all kinds of people do crazy things." The muffled laugh was followed by, "Like yours truly."

Ben was silent. It wasn't difficult to believe that many people could be bought—greed was epidemic. He believed her. It made sense now. "So, where am I going?"

"If we're not going to your place, we need a motel at least a half hour from the casino."

"Ok, I'll keep an eye out. We're about twenty-five miles out now."

"Something not too expensive but not too run-down either. I don't want the place to attract attention. Just some run-of-the-mill Florida tourist trap."

And when he did find one that Annette peeked out the window and thought would work, she asked him to drive past and then let her out several blocks from the place. He tried not to show it, but all the cloak and dagger secrecy was getting to him. Not being able to go to the police? What was that all about? Was he missing something? Trusting the wrong people? He didn't trust Andy with probably good reason, but others? Was he really being watched like both Robbi and Annette thought?

And then he knew what he had to do—get Annette to write out a confession saying everything she'd shared with him. A simple, 'I set up Sammy Longman.' Ben wasn't asking her to name names but to indicate that there were guilty parties out there and to own up to accepting money to lie. She could even make it sound like she was scared for her life. And wasn't that the truth? It took some forcefulness on his part—promises to say she had handed the note to him at the casino, no mention of taking her undercover, literally, to a hiding place. Ben would do everything she had asked him to do *if* she did this one thing for him—and for Sammy Longman. He played on her conscience. Hadn't she caused enough trouble? Sorrow, abject grief, really was the best way to describe it when you considered the effect Robbi's death had had on Sammy. She had wrecked his life; didn't she owe him?

And it worked. She agreed. Slowly, and with tears, she asked for pen and paper. He tore a page out of a notebook he kept in the glove compartment and handed it to her. It didn't take her long. She wrote, read it, added something, signed her name, and then handed it to him.

Ben read it and nodded. "I'm going to *find* your note later this afternoon. It's going to look like you slid it under my office door while I was gone."

Annette nodded. "Ok. I'm trusting you to keep your word."

"You have my promise. No mention of having seen you today." He drove around to the back of the motel and let her out in an alley. "Here. I only have fifty in cash. Are you going to be okay?"

"I have some cash, too."

"Then, be careful. You know how to reach me if you need to. Don't hesitate, I mean it. If you need help, use my cell." She nodded and walked quickly around the side of the building.

Ben waited just long enough to make sure she wasn't coming back before he started the Rover and eased down the alley to the street. To be on the safe side, and just in case, he decided to swing by his house on the way back to the casino. He needed to make this trip look fruitful, so he picked up a folder from his desk and then laughed at himself. What did he expect? Cameras in the house? Maybe outside? The garage, the porch? But some sixth sense said he wasn't being foolish, two deaths, a false imprisonment, another life in danger—he couldn't forget all that had happened. No, being careful needed to become as second nature as breathing. Had he already goofed up by trusting someone who wasn't on his side? Could he even trust his ability to tell the good guys from the bad?

* * *

They had five minutes in the hallway outside the contestants' lounge before Alana had to check in for final preparations—last minute dress alterations if needed, then a couple hours for hair and nails. The late morning hours had included a spa treatment. Zac wondered about a body salt-scrub. It didn't sound like fun but Alana seemed to have liked it. So, it was without much fanfare that he handed her the gift bag.

"I thought of you and how I wanted to say thank you. I saw this last summer and had my mom send it. I wanted you to have a reminder of how much your help meant to me."

Alana carefully slipped the box from the bag and opened it. The squeal of delight said it all. "I love it. Haida designs are my favorite. It's beautiful." She put the bracelet on her wrist, turning it several directions, letting the moonstone catch the light. Then, she threw her arms around him and kissed him. On the mouth. He didn't pull away but felt heat travel up his neck to his face. And he couldn't think of one clever thing to say so he just mumbled, "I'm glad you like it. See you at six." Dumb. He should have kissed back. Would he get another chance?

He knew Julie was going to pick up a silver chain for Nathan to turn his keychain fob into a pendant and he caught sight of a shiny Zia symbol with turquoise center hanging around Skyler's neck as she walked by. This had been a pretty neat summer after all. For him and his brother.

* * *

First thing Ben did when he got back to the casino was slip Annette's note under the door. The hall cameras still weren't working according to Andy. He could only hope that there weren't any cameras hidden in the office along with the mic in the lightshade. But did it matter? No one knew Annette was gone, at least, as far as he knew. And there shouldn't be any indication that he was the one handling the note. He had been careful. But he'd wait a while before he would unlock his office and *find* it.

In exactly one hour, Ben unlocked his office and picked up the single sheet of paper that was on the floor just inside the door. He took it to his desk, sat back, read it, put it down in front of him and leaned forward on his elbows. Enough of a show just in case? He was certain that if there was a camera, it had caught everything. He read the note again, pursed his lips and reached for the desk phone. A quick call to Oscar Billie.

Chapter 23

It felt a little bit like she was being banished, or, at least, being given time out. A desk and two chairs had been placed literally in the hallway to the side of the double doors to one of the busiest restaurants in the casino. When she questioned the arrangement, Julie was told that space was at a premium and this was the best they could do. The pageant's staff had simply taken everything available. One of the restaurant managers suggested that it gave her exposure, and that she should be pleased. She bit her tongue and merely nodded. It was apparent that he wasn't pleased at having her almost in their entry.

She had set up three interviews for the morning and would follow those after lunch with ten more. She opened her laptop and put her cell phone on the table beside it.

Still, it was almost an hour before her first appointment. Nothing like being early. Actually, it gave her time to go over her notes and brush up on the contestant's bio and time to get a glass of iced tea, unsweetened. She might live in the South now, but tea didn't need sugar to make it palatable—that is, not for her.

The restaurant's bar was in the very front. If you needed to wait on a table, at least there was a comfortable place to do it. Julie supposed that the bartender could arrange for a glass of tea. The restaurant offered brunch so the dining room was still full of people, but the bar was empty. Was ten o'clock too early to drink, even for a casino? She doubted it. Maybe being Sunday made a difference. The pious souls who might be drinking were instead at church? She doubted that, too. One look at the gambling crowd and her first thought wouldn't be church-goers.

"Would it be too much of a bother to get a glass of iced tea?"

The bartender turned away from rearranging the bottles behind the bar. "No, of course not. Is that it? Just tea?"

"Yes, thanks, I'm working. I'm the one in the hallway." She pointed back over her shoulder. "And that's unsweetened tea." She'd learned the hard way that you better say that upfront or your tea would be undrinkable.

He put a glass of ice on the counter and reached into an underbar fridge for a pitcher of tea. "Here you go. Sit here or take it back to your office." He was grinning. "That's a pisser they put you in the hall. You'd think the *Miami Herald* would have more clout. But all this will be gone by tomorrow night—out of our hair until the next time. Somebody said you would be interviewing the girls, or, at least, some of them?"

"That's right."

"Listen, I don't know how to ask you this, but I need a favor." He was watching her intently. Sizing her up? Julie wasn't sure.

"Of course, if I can be of help. The pageant demands a lot from all of us."

"Well, this has nothing to do with the pageant. And it's weird, I mean weird even to me."

He certainly had her attention, but what was going on? "Ok, just tell me."

"It's my little brother. Fifteen and totally a geek. Every time I make fun of him, my mother points out that when he's my age chances are he won't be tending bar." A sheepish grin, "She's probably right."

Julie waited. The guy seemed almost embarrassed to share whatever it was. Where was this going? She glanced through the front door and checked her makeshift office. Was it safe to just walk away from her computer like this? Maybe she could hurry things up.

"It can be a pain having a smart sibling." That wasn't very comforting but it might indicate she was on his side and help him decide to share.

"Yeah, you can say that again. My name's Ryan, by the way, and my little brother is Joey. I think he was born understanding algorithms. You probably know the type. Well, he belongs to a drone club, about twelve kids get together once a month to see what trouble they can get into by taking pictures through the neighbors' windows or dive-bombing some family's dog. I'm more or less kidding. There was an accidental peeping Tom episode but they're harmless for the most part, just aggravating for their parents." He stopped and poured himself a glass of tea. "Everyone was relieved when the club announced that they were going to design and build weather balloons. What could be more innocent? I think every parent silently cheered them on. I know my mom and dad did."

Where was he going? Julie was confused. So far, she didn't see a problem. "I'm assuming weather balloons had their own set of problems?"

"Unintended, and I can't even be more specific. Joey asked me to find someone at the *Herald* that he could talk to. Apparently, the balloon captured something that it shouldn't have—something that Joey feels is newsworthy. God help us if it's something embarrassing."

"Do you know if it's related to some kind of criminal activity? If so, he needs to be talking to law enforcement."

"I mentioned that but the kid's adamant that he can't go to the police. He insists that a reporter could help him. He specifically mentioned finding someone from the *Herald*."

"That's me. Okay, I'm in." And intrigued, Julie admitted to herself.

"Do you have time to talk with him before you start your interviews? He could be here in ten minutes."

"I have an hour before I meet with Miss Oklahoma."

"I'll call him."

Julie carried her tea back out to her makeshift office to wait, and Joey showed up right on time. But it was tough not to keep from smiling—he was the absolute epitome of a teenage nerd, backpack, rumpled plaid shirt, high-top sneakers, and thick, round-shaped, black-rimmed glasses. It could have been a Halloween costume, but Julie knew it wasn't. He'd ridden his bike over, and the helmet that he placed on the edge of her desk finished his look.

She instantly liked him. It didn't take any time at all

to realize that Joey was not only smart, he was also nice. He thanked her profusely for meeting with him and said he could explain why he was so insistent that his brother find him someone in the media to talk with. He pulled out a scruffy-looking laptop from his backpack, opened it and then moved the chair from in front of the desk to be parallel with hers behind the desk.

"We need to look at this together. But I need to give you a little background first." He cleared his throat and pointed to a decal on his backpack. "I'm a member of Flying High. No, it doesn't have anything to do with drugs. We're just a bunch of kids who play around with drones. I'm sure Ryan told you this already. The club works together on group projects. This month we ordered a weather balloon kit. It was like super neat. It was made of neoprene and was designed to be filled with either hydrogen or helium. Our balloon was filled with helium. A regular weather balloon only carries instruments. You know, ways to measure things like atmospheric pressure, temps, humidity, wind velocity ... our balloon could do all that but we also attached a camera. The joke was we hoped to run across ET."

Julie laughed, surely he must be kidding, an extraterrestrial? "And did you?"

"Well, not exactly ... we launched it three days ago and everything seemed to be going perfectly. I was the one monitoring it. I set up my laptop to receive photos, as well as text. We were getting all the reports we expected—heat, wind, pressure but it soon became obvious that something was wrong. Really wrong. The camera was only recording what appeared to be a location very close to ground. GPS tracking equipment helped us find the balloon, and what we feared was exactly what had happened. The balloon had lost its helium. It was stuck in the top of a pine tree some forty to fifty feet above ground by the edge of a holding pond outside town. One kid's dad is a volunteer fireman and he used a hook and ladder truck to get it back basically in one piece. But this is where it gets good. I want you to take a look at what was recorded." Joey opened a file and sat back.

At first the image jumped around. Must be wind, Julie thought. When the image smoothed out, the pond was clearly visible, directly below the balloon's camera. When the black Traverse entered the frame, it was going at a high rate of speed and just as Julie was about to comment, the SUV missed the turn and instead of moving away from the pond, it jumped the culvert, striking the cement guard rail and coming to rest at the edge of the water.

And then things got really interesting. A cop car with the county law enforcement insignia plainly visible along the passenger-side doors jerked to a halt just behind the Traverse. The car had no lights showing, not even headlights, yet, it had clearly been following the Traverse. Two uniformed men jumped out and approached the Traverse, one on each side of the cab's front doors. And the cop on the driver's side jerked open the door and dragged the driver out—a woman, but not just anyone. From the pictures Julie had seen, the woman was Brianna Walters. She appeared to be hurt or maybe just stunned and slumped against the cop trying to hold her up.

What happened next was murder. Julie found it hard to watch the bashing of Brianna's head against the edge of the open car door before tossing her into the back seat of the Traverse. Then with the drivers-side door still open, one of the men put it into gear, turned it, one hand on the steering wheel, lining the car up to face the water and began to push it forward into the pond. Julie sat quietly until the car had disappeared and the two uniformed men had returned to their car, backing up onto the road and taking off the way they had come.

"You've safeguarded this evidence?" Julie turned to Joey.

"Made copies including one for you. I can airdrop it to your phone or your computer and it's here on a thumb drive." He handed her the drive and she quickly slipped it in her purse. "It's a fantastic story—proof that there are bad cops out there. It could turn this county inside out and with elections coming up—the sheriff's on the ballot, I think. And that—"

Julie interrupted, "I hope I don't have to tell you how dangerous this is. *No one* can know you have this video. Maybe I should be asking if any other members of the club have seen it?"

"No, no one. I know it isn't safe even knowing it exists."

"You're exactly right."

"When my friend's dad took the balloon down from the tree, he gave the electronics to me. That was yesterday afternoon. The other club members are working on repairing the balloon. They just want it back in the air. I handle the surveillance results."

"Make sure you put all copies in a safe place, and sit tight."

"What are you going to do?"

Julie took a deep breath and slowly exhaled, "I'll be honest; I don't know. For starters, I'm going to share it with my husband. It may be that we have to seek federal help, bypass local law enforcement. The incident took place off the reservation, which narrows the number of people who might otherwise be involved. I just want you to know we'll do the right thing. And thank you. I admire your courage in coming forward. And you're right—it will make a great story. I'll credit you and the club." A quick handshake and Joey put on his bike helmet, waved to his brother through the restaurant's front glass and headed out the door.

Julie picked up her cell and dialed Ben. No answer. Would he check his voicemail if she left a message? She left a terse, "Need to talk" and hung up. Maybe they could meet at the house for lunch. She had one hour with Miss Oklahoma before being able to get away.

Chapter 24

S on of a bitch." Chairman Billie put the piece of notebook paper down, pushed back from his desk and stood up, then leaned forward, picked up the paper, folded it and slipped it into his shirt pocket. "Let's go get something to drink."

Ben nodded. Did the chairman think his office was bugged? Going someplace else to talk was probably the safest thing he could do, just in case.

"I vote for sitting outside. How about a soft drink?"

"Sounds great." Both men left the office and walked across the main floor and out the front door without talking. Ben could tell the chairman was angry. And who wouldn't be? What Annette had put Sammy through was cruel.

"Snag a table, I'll be back. Food trucks are always good for a cold drink. Coke, okay?"

Ben nodded and picked out a table to one side separated from the others. Looked like someone had moved it then didn't put it back among the others which made it perfect for offering a little privacy. When the chairman returned, he sat sipping his drink before commenting.

Finally, shaking his head, "Isn't there anything too sacred to be sold for money?"

"Probably not. Brianna, now Annette … ruining lives doesn't seem to carry the weight it should."

"I need to talk with Annette."

"She's in hiding and I'm not at liberty to say where she is. I guess I'd like to see you give her note to Chief Patrick. He'll know what steps are necessary to see that Sammy's released."

"Do you think Annette's life is in danger?"

"I think Robbi's life, Brianna's life … yeah, definitely Annette's life; all were or currently are in danger. I believe that Robbi was killed because she had some kind of information given to her by her grandfather. And Brianna? Did she really miss the turn by that holding pond or did she have help? We're probably never going to know for sure. Were you aware that she didn't go to the police and confess? Say that she was setting up my son so that she could demand money from me?"

"But that's what was leaked."

"Do you remember where you heard it?"

"Yeah, Andy came by and told me. I felt sorry for her. Her grandmother is seriously ill. I could understand the motivation."

"I think the motivation was to get rid of me. Someone had promised five thousand dollars for the totally fabricated rape scene and picked a good little actress to play the part. Care to know how many people jumped on the bandwagon threatening my departure? Before all the facts came out?" Ben didn't remind the chairman that he himself had given Ben thirty days to leave and had been pretty adamant about how disgraceful the situation was.

"I sent you a letter of apology, but hear me say it one more time. I'm sorry. I acted without even giving thought to there being another scenario. I didn't believe what your son said happened. It was foolish and inexcusable on my part not to give the young man a chance. I hope my apology is accepted?"

"It is—sorry, that's my phone again." Ben stood and reached in his pocket. "My wife wants me to call her. I need to take this. Must be something about the pageant tonight. Some last-minute change probably. Thanks for meeting with me. I'll follow up and turn this over to the lawyer who was working with Zac unless you want to handle it differently?" Ben thought the chairman was about to say something, then shook his head.

"I like your idea. Go for it. I can't wait to have Sammy back among us. The kid has suffered far too much. Thank you for taking this on and letting me know."

Ben had already dialed Julie before he reached the casino's front door. "What's up?" She'd answered on the first ring.

"Any chance you could meet me at home for lunch? I'll be finished with this interview in another fifteen minutes and be home in thirty. It's important or I wouldn't bother you."

"Don't I get a hint?"

"I need to finish this interview."

"So, that's a no."

"Yep. But you won't be disappointed."

* * *

"Who goes first? I've got some pretty interesting news myself." Ben pulled a stool up to the kitchen counter and held out a copy of Annette's confession.

"What's that?" Julie reached out to pick it up.

"Does that mean I go first?" Ben was teasing but he was anxious to share that Sammy's release was imminent.

"Sure." Julie took the copy and read quickly. "Oh my God, this is the best news ever. I'd almost given up. And we all knew that it would take something like this, the so-called witness recanting, to free him. How did you manage to get this?"

Ben quickly filled her in on Annette's decision to hide. "I won't share where she is with anyone from work, but I guess she may be difficult to find. I got the idea that she'll be moving around as much as she can. In fact, I hope that's the plan. I gather she didn't offer to tell you who paid her to lie?"

"No, that wasn't even on the table. My guess is the same person who paid Brianna, which means she needs to stay under the radar."

"Smart. Once she's discovered missing and the confession becomes common knowledge, her life is in danger. And let me prove what I mean." Julie set her laptop on the kitchen counter and plugged the thumb drive into a USB port. "Watch this."

Ben leaned in, watched the clip, and then replayed it before asking just one thing. "Cops?"

"Looks like they're for real. At least the car has the proper identification. The two men aren't familiar. And I'm not sure they're wearing uniforms, just dark clothing. It seemed obvious that Brianna knew they were following her. It appeared that she was trying to get away. I'm not sure she would have missed that corner if she'd been driving a decent speed."

"Obvious that the accident didn't kill her." Ben shook his head. It was difficult to get the image of Brianna's head injury out of his mind.

"I know. That is so hard to watch. After Robbi, it's another example of the ruthlessness of these people. And we don't have any idea who is behind it."

"Somebody trying to give the casino a black eye. I think what's been happening—including your would-be robbery in the parking lot—just underscores someone wanting to break up the Seminoles' monopoly on gaming in this part of Florida. All we have to do is prove it."

"You know, I think Annette was the plant that my boss said was working at the casino. I can't prove that, but she seemed to know a lot. According to Annette, gossip had Brianna and my boss as having an affair."

"Affair? I thought he was—"

"Don't say married with children. I said that and was called naïve."

"Kinda puts a new twist to things, doesn't it?"

"If it's the truth."

"Then that's a place to start. But you need to be careful. No heroics."

"I promise, but how do we prove his involvement? Find something that would put him in the mix?"

Ben shrugged. "I'm not sure, but diluting the tribes'

power would be big—especially if a person had an interest in an independent casino. I could do some checking."

"He doesn't strike me as someone who would leave an obvious trail. I'd bet there's nothing in his name to connect him to gambling in any way."

"You're probably right. My biggest concern now is what to do with the weather balloon tape. Do I give a copy to Chief Patrick? If he's a good cop, it's the only way to go; if he's a bad cop, then I'd be asking for trouble. The two of us could end up looking over our shoulders, waiting for something to happen."

"I know we can't make decisions now, and I have to get back. A few more interviews and then it's the big evening. I swear the excitement at the casino is palpable. The contestants are all so primed. It should be a great show. I'm at the press table down front. I'll see if I can wrangle a seat next to me."

Chapter 25

All the escorts would meet their contestants in the foyer. Then, one hundred and two young people in evening wear, plus another thirty pageant staff, would follow as they entered the auditorium. They would walk in two-by-two as couples only to split to sit on opposite sides of the stage. Actually, on opposite sides of the runway. This elevated platform was exactly fifty percent of the length of the room and was lined by TV cameras and operators. It would give the audience an up-close, personal look at each contestant. An assigned young man would escort his contestant to the side of the stage when it was that contestant's time to meet with the master of ceremonies and then after introductions, the contestant would walk down the runway, pause at the end to make contact with the audience by maybe waving before returning to center stage.

This maneuvering was something that the group had practiced even though Nathan thought it was a waste of time. Directions were written out along with a diagram and each contestant and escort got a copy. But why? Could anything be any simpler? As his dad would say, it wasn't rocket science. It was this micro-management that made Nathan decide he wouldn't volunteer to take part in something like this again. He was tired of being watched, clothing checked, told open-toed shoes weren't appropriate—really? Sandals outlawed? Wasn't this Florida?

But he'd met Skyler and that made things worth it … almost. She hated the constraints as much as he did. Her mother and father had flown to Florida for the finale and had taken the two of them out for dinner earlier. Nice people. Her dad was a sports fan. Nathan was kind of sorry that he couldn't sit with them during the final judging. Again, rules that couldn't be broken.

And he really thought Skyler had a chance to win. It made sense that the older girls had the edge. He knew that Zac was pulling for Alana. Tonight, each contestant would be introduced with a quick chat hosted by the emcee. A follow-up to the topic they had discussed during their individual interview would be featured with possibly additional questions. He thought both girls had solid topics—each emphasized community work and their contributions to supporting future generations to follow in their footsteps.

A local vocalist opened with *America the Beautiful* followed by the emcee introducing each girl with a few words about the state she represented. Then all hell broke loose.

The double-doors at the back of the auditorium were still open and suddenly the sound of gunshots rang out. The emcee dropped to the stage floor and, clutching the mic, ordered everyone to seek shelter—in place! That meant diving under tables, crawling under the platform runway. Some tried to run for the doors only to pushed back.

Nathan did as he was told amid the screaming. Those trying to leave the room ran the risk of being trampled and cries for help were almost as loud as those of panic. He scooted up next to a support propping up the runway and sat with his back to the stage. He'd pulled Skyler down to sit beside him and held her hand.

"Mom and Dad? Do you think they're okay?" She started to stand, but Nathan gently pulled her back to sit beside him.

"I think we have to wait to get the all clear. It's probably not safe to stand yet. I heard some guy on the other side of the platform say that there's an active shooter—maybe more than one. And someone said something about a hostage." He took her hand and positioned his upper body so that she was shielded. He hoped she couldn't hear his heart thumping in his chest. This was the real thing. Lives were in danger. He could hear the sobs of those closer to the stage. And there was nothing anyone could do, but wait.

* * *

The standoff lasted two hours before everyone was escorted by armed guards back through the casino and out into the parking lot. Ben quickly found Zac and Alana and

Nathan and Skyler and gathered them to one side to stand with him and Julie. Skyler's parents rushed up, hugged their daughter and thanked Nathan for keeping her safe. Alana's mother couldn't stop crying, saying over and over, "I was so frightened."

By now it was nine o'clock. Would the evening's event continue? It would be difficult to just pick up where it was left. The people in the parking lot had thinned noticeably. The minute there had been an all-clear given, throngs of people got into their cars and left. Finally, it was announced that with a ballroom in disarray, and based upon the points received by each contestant over the previous four days, four finalists would be selected to compete in a sadly truncated presentation, with Miss Teen USA's court consisting of three runners-up. Only these contestants would be allowed back into the ballroom with their escorts.

The final choosing would be televised, taped for later showing, but not before an audience. All other participants and their families were invited to wait in the foyer with the naming of the semi-finalists promised within thirty minutes. Bummer.

The disappointment was palpable, Ben thought. Some of the people remaining called out protests, but he was relieved to see that the crowd stayed orderly. Their reaction was just registering disappointment, not a precursor to action.

And, cops were everywhere. That, at least, offered a feeling of safety and brought home the fact that this hadn't been a drill. Ben hoped those in the parking lot realized they had escaped a death-threatening situation. The crowd quieted as Chief Patrick stepped up to the hastily set up microphone just outside of the casino's front entrance.

He told them the shooter who had barricaded himself inside the office of the CEO had been killed. The CEO had been wounded and would require surgery. He had been taken to the local hospital. It was not known if his injuries were life-threatening. The situation was reported as under the control of local law enforcement. Chief Patrick continued his report, assuring the crowd that what had transpired had been the actions of a lone gunman, apparently a disgruntled former employee who had recently been terminated. The chief's men had thoroughly checked and double-checked the area, including the parking lots and parking garage. He was relieved to report that employees could safely return to their positions inside the casino. Customers could likewise return to the gaming areas. As to the pageant, he would turn the microphone over to Mr. Holmes, pageant director, for further directions concerning the evening's event.

The pageant director was speaking to a greatly reduced crowd. Probably over half had left already. But those who waited heard the names of Miss Illinois, Miss Alaska, Miss Texas and Miss California called out over a loudspeaker. Skyler hugged Nathan, then her parents, before joining Alana and Zac to make their way back into the building to find out the winner.

Ben and Julie followed but waited in the hallway outside the ballroom and watched from the doorway as contestants and escorts were picking their way around overturned chairs and tables and torn bunting to reach the stage. Finally, with escorts standing to the side, four young women lined up to the right of the emcee who still looked shaken.

In quick succession, finalists four, three and two were

named leaving the contestant who was Miss Teen USA alone in the center. Skyler Thompson, Miss California, received a crown from a stagehand and the three girls standing next to her gathered around her, slipping the banner declaring her title over her shoulder, adjusting it and congratulating her. Zac and Nathan cheered and clapped their approval until they were told to tone it down by another stagehand as he was arranging a group photo to be taken with the emcee and the pageant director. Ben guessed the photo-taking would take some time and both boys would want to say their good-byes. Again, Uber would provide the boys' ride home.

"Ready to go?" Ben turned to Julie.

"You go on. Remember, I brought my car because I still have work to do. I need to get some comments from the winners. I don't expect to be long. See you at home." A quick kiss and Julie walked back into the ballroom.

She paused just inside the door. What a mess. Was there even one table or chair upright? What a terribly graphic reminder of the ordeal they had all been through. A photographer from the *Herald* and two assistants were talking with the girls on the stage. She decided that she wouldn't be in the way if she hung out close by. She needed to speak with each of the contestants individually and as a group before they left the auditorium.

"Hey, kiddo, I was hoping I'd catch up with you. You know Bert." Julie turned to see her boss standing next to an older man who was often rumored to be the best reporter on the *Herald*'s staff.

"Of course. I think everyone knows Bert. I've even heard the word idol bandied about." She smiled. She meant it to be funny and got the grin she expected, but she also wanted to point out his obvious place at the top of the hierarchy of the *Herald* writing staff according to those he worked with. There would be some cub reporters who would be genuflecting about now.

"Great. Then I take it you two wouldn't mind putting your heads together to come up with a piece for the morning edition. I've listed some selling points. I don't have a problem with it becoming an opinion piece. I don't know if you mind driving back to the office but it might be easier to work there. Anyway, here are my expectations. If you have questions, I'll have my cell with me." With that he handed each a sheet of paper, wished them well and walked back up the aisle and out of the auditorium.

"Have you looked at these?" Julie held up a copy of her list to Bert.

"I haven't read them all but I have an idea of what's there."

"Definitely some things we need to discuss. I need about a half hour to do some quick interviews here. I have my car and can meet you at the office in forty-five minutes. Will that work?"

"Sounds like a plan."

Julie continued on toward the stage. Question one to each girl would be what this award means, how she would use it in her community to encourage young women to accomplish their own goals, and question two, what would it mean to be a spokesperson for the pageant? What personal expectations, real or imagined, did she have? One of the stagehands placed five folding chairs in a circle and the girls' escorts, including Nathan and Zac, retreated to the foyer to wait there.

She recorded their answers to the more weighty

questions, and then threw in some fluff—what was your reaction to hearing your name called as winning the title? Aside from placing in the final four, what has been the most interesting or exciting part of this contest for you? The girls were bubbly and cute and forthcoming with their answers. It went quicker than Julie had expected. On the way out, she said good night to Nathan and Zac and mentioned that she'd be late, then continued on to the garage. It was a little after ten. She certainly hadn't expected to be working at that hour this evening.

* * *

Bert had an office, no cubicle for him. With the door closed and the plastic vertical blinds drawn, there was almost no noise from the room beyond. She was seldom at the office this late and was surprised to see a pretty full second shift in place.

"Take a few minutes and see what the boss is suggesting. Actually, I shouldn't use the word 'suggest.' I think his list is cast in stone. Let me know what you think. Coffee? I think there's a fresh pot in the lunchroom."

"I'd love some, thanks."

Julie pulled a chair out from a small corner table and unfolded the list. A cursory glance was all it took to realize the tone of what Ken Usher had written and it all came down to portraying the Casino corporation as incompetent—not able to police its own, endangering staff as well as patrons, in over its head and—she had to look at this part twice—it should be sued for misappropriation of funds.

Where had that come from? Was the tribe cheating its own people? Or did Ken have the community in mind?

Probably. He seemed to be using scare-tactics. Was that the gist of what she was reading? The casino made the area unsafe for its citizens? And what was the proof?

She expected and found examples--uncorrected examples--of the murder of Robbi Aponi by an Indian man, the assault on herself, and then the attempted rape ... ending with the evening's intended mass shooting that left one dead and the CEO wounded.

Mass shooting? Who knew that was really the intent? Had it been proved? The shooter was dead. Rumor was that the shooter was someone who had recently been fired. But was that even the truth? It seemed that he was looking for only one person, the CEO. But proof? None.

Agreement to any of the accusations would make her culpable. She couldn't be a part of this. There was simply no way that she could support these accusations. So much of what had happened recently had been proved to be other than what was originally reported or even observed. The whole story wasn't being told. And it was clear to her why.

This was simply supposed to be scare tactics used to manipulate the *Herald*'s readership, voters who would have a say in whether the Seminole's monopoly needed to be dissolved.

She looked up as Bert returned and handed her a cup of coffee and three small containers of creamer. "Bert, I'll be blunt. I'd rather turn in my resignation than be a part of lies. I didn't become a news person to mislead the public. I report honestly or not at all."

"You're probably right; it's going to cost you if you don't support the boss."

"You don't have a problem with all this?" Julie pointed

to the list for emphasis. "And what's this TD here at the bottom? We score a Touch Down if we follow orders?"

"Boy, you are a newbie. It's the initials that the boss likes to use—TD for Top Dog. He treats it like a joke but I think he secretly loves it. Look, don't go rushing out of here all mad. It's been a hell of an evening. Finish your feature on the pageant. I imagine you got some dynamite quotes from the girls. The guys should be checking in with photos anytime. Get that part of your assignment ready for the morning edition. Then, take a copy of the list here, and go home. Let's turn it into an opinion piece, an editorial for tomorrow's evening edition. That would give us some more time. I can come up with what he wants for the morning. I don't feel compromised. Get your thoughts together and give me a call—I'll still be here at midnight. I've got the particulars on the shooting. I'll get that part of the story in for tomorrow's headline."

Julie nodded. Probably sound advice. This wasn't the time to overreact, but at gut-level she knew she wasn't. And she wouldn't have a part in indicting innocent people— Sammy Longman, Zac … the truth needed to come out. She should be writing about Brianna's death, perpetrated by cops, Zac's set up, Sammy's false imprisonment. But right now, all she could think of was a hot shower and running all this past Ben. She needed an impartial voice of reason.

* * *

"And if I don't have a job? If refusing to go along with this costs me?" She pointed to the list in Ben's hand. He was sitting across from her at the kitchen counter.

"Hey, you're not out of one yet. I think you have sound reasons not to follow your boss's orders. I couldn't agree with you more. In so many words, he wants you to lie—at least color people's thinking about the Seminole holdings, make them rethink the status quo. Any idea at all about the misappropriation of funds accusation?"

"None. Not sure where I'd start but I'm tempted to do some digging."

"Promise me you'll be careful." Ben picked the list up again. "And what about this TD? Initials?"

Julie filled him in on what Bert had said. "Seems Ken likes it, refers to himself as Top Dog whenever he can."

"I'm going to borrow the list. I'd like to run the weather balloon material by Chief Patrick. I want to see or hear his reaction to what appear to be two cops killing Brianna and pushing her car into the pond. And I think he needs to know that your boss wants the truth, either hidden or slanted in such a way to screw over the casino, to set them up as unable to function in a safe manner, and, of consequence, the savvy voter will immediately decide the monopoly needs to be broken up. It's a fairly clever manipulation."

"Do you think that's wise—being so open with Chief Patrick?"

"Guess we'll find out, but I happen to think he's on the right side. He's been honest with us—and has kept us in the loop. I can't help but think he didn't have to be as straightforward as he's been."

"Any idea when the boys will be home?" She'd left while the photographers were still at work.

"Zac texted and said the pageant was opening one of the casino's restaurants for an after-party. Give the winners a chance to receive the well wishes of their fellow contestants. I expect it to be a late night—especially since both Zac and Nathan were escorting winners. It's really a shame that the ceremony had to be interrupted."

"Do we know how Chairman Billie is doing?"

"I just called the hospital. He's still in surgery but word is he's expected to fully recover."

"That's fantastic news."

"I agree."

* * *

"Everything on your end taken care of?"

"Got my best people on it."

"Shame that idiot couldn't stick with the plan and kill Billie before taking a bullet himself. Who could miss with a Glock at close range? We weren't paying him to play cops and robbers, we were paying him for a hit."

"Just be thankful that he got it—himself. I don't think we could have trusted him if he'd walked out of there. I think he would have spilled his guts at the first opportunity."

"Yeah, maybe. But what's the plan if the chairman survives?"

"Is he supposed to?"

"No word yet. I guess we'll deal with that when we know for sure."

Chapter 26

Oscar Billie was in the hospital for seven days. At least six too many, to hear him tell it. He'd been operated on, interrogated by the cops, and made to eat hospital food. No, he had no idea who the gunman was; no, he was not a former employee; no, the man didn't seem to be there to steal anything; no, he didn't ask for money or threaten him with a trip to an ATM to clean out the chairman's account. Chairman Billie wasn't any help.

The cops acted like they didn't believe him when he said it seemed like the guy just wanted attention, to shoot up the hallway and his office, wound him, and that was it. Could it have been suicide by cop? How was he supposed to know that? He didn't even think the gunman getting killed was part of the plan. But if not, what was the plan?

A few hundred people were scared to death, not to mention casino-goers who were evacuated, too. What kind of press would this get the casino?

But worst of all? Chairman Billie would have to use a walker. Maybe not forever, but for the time being. The femur that took the bullet was wired and stitched back together but not thrilled about supporting weight. He had months of rehab to look forward to. And if he complained? The docs and nurses both reiterated how lucky he was, how if he had to be hit, taking a bullet to the thigh that missed arteries was preferred to a chest shot or, God forbid, something to the head.

And in the middle of all this, he had been notified as a tribal elder that the body of a member of the Seminole tribe had been found at the edge of a game preserve in the Everglades, just south of Okeechobee. Park Rangers had made the discovery and the body had been excavated from a pit of quicksand and sent to a local morgue. According to a note left with his belongings in a nearby kayak, the act was suicide, and the man's name was Leonard Holt. The name was still just an educated guess because of the body's deterioration. Months in a pit of quicksand wasn't a good medium to preserve a body. They had an intact skull but with the flesh rotted or ripped away, it wasn't giving up its secrets. Any scent of carrion in the wilds and scavengers, usually birds, would fight over the spoils. Chairman Billie was asked to have the man's dental records forwarded to the mortician for positive identification. Only then would the body be returned to the tribe for burial.

At least, a bullet hole in his femur didn't keep him from working and the hospital provided a laptop, phone, and writing desk with a stool for propping his leg up. He called the IHS clinic near Tampa where Leonard used to live and had his dental records overnighted to Okeechobee. The actual records. In the meantime, IHS emailed copies to the office of the medical examiner. That would prove identity, but didn't solve the problem of signing to have the body released if it was, in fact, Leonard's. Indian protocol said that once the death of a Seminole member had been confirmed, the body had to be escorted by a fellow Native person to its final resting place. And Chairman Billie knew that Leonard would want to be with his granddaughter. Burial had to be in close proximity to Robbi Aponi. And there would be a ceremony. Something at the casino to honor a long-time employee. A eulogy, comments by family and tribe, other contributions by friends ... Leonard's favorite foods—wasn't he a corndog fanatic? It had to be special.

Since he was still in the hospital, Oscar Billie had a brilliant idea. If he couldn't go, he could send Ben Pecos to sign for the body and escort it back. The minute he knew for certain that the corpse was Leonard Holt, he'd contact Dr. Pecos. It made sense to involve Indian Health Service and bypass a lot of red tape by having a government employee step in and take charge. The doc could certainly meet the requirements for bringing the body home. Yes, a brilliant plan and now he only had to wait for the final ID.

* * *

Ben called ahead and made a nine o'clock appointment to meet with Chief Patrick. Monday morning, the start of a new week, and he was already apprehensive about how the week would unfold. He was curious to see the chief's reaction to the tape of Brianna's car being pushed into the holding pond. Even though he trusted the chief, he was secretly relieved that he was meeting with him in his office. He knew he'd feel better when names had been named, and those behind the recent events had been apprehended.

Per usual, he wasn't kept waiting. Bypassing a lot of small talk, Ben set up his laptop on the chief's desk and opened the weather balloon file.

"Gonna tell me what I'm supposed to be watching?"

"I think you'll find it self-explanatory." Ben dragged a chair up to the corner of the chief's desk, situated the laptop so that the chief had a clear view, double-clicked on the file, and sat back.

The chief watched the tape in its entirety, went back to the beginning and replayed it, then just sat there staring at the screen. Only the pursed lips and grim downturn of his mouth combined with the staccato tapping of fingers on the desk gave a hint of his reaction.

Finally, he turned to Ben. "Interesting use of salvage."

"Sorry? Salvage?" Ben wasn't following.

"Yeah, the cruiser. Reconditioning police cars as junkyard sweethearts is big business. They're stripped right down to removing the plastic seat covers on the back seats. I'd bet these side-door decals were reapplied. If you look closely, the edge of the word 'county' kind of drifts downward. The Dodge Charger, Chevy Caprice, Ford Taurus, and, of course, the Ford Crown Victoria—you can buy all of them off of car lots. Even through CarMax. Looks like this Charger has seen better days but the spotlight and metal brush guard are original issue. Nobody would have even given a police car a second glance as it followed another car. Isn't the first time a used cruiser has been part of a crime."

"Any ideas about the two guys?"

"I'll have the techs go over the tape—maybe enlarged, we'll be able to identify someone, but I wouldn't hold out hope. We'd have better luck going after who's behind the murder. Anything else you want me to take a look at?"

"Yeah, one more thing. My wife was given this list of suggestions by her boss at the *Herald*, how to structure features and/or editorials concerning the recent problems at the casino. Easy to see the paper is staking out a position—not necessarily the truth—and the problem is, the paper reaches millions. Many of those readers are voters. Julie is having a hard time being asked to misrepresent what really has happened there by casting the casino in a bad light."

"Yeah, a problem of ethics. Who's TD, by the way?

"Apparently stands for Top Dog. Ken Usher's little inside joke as a name for himself, I'm told. Likes to announce his position as Editor-in-Chief with a little humor."

"Same initials as those on the text by Brianna to the person who owed her $5K. I think this tie-in may come in handy. Can I hang onto this?" The chief was already slipping the paper into a folder on his desk.

Ben nodded. He thought he noticed a look of smugness but any comment was interrupted by his phone vibrating. "Sorry, I better take this. It's Chairman Billie." He stepped out into the hallway. "Yes, Chairman Billie, how can I help you? Of course, I would be honored to escort Leonard Holt home. Leave in the morning? That won't be a problem."

Chapter 27

Ben had a couple hours' drive ahead of him to just get lost in his thoughts. He'd be alone to sift through what might be called evidence in the multiple instances of criminal acts associated with the casino. He tried to imagine what a sense of closure might look like. Would there be arrests? There should be. Murders, lives potentially ruined? There had to be accountability.

Taking off at six a.m. after picking up a van owned by the casino, he stuck to major highways before cutting over toward Lake Okeechobee. This would be an exciting day if he were a fisherman. The lake boasted the best speckled perch and large mouth bass fishing in the entire state. And the scenery was breathtaking. He loved the mountains of New Mexico but here at twenty-four feet above sea level, every season was green and flowering. The lake's seven hundred and thirty square miles also boasted the perfect, natural bird sanctuary. And he wasn't even thinking of the true wildlife. Critters—bobcats, alligators, snakes—were also well known to inhabit the area.

With good directions from Chairman Billie's office, Ben drove directly to the morgue on the outskirts of the town. Okeechobee gave off small country township vibes. Posters of the upcoming music festival were plastered everywhere. The event apparently was yearly and held in a place called Sunshine Grove. It was as if he'd landed on another planet—this was a far cry from the Miami area and light years different from the Seminole Casino and Hotel. But could he ever live in a town this size? Doubtful.

Yet, the efficiency of the pathologist's lab was impressive. The paperwork was ready for Ben to sign, the man's assistant made copies of his ID, and then led him to an office at the back of the building with a plaque above the door which read: Thomas Fetteridge, MD.

"Welcome." A somewhat portly man invited Ben into his office. "I'm assuming this is your first visit to the area?" Ben nodded. "I'm sorry it couldn't have been under happier circumstances. My condolences to the tribe. Here, have a seat. I'll just take up a couple minutes of your time before I'm going to ask you to bring your vehicle to the back of the building. Just back up to the loading dock, and we'll get Mr. Holt settled in for his trip home. But first, I'd like to share something with you."

Ben wasn't surprised. There were probably personal effects that would need to be handled separately. He sat in the chair offered while the doctor rummaged around in the middle drawer of his desk finally pulling out an envelope.

"Here we go. This needs to go back with you." He handed the envelope to Ben. "To say this is important is perhaps, an understatement. I found this flash drive in the gentleman's mouth, safe-guarded against the elements in a tiny plastic bag. I haven't even checked to see if it's still working. I will have you sign that you have received it. I also have the note for his granddaughter, a pocket knife, spare pair of reading glasses—personal items that I'm certain the family will want. Well, everything is in this box, and if I could just get you to sign this annotated list."

Ben's mind was racing. If the drive was a duplicate of the one found in Robbi's locker, this might be the answer to all their questions. Wasn't Leonard Holt a member of the inner circle at one time? A financial officer? He would have had a front-row seat. And this was probably what got Robbi killed. Ben was thankful Leonard wouldn't know that. He thanked the doctor, slipped the envelope containing the drive into the box of personal items, and walked out to the parking lot.

Three young men loaded the triple-layer cardboard box containing the remains in an insulated body bag into the back of the van. They were respectful and careful. After the cargo was tied down, there was still room for Leonard's kayak. Within twenty minutes, Ben was on his way back to Hollywood and the casino.

* * *

Ben called ahead and left a voicemail for Chief Patrick, could they meet later that afternoon? Then, he double-checked with Chairman Billie. Should Mr. Holt's remains be brought to the casino and left in the van when he returned, as they discussed? And was it still the plan to take the body onto the reservation for burial that evening? Affirmative. Chairman Billie had already arranged for drivers and members of the Indian community to prepare the body. All was in order.

Ben had to admit his excitement was building; he couldn't stop thinking about the possibilities of what might be on the flash drive. Chairman Billie was as good as his word and two casino workers met him in the casino's parking garage to take possession of the van after first removing the kayak and loading baskets of food and gifts for the family's celebration later that evening on the reservation. Ben had slipped the envelope containing the flash drive into his own pocket earlier and had received a call from Chief Patrick that anytime mid-afternoon would be convenient to meet.

* * *

This was it—everything or nothing. Ben felt that certain about the drive as he handed it to Chief Patrick. It was going to contain something meaninglessly work related or it was a bomb just waiting to detonate.

"Let's walk down to the lab. I've got a couple techs standing by. If this is what we both hope it is, then it's got to be copied and handled carefully."

The room was set up with two chairs behind a computer table that held a desktop computer. An operator reached out, took the flash drive, and plugged it in. Ben and the chief both repositioned their chairs for a clearer view of the screen ... and waited. Almost instantly the directory listing the drive's contents flashed into view. And there it was. This drive would appear to be an exact replica of the one that Robbi had concealed in her locker—its name, The Noose.

"Now, if a little exposure to Florida's climate didn't do any damage." The tech opened the first file. Andy Thunderhawk was sitting at a table counting stacks of money, banding each and putting them into a suitcase. In the background April Bowlegs stepped forward and handed him several sacks of bills. And that was it.

"All the money could be explained. Putting it in a suitcase makes me wonder but it's not proof of a crime." The chief was taking notes. "Let's see what's next."

The tech opened the second file. Again, not a problem, it opened immediately. The file, Black Money, was instantly more interesting. Here the suitcase, presumably the one filled with money, was being put into the trunk of a car with a New Jersey plate.

"Stop for a minute, let me get that plate." Chief Patrick then waved for the tech to start the video again. Two men appeared to sign for their cargo and when one slipped off his jacket and bent over the trunk to shove the suitcase farther back, the gun in his waistband stood out clearly.

The third file was, at that point, the most incriminating. Spreadsheet after spreadsheet in minute detail spelled out who was on the take. And, yes, there was Julie's boss's name at the top of the list. Ben was not as familiar with those singled out, but the chief let out a low whistle.

"Worse than I thought. This is a community who's who list."

Again, he asked the tech to go through the pages slowly while he took notes. In almost every frame, two people stood out—Ken Usher and Dale Epstein, the casino's recently hired CFO, along with a local bank president and a real estate mogul. The file marked 'Legislators' included several leading political wheelers and dealers. There were even photos copied from room cameras of several men receiving payoffs. But payoffs for what?

'Where the Bodies are Buried' seemed to indicate safe deposit boxes, including access codes, two safes at the casino, again with codes, and literally a secret room behind the mechanic's closet in the garage.

Perhaps, the biggest shock was that 'X' contained carefully spelled out plans to kill Chairman Billie. It also explained what was worth so much money. Drugs, among other contraband. Plain and simple, the casino was being used to cover for a giant money laundering operation. Then there were pictures of yachts, lavish parties in Miami, girls … six-figure cars.

Busting up the Seminole's control would make sense. Then those outsiders behind the scenes could move into positions of authority—even establish other support entities, smaller casinos to siphon off some of the collected revenue. Keep the projects from attracting attention. This was a huge operation bursting at the seams to expand, and they hid behind the cover of a reputable business to do so.

"Wow." Ben wasn't sure he could find words to really do justice to the despicable information in front of him.

"Yeah, I have to admit I'm shocked at the scope of things. But I think we have more than enough to clean up this mess. Thank you, Leonard Holt. I can only think of what might have happened if the copy Robbi had hidden in her locker had been found by someone who worked at the casino."

"I don't envy you all the work."

"It will have to include the Feds, of course, and law enforcement from surrounding communities. But I'd like to say that leadership of the Seminole Casino and Hotel is safe with the Seminoles. By the way, we picked up Annette earlier. To keep her safe, she'll reside with us for awhile. We'll need her testimony."

* * *

Dinner that night was filled with everyone's stories. Zac and Nathan talked about seeing Alana and Skyler off at the airport. Copies of the *Herald* were everywhere at the casino with great pictures of the Miss Teen USA finalists and then several shots of Skyler wearing her crown. Julie's interviews were featured on the front page.

Ben shared a brief overview of finding a flash drive copy that matched the one that had gone through a wash cycle. He reiterated how important it turned out to be. He had talked with Julie earlier about her boss's involvement. They both expected him to be arrested. It looked like she still had a job, just a new boss.

Before Julie brought a couple cartons of ice cream and a scoop to the table for dessert, Ben offered to help her get out bowls and spoons and they both walked to the kitchen. Out of sight, they heard Nathan poke a little fun at Zac.

"So, how'd the kissing lessons go?"

"Huh? What are you talking about?"

"I heard that silver bracelet worked—got you some face time."

"I think you heard wrong. But I bet if it did, it worked better than a Zia key chain fob."

Both boys laughed and Zac called out, inquiring as to

where the ice cream was. Cookies and Cream or kissing? Ben guessed ice cream could still take priority at fourteen.

+ + +

Thank you for taking the time to read *Snake Eyes* If
you enjoyed it, please consider telling your friends or
posting a short review. Word of mouth is an author's best
friend and is much appreciated. Thank you,
Susan Slater

What's next up from Susan Slater?
Susan is stepping out of the mystery genre (briefly)
with another novel of women's fiction called *The Aunt
Farm*. All we can say is that it involves a group of ladies
"of a certain age" and it promises to be hilarious.
Watch for it in 2023!

+ + +

Books by Susan Slater

The Ben Pecos Mystery Series
The Pumpkin Seed Massacre
Yellow Lies
Thunderbird
Fire Dancer
Under A Mulberry Moon
The Thaw
Ghost Dust
Paper Arrows
Snake Eyes
A Way to the Manger (a Christmas novella)

The Dan Mahoney Mystery Series
Flash Flood
Rollover
Hair of the Dog
Epiphany
Widow's Walk

Standalone Novels
0-60 – contemporary romance
The Caddis Man – historical fiction
Five O'Clock Shadow – mystery-thriller

+ + +

**Get another Susan Slater book FREE! Visit her
website to find out how!**

Visit Susan's website at http://susansslater.com where
you can sign up for her free mystery newsletter and a
chance to win some very cool stuff.

Contact Susan: susan@susansslater.com
Follow Susan on Facebook

+ + +